SOUTHERN COMFORT

Amy Lillard

This is a work of fiction. Names, characters, places, and incidents are either the product of the author's imagination or are used fictitiously, and any resemblance to actual persons living or dead, business establishments, events, or locales, is entirely coincidental.

SOUTHERN COMFORT

Originally published Crimson Romance as Amie Louellen

Second Edition
Published in the United States of America

Praise for Amy Lillard

"Lillard's characters will tug at your heartstrings and leave you wanting to meet more!"

~Laura Marie Altom

"Amy Lillard's novels are funny, sweet, charming, and utterly delicious. Reading her stories is like indulging in gourmet chocolates: You'll savor every delightful page and when you reach the end, you'll always wish there was more!"

~Michele Bardsley,

"BRODIE'S BRIDE is funny, warm and thoroughly charming. Make room on your keeper shelf for Amy Lillard!"

~KarenToller Whittenburg

OTHER BOOKS BY AMY LILLARD
ROMANCE NOVELS

AMISH ROMANCE

THE CLOVER RIDGE SERIES

Saving Gideon

Katie's Choice

Gabriel's Bride

THE WELLS LANDING SERIES

Caroline's Secret

Courting Emily

Lorie's Heart

Just Plain Sadie

Titus Returns

Marrying Jonah

The Quilting Circle

A Wells Landing Christmas

Loving Jenna

Romancing Nadine

A New Love for Charlotte

More Than Friendship (e-novella)

More Than a Promise (e-novella)

More Than a Marriage (e-novella)

THE AMISH OF PONTOTOC

A Home for Hannah

A Love for Leah

A Family for Gracie

An Amish Husband for Tillie

THE PARADISE NOVELLAS

The Amish Christmas Sleigh

Amish Brides

THE PARADISE VALLEY SERIES

Marry Me, Millie

The Amish Matchmaker

CONTEMPORARY ROMANCE
  CATTLE CREEK SERIES
        Loving a Lawman
        Healing a Heart
        Besting the Bull Rider (coming soon)
  MAYHEM AND MAGNOLIAS SERIES
        Southern Hospitality
        Southern Comfort
        Southern Charm
  STAND ALONE ROMANCE
        All You Need is Love
        Blame It on Texas
        Brodie's Bride
        Can't Buy Me Love
        Forget Me Not, Baby (coming soon)
        Love Potion Me, Baby
        Take Me Back to Texas—sweet
        Take Me Back to Texas—sexy
        Ten Reasons Not to Date a Cop
        The Trouble with Millionaires
HISTORICAL ROMANCE
        As Good As Gold
        The Gingerbread Bride
        No Greater Treasure
        Not So Pretty Penny
        The Wildflower Bride
                MYSTERY NOVELS
AMISH COZIES
  THE KAPPY KING MYSTERY SERIES
        Kappy King and the Puppy Kaper
        Kappy King and the Pickle Kaper
        Kappy King and the Pie Kaper

This Little Pig (Kappy King and the Pig Kaper)

Any Way You Slice It (Kappy King and the Pizza Kaper) coming soon

SUNFLOWER CAFÉ MYSTERY SERIES

Dairy, Dairy, Quite Contrary

SUGARCREEK AMISH MYSTERY SERIES

O Little Town of Sugarcreek

Shoo, Fly, Shoo

Stranger Things Have Happened

OTHER AMISH COZY MYSTERIES

Unsavory Notions

CONTEMPORARY COZIES

MAIN STREET BOOK CLUB SERIES

Can't Judge a Book by Its Murder

A Murder Between the Pages

A Murder Like No Author

OTHER CONTEMPORARY COZIES

Pattern of Betrayal

DEDICATION:

To the great state of Mississippi. It's taken me a while and residence in another state to completely appreciate your beauty. My birthplace, my home.

Look away, look away, look away Dixieland.

CHAPTER ONE

"But what about the ghost?" Newland Tran balanced the tiny saucer of cookies in his too-big hands and nodded politely to his hostess.

Bitty Duncan gave him the sweetest smile, her wrinkled cheeks dimpling. If he had to guess, the woman was close to eighty-five, yet she had a spring in her step and a sparkle in her eyes that belied her age.

She was the quintessential grandmotherly type, if a typical grandmother had lavender-colored hair to go with her crocheted shawl and flowered housedress.

"Would you like another glass of tea, Mr. Tran?"

She said his name with the short "a" sound, but Newland didn't bother to correct her. It seemed that most everyone in the South wanted his name to rhyme with *ran*, and there was nothing he could do to squelch that desire.

"No, thank you. I would like to hear more about your ghost though." For someone who wanted a tabloid reporter to write an article about the ghost she had in her house, Bitty seemed reluctant to talk about it. Or maybe she just wanted someone to keep her company.

Great. That was just what he needed. To come all the way out here from Chicago to keep an old woman from being lonely.

Turtle Creek, Mississippi. And he had thought that Jefferson County, Tennessee was bad.

That was where he'd lost the only woman he'd ever loved. The woman he'd proposed to, albeit somewhat out of the blue, and who'd turned him down. He wasn't even supposed to be in Tennessee at the time—he was supposed to be in Arkansas, working on a story—but he found out that Roxanne was in Tennessee, accused of murder and digging up the story to end all stories. One that she wouldn't allow anyone to print after she got it.

Well, he understood that part. But what he didn't understand was how in three days she fell in love with Malcolm B. Daniels IV, state senator from District 27. He was a stuffed shirt if Newland had ever seen one, always wearing a tie and a coat and little wire-rimmed glasses. What was up with the small-town Southerners that made them put on airs like none other?

Itty-bitty Turtle Creek was twice as bad as tiny Jefferson County. He'd only been here two hours, and he was already itching to get back north of the Mason-Dixon Line.

"The ghost. Of course." Bitty nodded. "Well, he only shows himself on the last Thursday of the month."

He wished she would have explained that in her original letter to the paper. Newland resisted the urge to check the date on his watch. Today was Tuesday. He had a week and two days before the last Thursday of the month.

"Are you sure?" he asked as he wrote the tidbit in his notebook. No full moon stories or anniversary dates. Just the last Thursday of the month. "Why do you suppose that is?" He played along. What choice did he have really? He had nothing to get back to.

6

He'd lost his job at *I Spy* after he had gone off the deep end a little bit. But only just a little bit. So he had tipped Roxanne's desk over at the magazine. He'd been angry when he returned from Tennessee last year. But the editor-in-chief didn't like it very much—the tipping over of the desk—and the next thing Newland knew he was out on his can.

So he had taken a couple of months and nursed his broken heart but by then news of his "volatile nature" was all over Chicago. At any job he got, he was watched like a hawk, and every photographer who was sent out with him trembled as if he was going to smash their face in. Newland couldn't take it anymore so he went freelance. Didn't that sound better than "I quit"?

It had at the time. But now things were getting tight. He needed this story. He needed it badly. And that meant sticking around to see this alleged ghost in person.

Though at this rate he supposed he could leave and come back closer to the day the ghost would turn up, but that would cost gas and time. And it wasn't like he had any place else to be.

"I couldn't possibly know why." Bitty shook her head in a sad sort of way. "Who knows why Confederate ghosts do anything that they do?"

Newland wanted to write something in his notebook, hoping that taking down pertinent information would make him appear attentive and understanding. But he didn't know what the heck he would write.

"So it's a Confederate ghost. And you've seen him in the cemetery behind your house, correct?"

7

"He comes in too." Bitty pointed to an empty spot on a shelf across the room. "See those decanters there? I used to have the whole collection, and he knocked one of those down about…let me see, that must've been about two weeks ago. Just crashed onto the floor."

Newland studied the line of glass cars. He had never seen anything like it in his life. The backend of each one had a screw-off lid, like the kind that came on a toothpaste tube.

"So he comes into the cemetery on the last Thursday of the month, but he comes inside whenever he chooses?"

"Yes." Bitty nodded her purple-rinsed head. "That's right."

He stood and went over to the bookcase looking at each one intently. He turned back to Bitty. "Do you mind?" He gestured toward one of the cars.

She waved a hand. "Go right ahead. The collection's ruined now."

Newland picked up one of the cars and examined it. It was made of dark glass, sort of brown, almost black. It had red painted accents and a matching red lid on the back.

He flipped it over and looked at the bottom. It came from one of those makeup catalogs. He didn't know how he knew that. Maybe some joke from high school or something because there'd never been any makeup in his house. After his mother, father, and brother died in a car accident when he was five, he'd been raised by his uncle with no women around to speak of. Unless he counted his uncle's occasional dates, but Joey Tran was not the kind to date women who wanted to hang out with kids. Though they all wore *a lot* of makeup.

Newland placed the decanter back on the shelf as gently as possible—careful not to set it too close to the empty spot that Bitty seemed to have reserved in memory of the broken decanter—and returned to his seat. The chintz sofa boasted a print made up of two-toned pink roses the size of dinner plates and a crocheted throw tossed across the back.

"You were in the room when it fell?" he asked.

Bitty shook her head. "I don't ever see him in the house."

Newland had picked up his notebook and pen ready to record all the details of her paranormal experiences. He let it fall again. "If you've never seen him in the house, how do you know he's ever *been* in the house?"

"It's the little things that tell me he's been around. The stove will be on and water boiling or the refrigerator door will be left open. And then my Stanley's decanter. God rest his soul. He collected those for years."

"I see," Newland said. But he didn't. He was not a collector of anything really. Maybe because his life had been sparse, growing up without parents. Or maybe it was just a personality thing. But most of his possessions would fit in a duffel bag, or at the very least in the trunk of his compact car. He never saw the need to hold on to things. It just weighed a person down.

"Let me make sure I have everything correct." Newland looked at the sparse summaries he had in his notes. Most everything that Bitty Duncan had told him was stored in his brain. "You have a Confederate ghost. He shows himself in the cemetery the last Thursday of the month, but he comes into the house on other days and wreaks havoc."

"He's not dangerous or destructive. Just sort of mischievous."

"I see," Newland said again.

Bitty nodded approvingly. "So you'll do it? You'll stay here until my ghost appears and then write a story to tell the world?"

Newland nodded. "Of course." It was the very reason he had come here after all. This was the story that was going to put him back in the game. And he would stop at nothing to get it.

****

Oskar barked out his welcome as Natalie pulled her little red convertible into the familiar driveway off Sycamore Lane. She'd been shocked when she got the call from her aunt's neighbor, Josephine, telling her that there was a strange car at her aunt's house. Natalie had an uneasy feeling she knew exactly who it was. She had to put a stop to this. And now.

"Come on, baby." She hooked Oskar's leash onto his red-studded collar and carefully set him on the uneven sidewalk. She had other things to do today besides get rid of the stranger her aunt had invited into the house. Again. This had to be the third reporter she'd invited in to write about her 'ghost.'

These days Natalie's life consisted of going around and cleaning up after all the members of her family. What she wouldn't give for just one day of no drama, no craziness, and no ghosts.

She gave one courtesy knock and let herself in. The house smelled like it always did, like old wood, furniture polish, and lilac. If she had her way she would bottle that scent and keep it with her forever. But today she didn't have time to bask in that glorious aroma. She had things to do.

"Aunt Bitty, it's me, Natalie." Her shiny red heels clicked against the hardwood, the sound echoed by Oskar's toenails. She still had to attend Gerald's sister's wedding tea this afternoon, so hopefully this wouldn't take very long. How long did it take to kick the paparazzi out of one's elderly aunt's house?

She wound her way across the waxed wooden floors and threadbare rugs until she made it to the parlor. Her aunt always entertained in the parlor.

"Just as I suspected," she muttered under her breath.

Sitting across from her aunt, dressed in an unlikely corduroy blazer, some sort of t-shirt, and jeans that had seen better days, the two-bit reporter who had come to take advantage of her aunt balanced a glass of iced tea and a small saucer of sugar cookies.

Her aunt pushed herself to her feet, and to his credit, so did the reporter.

He had to have been the tallest Asian man she had ever seen. He was at least six foot, with blue-black hair and dark, exotic eyes. And when he smiled, a tiny dimple winked at her from one corner of his mouth.

He took a step forward, extending his hand as he approached. "Newland Tran."

Natalie looked at his hand, then back up into those deep brown eyes. She searched her brain for something pithy to say, but before she could come up with even the smallest remark there was a flash of white, a growling howl, and a whimper.

"Aunt Bitty! Do something!" Thank heavens she hadn't taken Oskar off his leash. She used the strap attached to the harness to swing the poor pooch into her arms. But it was the handsome reporter who picked up the wallowing bundle of white Persian cat.

"Poor baby," Natalie crooned to Oskar. "I don't know why that mean ol' Mr. Piddles doesn't like you."

As if in answer to Natalie's words, Mr. Piddles hissed. Though Natalie wasn't much of a cat person, she didn't mind them normally, but Mr. Piddles was in a league all his own. He got along with Oskar some days—usually when Piddles was put in the sunroom for Oskar's visit— but there were times when he attacked for no good reason.

"Aunt Bitty, would you please get your cat?"

Her aunt took the spitting white bundle from the reporter and cuddled him close. "He's not normally like this, you know," she said.

Natalie shook her head and mouthed to their visitor, "He is, too."

Except the cat didn't seem to mind this tall stranger.

"Won't you come in, dear? I'd like to introduce you to—"

Natalie interrupted. "Can I talk to you for a minute, Aunt Bitty?" She looked pointedly to the reporter. "Alone."

If she had offended him he didn't show it. He merely stood there looking back at her. It was as if he had already won.

Won? There was nothing to win. This was not a competition. So why did it feel that way?

"I don't know, dear. I don't think we should—"

"He'll be fine, Aunt Bitty." Natalie took her aunt by the arm and led her out into the hallway. She scooted her down a couple more steps for good measure, then asked, "Why is he here?"

"Why, the ghost of course." Her aunt said the words in such an offhand manner that sometimes Natalie believed there might actually be a ghost in the house. But they all knew that wasn't true.

"Aunt Bitty," Natalie started, her voice softened with love and compassion. "There is no ghost. We've been over this."

Her aunt narrowed her gaze. Although her blue eyes still twinkled, Natalie knew this was the closest she got to angry. "There is so a ghost. And that's why Mr. Tran is here. He's going to help me prove it."

"There is no—"

Her aunt shook her head. "If there's no ghost, how do you explain my stove being left on and the refrigerator door being open and doors shutting throughout the house? And things falling off the shelves when no one's in the room?"

Natalie bit back a sigh and tried to keep her understanding tone. "You own a cat. He knocks the things off the shelves. The house is drafty and one good gust of wind through the front window will pull doors shut on the second floor. And…" She chose her words carefully as to not hurt her aunt's feelings, but something was going to have to be done about this and soon. "Are you sure you're not the one leaving the stove on and the refrigerator door open?"

"Posh." Aunt Bitty waved a dismissive hand at her. "I know y'all think that I'm going senile, but that's not true. I'm as sharp as I ever was, and I have a ghost." She said the words with a staggering finality and left Natalie standing in the hallway all alone.

"Now, Mr. Tran, about those cookies…"

Natalie shook her head and followed her aunt back into the parlor.

They were seated in the same places they had been when Natalie had burst in and all hell had broken loose between Mr. Piddles and Oskar. Except now her aunt held the cat in her lap stroking his fat, furry head. Even from this distance Natalie could hear the beast purring. She didn't know what her aunt saw in the beast.

"Natalie, dear, there you are."

Where else would I be?

"I was just telling Mr. Tran here all about my ghost."

Somehow Natalie managed to bite back the words "imaginary ghost" and found a seat across from the reporter. That way she could keep a good eye on him.

"So you've never actually seen him, is that correct?" Newland Tran asked.

"I told you I've seen him in the cemetery."

"But never in the house, correct?" he asked.

"Just what are your credentials, Mr. Tran?" Natalie broke in.

Tran looked up at her with those exotic brown eyes and shot her a fake smile. "You want to see my press pass?"

Natalie felt the heat rise in her cheeks and knew that she was turning as red as her shoes. "That won't be necessary. But who exactly do you work for?"

"I'm freelance."

A euphemism for *can't keep a job*. "Freelance?"

"That's right." His voice had turned to steel.

14

"Who do you plan on selling this story to, Mr. Tran?"

"Whoever offers the most, of course." His eyes turned as hard as his voice.

"I see. So this is all about money?"

"No dear," her aunt interjected. "This is just to get the word out. I think people should know that ghosts exist."

Natalie refused to roll her eyes at her aunt's insistence that ghosts were real and that one resided in her house. Right now she just needed to convince her aunt that there was no ghost. That she was becoming forgetful in her advancing age and needed to go live in an assisted living home. Why, Meadowbrook was just down the road from there, and it was a perfectly fine place to live. Natalie had checked it out herself, on the insistence of her parents of course.

"That's why I called *I Spy,*" her aunt continued.

"*I Spy*? Like at the checkout counter at the grocery store *I Spy*?"

Her aunt nodded. "Yes, of course. They always have stories about Big Foot and aliens and all sorts of things like that. I figured they would be most interested in my ghost."

Natalie shot the reporter as hard a look as she could muster. "If she called *I Spy*, how did you get the information?"

Tran shifted uncomfortably on the Louis Some-teenth divan and cleared his throat. "I, uh, used to work for them."

"Used to?"

"That's right." He seemed to regain back some of his confidence and managed to straighten his spine and meet her steady gaze.

"Why don't you work for them any longer?"

"I decided to go out on my own," he said, teeth clenched.

"I see."

"I don't think you do."

"If you don't work for them, then how did you hear about my aunt's story?"

He shifted in his seat. "I just remember seeing it one time."

Hacked into the company computer was more like it. People just didn't change their passwords like they really should.

"Have we forgotten about the cookies?" Aunt Bitty interjected.

"No, Aunt Bitty." Natalie chose a cookie and took a bite to show her enthusiasm for the treat.

Her aunt smiled. Just the reaction she wanted.

"Since that's all settled, I'll show you to your room." Aunt Bitty stood and placed Mr. Piddles on the chair where she had been just seconds before.

Tran stood as well.

Natalie jumped to her feet. "What do you mean 'show him to his room?'"

"Mr. Tran's going to be staying here, dearie."

"What? There's a perfectly good motel just down the road." This was going too far.

"Natalie, you know he can't find the ghost if he's not in the house."

"There is no ghost." Natalie's diplomacy where the specter was concerned was running thin.

"You don't believe in the ghost, Miss... I don't think I got your name."

"No, I don't," Natalie said. "And it's Coleman. Natalie Coleman." She didn't bother to offer a hand out to shake.

Tran made no move to greet her in such a manner either. Instead he wrote something in his little notebook. But she couldn't read it from this angle. Or maybe it was some sort of shorthand designed to hide secrets from the eyes of others.

She shook the thought away. She'd been watching too many late-night detective movies.

She turned to her aunt. "Aunt Bitty, surely you realize that he cannot stay here with you."

"Who else is he going to stay with, dear? I already live here after all, and if he's here and I'm here…" Her already wrinkled brow creased with her confusion.

Natalie took her aunt by the elbow and pulled her slightly away from the prying eyes of the reporter. It would do no good to take her out into the hallway again. She was certain that he would follow behind and hear every word.

"You don't know him, Aunt Bitty. You can't invite him to stay here at the house with you. He could be a murderer or a rapist—"

Aunt Bitty patted her on the hand reassuringly. "He's none of those things, dear. He's a reporter."

****

Newland bit back his laughter as he watched the spunky Natalie engage with her aunt. Despite her obvious animosity toward him, he found her somehow…cute, with her brown hair pulled back into a perfect bun and her blue eyes flashing with distrust. She was feisty and loyal. And he was glad that sweet Miss Duncan had someone like Natalie watching out for her.

"I don't care what he is. He can't stay here," Natalie said, her voice firm, as if she were talking to a five-year-old instead of an eighty-five-year-old.

Newland moved a little bit closer, trying to get more of their conversation.

Her aunt gave a firm nod. "See, I own the house, and I have invited him to stay."

It was obvious where Natalie Coleman got her spunk.

Once again he hid his laughter. He lowered his head and rubbed his eyes hoping the motions would conceal his mirth.

Natalie sighed. "Aunt Bitty…"

But the old woman shook her head. "I have decided."

Another sigh. "Then you leave me no choice."

"You do what you have to do. And I'll do what I have to do."

Bitty Duncan moved away from her niece and came to stand by Newland.

Once again, he flipped his notebook shut and gave her an understanding smile. "Come, Mr. Tran. I'll show you to your room."

He picked up his duffel bag and gave Natalie a quick nod before following Miss Duncan out of the room.

As he left he thought he heard a growl of frustration. Certainly not. A girl as pretty as Natalie Coleman surely didn't growl.

CHAPTER TWO

Other than Malcolm Daniel's place in Jefferson County, Newland had never been in such a house. It wasn't as big as Malcolm's plantation home by far, but somehow the walls had seeped up the history of the place. It seemed to hang around like an aura of good intentions and past deeds.

"How old did you say the house was again?" he asked as he followed Bitty up the stairs.

"Let's see now… We bought the house in 1950 and it was over a hundred years old then. It was built in 1824, then part of it burned in 1845, I believe. They rebuilt it. That's the wing on the back where the kitchen is. Nasty kitchen fires in that day." She spoke as if she'd been there to witness the whole thing.

Newland bit back his smile. There was just something about Bitty Duncan that made him happy. Maybe because he'd never had a grandmother of his own. Or maybe she just had that kind of personality. Whatever it was, he was going to enjoy his stay here.

"So that makes it almost two hundred years old, right?" She gave him an apologetic smile. "Math never was my strong subject."

But he was sure she had excelled at charm school.

"Now, you can stay in this room here." She opened the door to a large suite. The furnishings appeared to be straight out of the Civil War, and given the history of the house, it was a strong possibility. There was an antique washstand with a pitcher and a bowl, though he didn't think it had seen water in half a century. The four-poster bed stood majestically in the center of the room raised up enough that it required a small stepladder. He could only hope he didn't have a bad dream and roll off in the middle of the night.

Cabbage rose wallpaper, gilded frames containing black and white photographs, even the rugs in soft hues of rose and cream added to the delicate yet long surviving core of the room.

"This is your closet." Miss Duncan flung open the doors of a freestanding cabinet, revealing shelves and a hanging bar. It looked like an extra-large jewelry box.

He had seen things like that in the movies, but never knew they really existed. Of course, he and his uncle barely had furniture, much less antiques.

"And the bathroom is there. That's why the room is so small, dear. We had to take out part of it to make the bathroom." She gave him a wink. "But it's worth it."

She moved toward the door and paused, one hand on the cut glass knob. "You just make yourself at home now, you hear? I'm going to see about Natalie, but you come down whenever you're ready." She shot him that Southern beauty queen smile, then let herself out of the room.

Newland was hesitant to place his beat-up duffel bag on such a beautiful lace counterpane; in fact, the whole house felt a little untouchable. The parlor had been bad enough, but somehow with Aunt Bitty's collection of Avon car decanters, it had at least appeared lived-in and comfortable. This room looked like something out of Antiques Anonymous.

He sat his duffel bag on the floor by the freestanding closet. Even left it pulled closed. He didn't need anything from it. It wasn't like it mattered if his clothes were wrinkled. Most of them were T-shirts anyway. His long-standing indulgence.

Bitty Duncan might collect glass cars, but concert T-shirts were his weakness. Shirts from every concert he had ever attended, shirts he'd found in thrift stores, it didn't matter. If it had a name of the band on it, he wanted it.

The one regret in his life was that he'd never learned to play an instrument. Something always seemed to hold him back. He'd always had to work, to get a job mowing grass or carrying somebody's groceries. At night he fell into bed exhausted from trying to make his lunch money for the next day. But if his life had been different—if his family hadn't died—who knows what might have happened. He could've been the greatest rock star ever known.

Instead he was a freelance reporter, talking to an eccentric old lady about a ghost that may or may not exist.

Newland shook his head. How had his life slipped into this?

****

Natalie enjoyed her convertible, probably more than she should. But she loved to ride with the top down and the wind blowing her hair. Okay, so her hair was usually put up in a tidy bun, but she still enjoyed it.

Today was no different. It was warm outside, and she had turned on the air in her car to cool her while she enjoyed the sun and the wind.

She pulled up in front of the apartment she shared with her sixteen-year-old brother Aubie. She knew he hated the place. But she liked it. He thought they should move on up and buy a house in town, but the apartment was just perfect as far as she was concerned. She grabbed Oskar's leash and led him out of the car and down the sidewalk. She rounded the corner to their apartment door and let herself in.

"Aubie?" she called as she shut the door behind her. He should be home by now. School was out, and the city council didn't have a meeting today. "Aubie?"

She headed for the kitchen knowing that as much as he was not the typical teenager when it came to hobbies, he definitely was when it came to food. That was where she found him, stuffing his face with peanut butter and crackers while thumbing through something on his phone.

"Aubie," she said. "You need to get up and pack a bag. We're going to Aunt Bitty's."

"What?" Dry bits of cracker flew out as he tried to talk with his mouth full. Another typical teenager thing that kept him just this side of savant.

"I said we're going to Aunt Bitty's."

Aubie swallowed, then took a big drink of juice. "I heard what you said. But why?"

Natalie rolled her eyes. "She's got some reporter over there going to help her find the ghost."

"Again?" Aubie shook his head and went back to his snack. "I don't see how this affects me."

"It affects you because we're going over there until he leaves. She can't stay there with some stranger."

"Sure she can."

"No. She can't." She said the words succinctly hoping that this time they would sink in. *Nice try.* He was a teenager after all.

"Why do I have to go?"

"Because I do."

"I can stay by myself."

"Aubie, you're sixteen. I can't leave you here by yourself."

"Sure you can. My friends stay by themselves all the time."

It was an age-old argument between the two of them. How could Natalie explain to him that he was her responsibility since their parents were off in the Mediterranean, yachting and soaking up the sun on some tiny island? He was her charge, and she would not be able to forgive herself if something happened to him because she had left him alone.

"Go pack a bag, Aubie."

With all the drama that only a teenager could produce, Aubie stood, flung his chair back under the table, then flounced from the room. He couldn't have executed the exit better if he'd been a girl.

Natalie sighed, fed one of the peanut butter crackers to Oskar, then let him off his leash. She would give him a few minutes to run around the house before she packed her own bag.

The last thing she wanted to do was stay with her aunt and this reporter, but she had to. Somehow she had been left as guardian of the family, and though the job was full-time, it didn't pay well in appreciation.

She padded her way to her room, Oskar clicking behind her. She had a downstairs bedroom just off the kitchen, while Aubie's room took up most of the upstairs. She figured that was fair since his home office was up there as well. All she did in her room was sleep.

She grabbed her leopard print suitcase from the bottom of her closet, then started piling in her clothes. She had a couple of things to do this week.

Lunch with her boyfriend Gerald tomorrow. She tossed in her green silk dress and camel-colored heels. The town meeting tonight. She looked down at herself. Her polka dot dress and red patent shoes were a little over the top for a town meeting but had been just right for a high tea...

"Crap!" She had forgotten all about the wedding tea. Gerald would be furious with her. After all, it was for his sister's wedding.

As much as Natalie loved Gerald Davenport, she disliked his sister twice that much. Vanessa Davenport would have her name officially changed to Princess if she thought it would get her further in life. Unlike the Colemans, the Davenports came from new money. Though Natalie watched every penny in and out of the family coffers, her parents treated money much like the Davenports did. Like it was a toy to be enjoyed instead of the burden that it truly was. Natalie spent her days going to fancy lunches, high teas, and meetings of one sort or another as she ran the Coleman Foundation. Their money had been made eons ago when her great-great-great-great and maybe even one more great grandfather, Arvest Coleman, had gone to Texas after Davy Crockett. But instead of dying in the Alamo, Arvest had discovered oil in a land that he loved more than Mississippi.

He stayed in the Republic and sent money home to his wife and children. Now, generations later, that money had built on itself. All Natalie had to do was make sure that it went to the appropriate places. It was a meaningless job, really. Though she couldn't turn it over to anyone else. It was her responsibility to watch over Arvest's hard work and discovery. Lord knew her parents weren't going to.

She picked up her cellphone and dialed the number from her contact list. It rang twice before he picked up.

"Hello?"

She almost melted to hear the sound of his voice. "Gerald."

He was by far the handsomest man in Turtle Creek. And even though the town was small that was saying a lot. There were some good-looking people in this town. Suddenly the image of Newland Tran popped into her head. She pushed it away and concentrated on the man on the other end of the line. He was her type—not tall, dark, and Asian, but blond and oh-so considerate.

"You never made it." His words were clipped.

"Gerald, I am so sorry. I had to go to Aunt Bitty's real quick. She had a reporter there." She shook her head even though she knew he couldn't see her.

"Is this about the ghost?"

"I'm afraid it is." Natalie folded her blue dress into the suitcase and went in search of her matching shoes.

"Why is she still living there?" Gerald asked.

Natalie tucked her phone in between her shoulder and her ear, so she could fold her black pencil skirt and white silk blouse. That should do fine for tonight's town meeting and any other casual excursion that might come up. "It's not like I can have her committed." Though she suspected that if Gerald had his way that was exactly what she would do.

For all of his physical beauty, wealth, power and mostly charming demeanor, his one flaw was his aversion to her aunt. Natalie wasn't sure why, but not everyone got along with her eccentric Aunt Bitty.

"I was just calling to say sorry about that tea. I'll try to make it up to your sister." Natalie managed not to gag as she said the words. She wasn't even sure why Vanessa would want her there except so that she knew that she had the attention of everyone in town.

"I made an excuse for you," he said, his voice sounding a little on the exasperated side. How she wished she could look into those green eyes and see what he was thinking at that exact moment.

"I appreciate that." She worked hard keeping up with everybody, making sure that her parents' account had money in it when they needed it, that her genius brother made it to school on time, and that her aunt didn't burn her house down and blame it on the ghost. She didn't mind the work per se, but she hated that Gerald didn't seem to value her efforts at all.

"I don't think I'll be so lucky next time."

"With any luck there won't be a next time, right?" Natalie said the words with a lighthearted tone, but they both knew they weren't true. There would be plenty of next times. In fact, her life seemed to be a series of next times, unfortunate happenings, and outright craziness. As much as she tried to keep everything under control, smoothed out, and wrinkle free, it seemed that everything crinkled at the same time.

"Yes," he said. His voice sounded distracted, and Natalie knew that she was losing him to whatever was on his desk just then. A new fundraiser or charitable promotion. Like her, he managed the family fortune.

"I'll let you go now. I've got to get packed for Aunt Bitty's."

"What?" That got his attention. "You're staying there?"

"I can't leave her all by herself with a strange reporter. I don't know this man from Adam's house cat. How can I let him stay at my aunt's house alone with her?"

"So you and Aubie are going to stay there so he can kill three of you in your sleep, is that right?"

"Gerald, stop saying things like that. Everything is going to be fine. I'm more concerned about the family silver than I am a triple homicide."

"Uh-huh."

She had lost him again. "I'll talk to you later, okay?" She turned off the phone without waiting for his answer.

****

On any given day, Natalie found dinner with her aunt to be odd, but tonight it was even more so. Bitty sat at the head of the table chatting nonstop. Newland Tran sat next to Bitty on the left, while Natalie was on the right. Aubie sat across from his aunt. The cat wound in and out of their feet waiting for someone to drop a morsel that he could snatch up. For all his pedigree and breeding, the cat was an alley cat straight up.

Being directly across from Tran at the table was a tad on the trying side. Natalie told herself it was because she wasn't used to having somebody sit in that chair when she ate with her aunt. Truth was she wasn't used to anybody being in attendance when she ate with Aunt Bitty.

"Aubie," she started with a frown. "Put your phone away at the table."

"Uh-huh." He didn't bother to look up from what was coming through. Knowing him it could've been an online comic or the city charter.

"Aubie." She said it louder this time.

"Yeah, yeah." He didn't bother to look up from the screen.

Natalie sighed. Was it too much to ask to have his attention at the table?

She reached across the table and plucked the device from his fingers, setting it in the chair next to her.

"Hey!"

Natalie shook her head. "Eat your supper, and I'll give it back to you." If he hadn't eaten so many peanut butter crackers this afternoon he might be hungrier for supper. As it was, the southern-cooked meal on his plate was much more nutritious than the snack he'd scarfed down earlier.

He looked as if he was about to protest, then thought better of it and picked up his piece of cornbread. He took a bite and chewed, glaring at her all the while.

Natalie looked back at her plate. She was used to such behavior from Aubie. One day he would miss her when she was gone. When she... Well, when she married Gerald she wouldn't leave; she would stay right there in town. But there would come a day when she wouldn't be making sure Aubie's socks matched or that he went to study hall with as much regularity as he did the town meetings.

"So, Mr. Tran," Aunt Bitty started. "What do you think of our little town?"

"Please, call me Newland," he said. To his credit he didn't choke when he had been asked what he thought of Turtle Creek, Mississippi.

Natalie had looked him up online right after she finished packing her suitcase, and although he seemed to be legitimate and completely on the level as a reporter, he was a Yankee.

Aubie checked his watch, then stood with haste. He grabbed his phone from the table where Natalie had left it, then shoved it into his pocket as he continued to nibble on his cornbread. "I've got to go now."

Natalie barely had time to register Newland's bewildered look before she pushed herself back from her place as well. "You need to stay and finish your supper."

"No time." He threw the words over his shoulder as he continued toward the front door.

Natalie turned back to her aunt and their wonderful houseguest. "I've got to go, Aunt Bitty. I'll help clean up when I get back, okay? This shouldn't take more than a couple of hours." So much for changing into something less polka-dotty before the meeting.

"What shouldn't take more than a couple hours?" the reporter asked.

"Why the town meeting, dear," Aunt Bitty said. She patted his hand where it lay on the table.

Newland nodded to where Aubie had just made his exit. "He's what? Thirteen? Twelve?"

"He's sixteen," Natalie said. *Going on eight when it comes to video games and thirty on the matters of politics.*

"He's sixteen, and he's going to the town meeting?"

Natalie shrugged. "He sort of has to. You see, he's the mayor."

CHAPTER THREE

The mayor?

Newland stood, tossing his linen napkin onto the table beside his plate. He almost felt guilty using the piece of cloth to wipe his mouth. Who these days used linen tablecloths and napkins for an everyday dinner?

Scratch that. He was in the South now, and they called it supper.

"He's the mayor?" He turned back to Natalie, but she was already striding toward the front door. He gave his hostess an apologetic smile. "I think I should go to this. In the interest of back story." He nodded reassuringly, hoping she would buy the excuse. This was just one more story he could add to his profile. Small town mayor at sixteen? It was beautiful.

"Go right ahead, dear." Bitty Duncan waved him away as if she was prepared for such abandonment.

Newland wasn't sure if she had suspected all along that he would follow behind, or if she was just clueless to the tension that surrounded her niece and nephew.

He gave her another small smile, then hurried toward the door.

Newland cleared the house just as Natalie was getting into some sort of low-slung car. He didn't know the make right off, but it was expensive and seemed a little out of place in this dusty southern town.

Maybe there's a story there too.

"Hey… Natalie…" He rushed over to her car. "Can I catch a ride with you to the meeting?"

He could drive himself, but if he rode with Natalie, he would have that many more opportunities to talk to her, plus save on his own gas. Funds were getting mighty low in the Tran Fund.

She seemed to mull it over for an eternity before she finally gave him a stiff chin nod.

"Okay." Her voice ended on a note that sounded like she was about to say more, like maybe give him a list of rules of things he could and couldn't do in her car. But she just jerked her head toward the side and waited for him to get in.

Newland wasted no time.

She backed out, and they were off.

"How's your brother getting to the meeting?"

Natalie didn't bother to take her eyes from the road as she gave a one-shoulder shrug. "He either rode his bike or took a cab."

"He doesn't have a car?"

This time she did look away from her driving and shot him an incredulous look. "Of course not. He doesn't know how to drive."

"But you said he was sixteen."

"Do you think I'm really going to let my immature baby brother behind the wheel of a car?"

Newland bit back a chuckle. "But you let him run the town."

He wished he could see the look in her so-blue eyes, but she had already turned back to the front. "That's different. There aren't nearly as many lives at stake with him at the helm of the city."

This time Newland did laugh. But it didn't draw any attention from Natalie. He supposed she expected it.

They drove in silence for a few moments before Newland ran a loving hand across the dash of her car. "Nice ride."

Natalie made a noise that sounded like some sort of agreement, but he couldn't be sure.

"You don't see many cars like this in small towns. This had to have set you back a pretty penny."

"Listen, Mr. Tran—"

"Newland," he corrected, but at least she said it correctly, with the "ah" a sound.

She coughed. "Newland," she acquiesced. "I've had more than my fair share of dealings with the press, and I know every trick in the book."

"What's that supposed to mean?"

"It means that I'm not going to answer a bunch of questions about my family or my life here in Turtle Creek, my brother as the mayor or the nonexistent ghost in my aunt's house just because you complimented my car."

Newland threw up his hands in surrender. "Whoa, all I said was you have a nice ride."

She chanced another look in his direction. "Thank you." Her tone was unreadable. He didn't have time to start another conversation as they pulled up in front of the school.

"The town meeting is here?"

"In the gym, yes." Natalie got out and dropped her keys in her purse but didn't bother to lock the car. Now that he'd sat in it, he knew it was a Jag and cost upwards of a hundred thousand dollars. But he supposed in a town the size of Turtle Creek, if anyone stole it, they would be easy to find. It had to be the only one around.

"So what's on the agenda for tonight?"

"Agenda?" She seemed distracted. "You mean the meeting? I believe tonight we'll be talking about whether or not to change the school colors and if something should be done about Harvey Johnson's hound dog."

Newland stopped as sure as his feet had been glued to the parking lot. He looked around at the milling faces. It seemed half the town had turned out to discuss these important matters. "You mean everyone is here to talk about the school colors and a hound dog?"

Natalie nodded. "Of course. We take politics very seriously around here."

Evidently, Newland thought as they walked into the gymnasium. Rows of chairs had been lined up on the gym floor, and a table had been placed in front with a line of chairs waiting behind it.

He had seen enough to realize that the chairs were for the townspeople who didn't want to sit in or had spilled out of the bleachers, and the table and chairs under the basketball goal were the places where the town council and the mayor would sit.

Aubie Coleman sat in the middle of that long, white, cloth-covered table—the honored seat reserved for the mayor—awaiting the meeting to start.

Natalie slipped out of her red shoes and hooked them on the fingers of one hand before walking smartly across the gym floor. She perched on the edge of one seat in the front row. Newland was forced to follow behind her, noticing that the other women who wore heels had, out of consideration for the wooden floor, removed their shoes as well.

She sat ramrod straight in her chair looking straight ahead. He supposed she was serious about not giving him any more information about anything at all.

I wonder what has her so up in arms. But he doubted he would be there long enough to find out. He had ten days before the ghost turned back up and after that he planned to hit the city limits as fast as he could.

Until then... He allowed his gaze to wander around the gym. Things were painted in an unfortunate combination of green and black. Though most of it was simply black. The center ring on the basketball court, the wall in front of the far-end bleachers, the doorways leading into what had to be the locker rooms, everything black, with touches of green, reminiscent of that of the famous tractors.

No wonder they wanted to change the school colors. He looked to one wall where a huge green and black turtle had been painted. Someone had drawn a ferocious looking face on the turtle, or at least they had tried to. On him, it just looked constipated.

Newland leaned closer to Natalie. "Instead of changing the school colors, how about the mascot?"

She cut her eyes in his direction with a look that clearly said, *"Will you shut up?"*

He didn't know what her problem was. The meeting hadn't even started yet.

About that time Aubie stood, rapping what looked to be the end of a croquet mallet against the table.

"Here he, hear ye," he said in that same singsong voice he'd used earlier. "I declare this town meeting now in session."

Aubie called forth the secretary to read the minutes from the last meeting. But since at the last meeting they had talked about making Earl Rogers paint his gas station to help spruce up Main Street and figuring out how to tear down Jude Maness's barn before it fell on top of some unfortunate cows, Newland once again allowed his attention to wander once around the room. It seemed that most everyone there was a farmer of some sort, all dressed in overalls with mud-caked work boots. There were a few suits among the people, but not many. Most of the women had the same uniform of dress as women everywhere. He could almost pick them out as they sat there. Yoga mom, baseball mom, cheer mom. Some things were the same North and South.

He cut his glance toward the woman at his side. She was the one he couldn't figure out. Dark brown hair pulled back into a smart bun. The tresses hadn't dared loosen as they drove, even with the top down. He wanted to reach out and touch it and see if it felt as soft as it looked. Her makeup was light, but immaculate and precise. Perfect eyeliner, perfect amount of mascara, perfect shade of shadow. Just a tiny bit of blush on high cheekbones, and maybe a dusting of powder across the nose that might have had freckles on it. He couldn't quite tell from this angle, though he hoped it was true. That was what she needed to break that I'm-so-perfect-I-don't-know-what-to-do-with-myself attitude. Freckles. Yeah.

Her diamond-studded earrings twinkled in the overhead lights when she turned slightly in his direction. As if sensing his gaze, she turned around to face the front once more. Everything about her from her car to her fingernails screamed money, but where did such money come from in a small town? Did it really matter?

Anything could matter at this point, as far as Newland was concerned. A story was a story. If there was a story dealing with the town, he would walk away with that one as well as this ghost—existent or nonexistent—in Bitty Duncan's graveyard. He didn't care. All he needed was one good story, one *really* good story. Between the ghost, the sixteen-year-old mayor, and the old money sitting next to him, surely that story was in Turtle Creek.

****

Natalie could feel his eyes studying her as she tried to listen to the town meeting. School colors and hound dogs might not be important to him, but they were important to Turtle Creek and that meant they were important to her.

She sat with her chin up and pretended she couldn't feel his gaze roving over her. Almost like a touch, a caress.

After what seemed like an eternity, they agreed to take the black out of the school colors, and just leave them green and white for the time being. Mainly because no one wanted to buy new uniforms for the school. She'd have to talk to someone about some donations to the school to help jump-start that program. Every time the teams went somewhere, they looked as if they were in mourning instead of playing high school basketball. The cheerleaders looked like generic cans of peas all lined up in a row. White uniforms, blocky black letters, a big TC across their chest. It was sad really, but it had been that way since Natalie had been a cheerleader here in this very gym.

But she didn't have time to think about that right now. She had to make sure that her brother knew—mayor or not—that he was spending the night at Aunt Bitty's house tonight. She started toward him where he stood talking to the principal but didn't make it more than two feet before she was stopped.

"Natty Nat."

She closed her eyes at the sound of that voice. The last person that she wanted to talk to. Ever. She whirled around and opened her eyes. "Darrell Hughes. So nice to see you." She almost choked on the words. And where Darrell was, there was also, "Gilbert." She nodded to his twin. She had been at odds with these two fellows since high school. They teased her mercilessly and in general made her life harder than it needed to be. They were always asking for money for one project or another trying to get her in on the "ground floor" of whatever big scheme they had going on at the time. There had been the plastic cow vomit prank idea they had come up with, along with the skunk-flavored gum and the spun-sugar T-shirts for spring break. That had been a doozy. The girls would be hosed down and the T-shirts would melt. Natalie rolled her eyes at the thought.

"Listen, fellows," she stated as nicely as she possibly could, "If you have another product idea, then bring it to the office tomorrow, okay? I have some business to take care of here tonight, and I don't have time to listen to your pitch." If they brought something in tomorrow she doubted very seriously it would be a product she could get behind. But still she would listen. She always did.

"We ain't here to talk about that," Gilbert said. Neither one of them had the sense God gave a goose, but they were good old boys at heart. They were slightly mischievous, a little on the ornery side, but thank heavens they weren't mean. Each one was like a mountain and both were strong enough to crush rocks.

Natalie somehow kept herself from wilting in relief. "Oh?"

"Yeah, we got this other thing going—" Darrell broke off as Gilbert elbowed him hard in the ribs. "Hey, why'd you do—" but he didn't finish the sentence as his brother's look cut him off but quick. Natalie was sure all the secrecy had to do with it being such a fabulous idea that they didn't want anyone else within earshot to hear it. But she didn't say as much.

"Well, that's nice then." She smiled at each of them in turn, so very aware that Newland Tran was right behind her, absorbing every word of their exchange.

"Hey, you that reporter from Chicago?" Gilbert asked.

Newland nodded. "I am."

Darrell dragged a hard gaze over Newland, starting with his tan corduroy blazer that had seen better days to his Falling in Reverse T-shirt and ratty blue jeans, and on to his equally ratty Converse Chuck Taylor All Star shoes. "You don't look like a reporter from the big city."

"Gotta keep things interesting." He chuckled, and Natalie hated that she liked the sound.

In fact, there wasn't a whole lot about Newland Tran that wasn't likable, except that he was here. And breathing the air around her. And surely out to exploit her aunt.

She knew something had to be wrong with him. He seemed legit enough on the Internet, but if he had gotten released from his job at *I Spy* and then decided to go "freelance," then why would he pick a story like this to get himself back on his feet? The chances of there even being a story were slim to none. And yet he seemed to be basing the return of his career on it? Not a smart move as far she was concerned. And if there was one thing Newland Tran looked it was smart. At least smarter than Darrell and Gilbert, for sure. No, there was something else to Tran. And she vowed to keep an eye on the family silver until he was gone.

****

Natalie leaned her head back and let the nighttime breeze wash over her. She had let Oskar out in the grass for one last potty break before bed. But she couldn't allow herself a break. She ran over in her mind her schedule for the next day.

She needed to talk to someone about school uniforms, needed to figure out what Darrell and Gilbert were up to, needed to run an inventory on the things in the house to make sure Tran wasn't walking off with anything more valuable than one of her aunt's perfume bottles. And a host of other things that kept the foundation going.

After the argument with her brother over returning with her to Aunt Bitty's house, Natalie's head was pounding. It felt good to be out in the air, breathing in the familiar smells of the night-blooming jasmine and the gardenias that her aunt kept at the end of the porch.

The screen door creaked open, and then shut quietly behind whoever came out onto the porch. Natalie didn't bother to open her eyes and look to see who it was. It couldn't be Aubie; he never shut the door quietly behind him, and her aunt was more than likely inside still watching *Dancing with the Stars*. That left only one person, and she wasn't sure she wanted to see him.

"You don't trust me."

Well, give him extra points for getting right to the point.

"Why should I?" Again she didn't bother to open her eyes. She kept her head back, trying to relax as much as she could while she waited for Oskar.

Okay, the truth of the matter was she had a hard time relaxing any time of day. She had too many responsibilities to let her guard down much and at the end of the day it was hard to let it go at all. But hopefully soon Gerald would ask her to marry him, and Aunt Bitty would agree to go live in Meadowbrook, and by some miracle Aubie would become as mature in all matters as he was in matters of city affairs. But until then...

"Hey, I'm a nice guy. I mean, what's wrong with me? You were nicer to those two lumps at the gym than you are to me."

Natalie pushed herself upright in the big wooden rocker and finally turned to look at him. "I've known those two lumps my entire life. We started kindergarten together. And as far as being nice to you, I've been nothing but cordial to you ever since you got here."

"Wow, you are uptight."

"I am most certainly not uptight." He'd hit a nerve, but there was no way that she was agreeing to his assessment of her. He didn't know anything about her. He didn't know what she did every day and how she managed to keep everybody's lives in order. He didn't know what kind of effort and energy it took to make sure that things got done. Or that she was the only one who could do it. She was the last Coleman left who had sense enough to make sure that the fortune was kept intact.

"So you're not uptight. Got it." She heard him chuckle, and the sound went right through her.

"I don't see what's so funny. You're the one here searching for a ghost. And yet I don't see any ghost-searching equipment."

"I beg your pardon?" This time his voice turned from filled with humor to a little on edge. Good, that was exactly how she wanted him.

"I did some research today, Mr. Tran. And I know that there are all sorts of ghost-hunting equipment. So if you are serious about hunting this ghost, why don't you have any of those plasmatic meters or those temperature gauges that show that a spirit is in the room, huh?"

He didn't seem so confident then. And Natalie wondered if she had hit her own nerve with Newland Tran.

"So just because I don't have some sort of meter or a temperature gauge you think I'm a fake?"

"You said it. Not me."

"I came here because your aunt told me a story, and I believed her. You're the one who doesn't. I don't need plasmatic meters and gauges that check temperature and all the other things that people on TV think a person needs to hunt ghosts. I have the word of a beautiful lady who assures me that the last Thursday of the month a ghost will appear.

We should see him next week, and that's all the proof I need."

CHAPTER FOUR

Tran stood and stretched his legs. Natalie was torn between standing just so he wouldn't tower over her and sitting back and waiting to see what he would do next.

He started down the porch steps.

"Where you going?" Natalie almost slapped a hand over her mouth. What business was it of hers where he was going? Except that she felt a little responsible for him since he was there and staying in her aunt's house.

He turned and shot her a grin. In the dying light of the day she couldn't tell if it was mischievous or just a grin. "I'm going over to the cemetery. You want to come with me?"

Natalie shook her head, then thought better of it. "Okay." She stood and started down the porch steps after him.

The cemetery sat behind her aunt's house and took up most of the back side of the block. It was an old cemetery, the kind in horror films with a wrought-iron fence made of spear-shaped posts and a creaky old gate that led inside. And she had never, ever gone into the cemetery. Not even in daylight. So what made her think it was a good idea to go at sundown? And with a man like Newland Tran?

"What do you expect to see here?"

He didn't stop walking as he answered. "I don't know. But it seems like the best place to start if this is where the ghost usually is."

"There is no ghost."

Newland stopped and whirled around to face her.

Natalie came to an abrupt halt as well, craning her neck back to look at him.

"Let's get one thing straight right now. You don't believe in the ghost. I do. So let's just agree to disagree. Every time I mention the ghost, how about you not deny his existence? Then come the last Thursday of the month, we'll see. Okay?"

Natalie nodded mutely. She supposed that was the least she could do. She had to keep up with Newland, find out what he was doing and make sure he didn't take advantage of her aunt and rob them all blind. If that meant admitting there was a ghost, or at the very least not denying the ghost, then she would do it.

"Good." He turned back around and started toward the cemetery once again.

The grave markers were old, some of them dating well before the War of Northern Aggression. A few were barely legible, while others seemed to have somehow escaped the erosion, still showing off names, dates, and relationships the person had enjoyed in his or her life. Several of the stones had sunk in recent years leaving them drunkenly crooked, turning this way and that as they tilted toward the earth.

"So do you think the ghost is buried here?"

She could do this, Natalie coached herself. "He might've been at one time." See? That wasn't so hard.

"What do you mean at one time?"

Natalie walked over to one grave staring at the arched tombstone with its eroded etching. "Back in the '60s, I think it was. Maybe the '70s. They came through and exhumed a lot of the Confederate soldiers from cemeteries like this. Some of them had even been buried out in the open on people's land and property and things. One farmer had three graves in his pasture. They dug them up and took them to the national cemetery."

"They?"

"The government. They decided that the Confederate soldiers deserved as much respect for fighting for their beliefs as the Union soldiers did fighting for theirs. So they exhumed their bodies and took them to a national cemetery. Some went up to Shiloh, some over to Corinth. There's a big cemetery there, you know. Anyway, the ones that were buried here were dug up and taken elsewhere. So if he had been buried here before, he's not here now." She pointed to an indention in the earth, almost like a shallow hole dug in between two graves. There was no stone marker, yet the ground still showed where it had been. "Like there."

Newland walked over to look at the indention in the earth. He studied it from this angle and that, and Natalie wondered what he was looking for. It was nothing more than a hole. At least now anyway. Once upon a time it had been a grave.

"So why would a Confederate soldier hang out in a graveyard where he wasn't buried?"

"Why does a Confederate ghost do anything?" She quoted her aunt with a smile.

Newland chuckled. And Natalie liked the sound. Wait. No, she didn't. The sound was neutral. It didn't dance upon her skin like the wind at night. It was just a chuckle.

"So why do you think he shows up the last Thursday of the month?"

Natalie thought about it a minute. She had no idea why a ghost would haunt a cemetery one night of the month. Again, further proof that there was no ghost and there was no haunting, but she had said she would play along, and she would. "Maybe that was the day he died?"

He nodded. "Or the day he was buried?"

"What about the day he was exhumed?"

"All good theories," Newland said.

Despite the fact that it was May in Mississippi, a cold wind blew through. Natalie shuddered. Ghost or no ghost, being in an old cemetery after dark was a little creepy.

"So do you have what you need? Can we go back now?"

He turned to study her with those dark eyes. "You're not scared, are you?"

Natalie somehow kept her teeth from chattering. Okay, so she was scared. But she wasn't admitting that to him. "Of course not. There's no ghost, remember?"

Tran nodded. "I was just fixing to remind you of that."

"Fixing?" she asked. "Did you just say 'fixing to'?"

He nodded and despite the dwindling light she could almost see a blush rise to his cheeks. "I spent some time in Tennessee last year."

"I see," Natalie said. So Mr. Chicago had spent time in Tennessee. Enough time that he picked up a little bit of the slang. Maybe he wasn't all bad. "What brought you to Tennessee?"

Tran winced. "It's sort of complicated, but you could say a girl, a murder charge, and a story about Elvis."

"Sounds reasonable."

The two of them laughed.

"Seriously, though, can we go back now?" she asked.

"Sure."

Newland said the words, but he made no move to leave the cemetery. Instead he turned away from her and looked at the lot as a whole.

Natalie tried to imagine it from his point of view. She had seen it time after time over the course of her life. It never changed, except maybe a few of the graves were a little deeper and a couple of the tombstones were a little more slanted, but there were no new graves here, no new tombstones. They were all weathered and beaten, most of the graves slightly overgrown with weeds and grass. There were no flowers, no flags, no mourners for these ancient deceased.

A large oak tree stood at one end of the cemetery, and Natalie wondered if the mighty oak's roots had caused the tilting of the tombstones closest to it. Despite the majestic oak's beauty, somehow the big trees lent an eerie air to the place.

"What's over there?" Newland pointed to a spot on the other side of the tree.

Natalie couldn't see it from her angle and stepped a little closer to him to get a better view.

Mistake. The closer she got to Newland Tran the more he was like a magnet, pulling her in. He was scruffy and rough looking, his hair a little too long and his clothes a little too disheveled, but he smelled good. Like manly aftershave and fabric softener. On the outside he might appear rough around the edges, but he took care of himself. She tried not to breathe

47

in that smell and instead focused on the spot where he pointed.

A mound of dirt lurked on the other side of the oak tree just barely inside the iron fence. It was so far off to one side and so far to the back of the lot, that she would have missed it had he not pointed it out to her.

"It looks like…" She didn't want to say the words. She swallowed hard. "It looks like a new grave."

"I thought you said the cemetery has been closed for decades."

Natalie nodded. "I can't tell you how long it's been closed. Aubie probably can. He's something of a historian for the town. Him and Gerald."

Newland turned toward her. "Gerald? Who's that?"

The cool night air stung her heated cheeks. "Gerald Davenport. He's my fiancé. Well, almost. I mean, boyfriend. He's my boyfriend."

Newland's eyes narrowed. "I see. And why would he know something about that grave or the cemetery?"

"He's part of the historical society here in town. In fact, he's the chairman of the society."

"I see."

"Yes." Natalie started rambling, a sure sign that she was nervous. "Aunt Bitty's house is not part of the historical tour, though it should be. I've been trying to get it on the national historic registry for years. That's how I met Gerald." As much as she tried to stem the flow of words, they just kept coming. "He's the chairman of the local historical society, and I've been trying to engage his help to get the national organization interested in Aunt Bitty's house. It was built long before the war. I'm sure she told you." She stopped to take a breath.

"She did mention something to that fact," Newland said. "But if her house was built so long ago, why isn't it on the historic registry already?"

"It was built by a northern sympathizer." She shrugged. "Some wounds take a long time to heal."

Natalie looked around, the wind kicking up and blowing her hair. At least it was pulled back and out of her face. She was still able to see anything if it was coming. Not that there was. Because she didn't believe in ghosts. "You want to head back to the house?"

"I'd like to look at this big mound of dirt first."

"Of course you would." Natalie nodded. "Okay, I'll wait for you here."

He started off toward the oak tree.

Natalie hadn't realized how dark it had gotten. The only reason she could see Newland was because he had taken out his cellphone and was using his flashlight app to lead the way. Where she was standing, it was totally dark. And her phone was all the way back at the house.

She could barely see two feet in front of her own face. Well, two feet and then Newland.

The wind brushed her again and set Natalie into action. "Hold up, Newland. I'm coming. You're not going to discover all this great evidence without me."

She thought she heard him chuckle, but she didn't comment. Instead, she started off toward the flashlight, thankful that she had put on walking shoes before she had come out here. Any of her normal footwear would be sinking into the soft ground. The thought made her shudder.

She finally drew even with Newland. He was standing near the mound of dirt which was half-covered with a black tarp.

"Where do you suppose the dirt came from?" Newland shined his flashlight around, but there was no new digging near any of the graves close to them, though one of them looked to be a little bit deeper than the others. Still it had a headstone, which as far she was concerned meant somebody was buried there and it was completely off-limits.

"I don't know. I guess that's the mystery, Scooby-Doo. Come on. Let's go back to the house. Now." She grabbed his arm, tugging him toward the cemetery entrance. They were so far away from the gate now that it would definitely be completely dark—super dark—by the time they got out and back onto the sidewalk.

But Newland was too strong and barely moved as she jerked on his elbow to get him to follow her. "It just doesn't make sense. The dirt had to come from somewhere."

Natalie looked over to the mound. It was a big mound. Bigger than what would be there if somebody had dug a new grave. She thought. It wasn't like she went around measuring mounds of dirt before someone was buried. "Maybe they brought it in for some reason," she said. "I mean, look at all the sunken graves. Maybe they're trying to level the place out. That's an awful lot of dirt."

"But why would they level off a century-old graveyard?"

"Well, it is sort of an eyesore. I mean, even in the light."

Newland seemed to think about it a second. "But wouldn't your brother be in charge of a project like that?"

"Of course." As the mayor he was in charge of all sorts of projects like that.

"Do you miss any of the town meetings?" Newland asked.

"Of course not," she said. "I'm my brother's guardian, and he is underage."

"About that..." Newland said. "How is it that he doesn't even have a driver's license and he can't vote, and yet he's the mayor of this town? I mean, he was elected?"

"Of course, but the town charter doesn't set an age limit on being mayor, and it doesn't delineate that the mayor has to be able to vote in a national election."

Newland laughed. "That's the funniest thing I've ever heard."

Natalie shot him a look. "Then you need to get out more. But for now, let's go home."

****

Newland took one last look at the large mound of dirt, wondering why no one had seen it before now. It wasn't fresh dirt, and it hadn't been completely protected by the small black tarp. In fact, only half of it had been covered. He would have to go check tomorrow and see, or maybe talk to Aubie tonight. If they got back before his bedtime.

Something was definitely going on here. He just couldn't figure out what. Or if this big mound of dirt had anything to do with this ghost.

Finally, he allowed Natalie to tug on his arm and move him back away from the dirt. He wasn't sure, but he thought she sighed with relief as he started toward the cemetery entrance gate. He shined his flashlight to lead the way, hoping that his battery held out. He needed to charge his phone, but with any luck they would at least make it to the sidewalk. He didn't think Natalie could take it if they didn't.

For all her talk about not believing in ghosts, she seemed really spooked to be in an ancient cemetery after dark.

He moved the flashlight up to look at the entrance. They were still far away. And his flashlight seemed to be getting dimmer. "Watch the ground, okay? I'm afraid we're about to lose the light, and I don't want you to trip."

"Lose the light?"

"My battery's about to die."

Maybe a bad choice of words.

"Oh…Okay… I guess—"

The light went out.

She stopped, and Newland pulled her a tad closer to keep her feeling safe, just in case there was a ghost out here—and he truly believed that there wasn't. After all, didn't Bitty say that the ghost only came out the last Thursday of the month? That in itself was weird, but he didn't have time to examine it. Right now he had to get poor, shaking Natalie out of the cemetery.

"Just watch the ground. Look at your feet and make sure you don't step in a—"

She crumpled like someone had removed all her bones. "Ow!" she cried.

"Are you okay?" He could barely make out her outline in the dark. If it hadn't been for the light-colored shirt that she wore, he might not have seen her at all.

"Yeah, it's my ankle. I think I stepped in a hole."

Grave, he silently corrected. But he wasn't about to say that to her. "Come on. I'll help you." He hoisted her to her feet, taking most of her weight on his shoulders as he wrapped one arm around her. "Can you walk?"

"I think so."

But he wasn't taking any chances. He kept his arm anchored firmly around her as he helped her maneuver through the staggering tombstones.

"Really…I'm okay. It just scared me more than anything."

"I don't mind helping you." He said the words, but the truth was he didn't want to let her go. She smelled good, she was soft against him, and it'd been a long time since he'd held a woman. Way too long.

She pushed against him "Seriously. I'm fine."

He might need to get back into the dating scene. Not that he wanted to date the sassy Miss Everything's-Got-to-be-Perfect Natalie Coleman. That was just asking for trouble.

"Almost there," he said as the sound of the creaky gate drew closer to them. The streetlights added a little illumination and now their walk wasn't quite so hazardous. Natalie limped a little on her left ankle, but he made no comment. For some reason she didn't want him touching her and that was fine. He didn't want to touch her anyway.

"We'll be home soon," he said.

"What are you doing here?" The voice came out of nowhere. Deep, strong, and without form.

Natalie stumbled again.

Newland caught her just in time.

CHAPTER FIVE

Natalie knew that voice, but it wasn't clear. And it had nothing to do with the warmth of Newland's body next to hers or the comforting weight of his arm around her. The flashlight shining in her face didn't help. She used one hand to shield her eyes. "Who's there?"

"Natalie, I would think you'd know my voice by now."

"Gerald?"

"Of course." He gave a discreet cough and lowered his light toward the ground, allowing Natalie to see the disapproving frown he shot her.

She moved away from Newland, quickly realizing that being snuggled up to one man while faced with one's almost fiancé was not the best situation to find oneself in.

"What are you doing out here?" Gerald asked again.

Newland took that time to speak. "I think we can ask you the same thing."

Natalie smoothed her hands down over her navy slacks and hoped her blouse hadn't suffered too much trauma at the fate of the graveyard. Still she knew she looked disheveled and disheveled was not one of her best looks.

"If you insist. I have some interest in this graveyard being president and chairman of the historical society. Someone saw something out here and called me."

"Of course," Natalie said, moving to stand by him. Strange as it was, she felt like she had deserted Newland in going to stand by Gerald. But he was her almost fiancé, and it wasn't like she picked sides. She was supposed to stand by him, right? Even if she would rather stand by Newland. Which was weird. Why would she want to stand by a man she had just met?

"Your turn." Gerald gave Newland a swift nod.

"I'm here at the request of Bitty Duncan."

Gerald rolled his eyes. "You're not here about the ghost, are you?" His voice turned derisive even as he shook his head. "She's been going on about that nonsense for years. Tell him, Natalie."

"I did," she said, though her words were not convincing. "But I'm hopeful that she'll eventually give up the idea and move into the home."

"Wait," Newland said. "What do you mean move to the home?"

"She needs to live someplace where she can get assistance," Natalie explained. Somehow when Newland said it the plan seemed cruel. But they were only watching out for her. "I'm sure she told you all about how the ghost leaves the stove on and the refrigerator door open." Natalie shook her head. "None of these things are the result of the ghost. She's starting to lose it." As she said the words tears stung in her eyes. She loved her Aunt Bitty with all her heart. She was the closest thing to a grandmother that Natalie had ever had. Her own grandmothers had died long ago. Bitty had taken over that responsibility. After Natalie's parents had flown the coop, it was Aunt Bitty to the rescue, always there for Natalie and Aubie whenever they needed her.

Newland shook his head again. "You mean to tell me that you're trying to convince a sweet old lady to give up the house she loves and go live with a bunch of strangers who won't allow her to do anything for herself?"

"Meadowbrook is not like that." Natalie's hackles rose. He had no right making accusations about her decisions for her aunt. She had nothing but Bitty's best interests in mind. She couldn't stay with Bitty twenty-four hours a day. She had responsibilities. And then there was Aubie. She had to take care of him. On top of that, she would be married to Gerald soon. It was best this way. Aunt Bitty could go live in Meadowbrook and even take Mr. Piddles with her. It was the perfect solution though Natalie had yet to convince her aunt that the ghost wasn't real and that her cat was the one knocking down her treasured collectibles from Avon.

"I thought better of you." Newland pinned her with those dark eyes, then turned to leave.

As she watched, he stomped out of the cemetery and down the sidewalk, not waiting for her to follow. Not that it mattered. She was a big girl, and she knew her way around. This was her hometown, her neighborhood. Let him think what he wanted. In a few days he would be gone, back to Chicago or wherever that rock was he'd crawled out from under. And she would still be in Turtle Creek taking care of things. Like she always did. She turned back to Gerald.

"Charming fellow," he said. Then he gave her a perfect kiss on the cheek.

It was the closest to a PDA she could get from him. But she would take it. He was reserved, and there was nothing wrong with that. She accepted his decorum and his standards. He didn't slobber all over her in public, didn't wrap his arms around her like Newland just had. Gerald didn't slobber all over her in private either. But all that physical, that wasn't what was important. The deep bond of sameness that brought two people together was the most vital. Not that crazy wild we-have-to-be-doing-something-all-the-time love that her parents shared. This was better. This was deeper. A love of the town, love of the same things, and a certain standard of social propriety that would carry them both through the rest of their lives. That was what was important.

"He'll be gone in a few days." She almost choked on those sad words. Sad? That was insane. She must be losing her mind. Was it any wonder with everything that was going on around her?

But she only had a little over a week before the ghost would appear in the cemetery—or not—and Tran would be on his way.

"I'll walk you home," Gerald said.

He didn't take her elbow or touch her in any way but somehow managed to spin her around and lead her past Myrtle's house and back toward her aunt's.

Myrtle Meeks was one of her aunt's longtime friends. Actually there were three other ladies around the same age who lived in the same neighborhood, though none had a house like Aunt Bitty's. As they passed, Natalie looked in to see if Myrtle might possibly be awake, but all the lights were out.

I wonder if she's seen the ghost. She immediately pushed the thought away. There was no ghost. Yet maybe Myrtle saw what her aunt saw. Or Josephine or even Selma. After all, they all lived close to the cemetery. Any of them could have seen anything at any time. Maybe her aunt's dream that the ghost only came the last Thursday of the month was just because that was when she expected him and that was when she looked. She would have to mention that to Newland later.

Gerald didn't say a word as they walked, but she could feel the disappointment coming off him. What had she done this time?

"I don't think you should be running around with him after dark, Natalie. I don't think it shows well on your breeding."

"I only went because I didn't want him running around without a local with him."

"Next time call me. I can escort Mr. Tran around town and show him what he needs to see rather than letting him dig through and find ghosts that don't exist and skeletons in closets that should've disappeared long ago."

For a second she thought she heard a note of panic in his voice, but that couldn't be right. What did Gerald Davenport have to fear from a tabloid reporter from Chicago? A freelance reporter at that.

She must have been mistaken.

Instinctively her steps slowed as she neared her aunt's house, partially because she was almost home and partially because the sidewalk became lumpy and bumpy the closer they got. A big sycamore tree sat in her aunt's front yard, its roots wreaking havoc on what had once been a nice sidewalk. There were also rumors of tunnels underneath her aunt's house. She didn't think that would affect the sidewalk. But it was just a rumor, like that of the ghost.

"Here we are." Gerald drew to a stop, nodding toward Bitty's house. "I take it you are still plan on staying here tonight?"

Natalie nodded. "I can't leave her here, I explained that. What if something were to happen to her?"

Gerald shook his head.

"It wouldn't have anything to do with that reporter, would it? More than just protecting your aunt from him?"

Natalie thought back to one arm slung around her waist and his strong presence at her side. She wanted to melt into his warmth. Which was totally ridiculous seeing as how she was almost engaged to the man standing in front of her. Good-looking, urbane, and cultured. At least he didn't go around in concert T-shirts and Chucks.

"Don't be ridiculous. He is so not my type." She lightly touched Gerald's arm, another of their accepted public shows of affection. "You know how I feel about you."

Gerald nodded, but the shadows from the sycamore tree hid his face from view. "Okay," he finally said. "Just lock your door tonight. I don't trust him." He squeezed her hand, then turned to go to his car.

Only then did she notice that it was parked at the end of the street. They had walked past it on their trip back to Aunt Bitty's front door.

She watched him go, her mind whirling with this unusual encounter. Then she gave a sigh and turned toward her aunt's house.

"He's quite a cold fish." Newland's voice came to her from the shadows of the porch.

She staggered back a step and placed a hand over her heart. She hadn't expected him to be out here still. "What are you doing hiding on the porch?"

"I'm not hiding. I've been here the whole time. Just because you were so wrapped up in your boyfriend doesn't mean it's my fault you didn't notice me sitting here."

"Really? That's just like a reporter to say, 'I'm not hiding in the bushes. So sorry you didn't see me.'"

"What do you have against reporters?"

Where did she begin with that? "Let's just say that I know reporters who feel it's okay to stop at nothing to get the story, including making it up. And that is something you had better not do."

"Why, Natty Nat, I'm injured. I have never made up a story of my life."

"That talking dog in Nebraska? That was a real story?"

"He did talk. It was creepy, but he talked."

Natalie rolled her eyes. "What about the twenty-pound newborn in Canada?"

"Hey, I can't change the weight of babies. It's all documented at the hospital."

"And the levitating rug in New Orleans?"

Newland stopped. "That was scary. Like voodoo."

"But not true?" Natalie pinned him for the answer.

"What are you getting at?"

"My family has a reputation to uphold. And it's awfully hard to keep everything on the up and up if we have paparazzi and reporters here making up stories about ghosts that don't exist. If there's a ghost, fine. Report the ghost. If there's not, there's no story, *capice*?"

Newland saluted her with one hand and clicked his heels together. The effect was lost on the rubber soles of his Converse. "Aye-aye, Captain."

Natalie rolled her eyes and started up the stairs. "Did you see Aubie come in?"

"Not while I was here. Are you having trouble keeping up with your brother?"

Natalie shook her head. "That boy…He needs his own keeper."

She started up the stairs to the room where she knew Aubie stayed when he was here. She could hear Newland's footsteps behind her, but she didn't care that he was following her. It had nothing to do with anything. Nothing at all.

She opened the door and peered inside.

"That's my room, and I consider that a bold invasion of my privacy."

Natalie shut the door and leaned up against it, staring up at Newland as he drew nearer. "I'm sorry. That's where Aubie usually sleeps when he's here."

Newland shrugged. "That's where your aunt put me. I can move if you like, but Aubie's not in there."

"I guess she didn't expect us to stay here."

"Why should she? She's a grown woman."

"Don't you say she can take care of herself. She is eighty-six years old."

"I guessed eighty-five."

Natalie rolled her eyes. "You can sleep here, but I have to find Aubie." She started going down the line of bedrooms. Aside from the one downstairs, there were four bedrooms upstairs. Her stuff was in the pink room up front, Newland's stuff was in the yellow room, the blue room was empty, and the white room had nothing in it as well. Why Aunt Bitty called it the white room Natalie could never figure out. There wasn't much in there that was white except for the walls. She supposed that was enough for her aunt.

Natalie shut the door and leaned against it. She tilted her head back, closed her eyes, and let out a low growl.

"I take it he's not in there?"

Without opening her eyes, Natalie shook her head. There were several places he could be, but she knew exactly where he was. Home. At their apartment. She stood there for a moment, eyes closed, but she could tell as Newland drew nearer. It was his warmth, his scent, or maybe just his presence that stuck in her head like an annoying song.

"I guess I should go get him." She pushed herself off the wall.

"Go get him? Where is he?"

"At home. At least I think that's where he is."

"If he's at home, why not let him stay there? I mean, he's sixteen and he is the mayor, you can't let him stay by himself for one night?"

"You have no idea what you're talking about, and I'd appreciate if you didn't jump into my family matters."

He looked around as if pointedly saying he was already in the middle of her family matters if he was standing on the second-floor landing of her aunt's house.

"More than you already are," she qualified.

She started down the stairs, intent on getting her brother and bringing him back to Aunt Bitty's house. Once again she could hear Newland behind her.

"You want me to go with?"

She shook her head. "No, and it's go with *you*."

Newland shrugged. "I said I spent some time in Tennessee. I didn't say I moved in."

"Spoken like a true Yankee."

He laughed. "I'll go with you."

She shook her head. "Not necessary. This is my responsibility."

****

It took some convincing on Natalie's part, but she managed to get Aubie into the car and back to Aunt Bitty's house without too much fuss. Threatening to cut off his allowance usually did the trick, and this time was no different. She knew he was angry as she pulled her car into Aunt Bitty's uneven drive. Aubie was out the door before she had completely stopped the car. He slammed it behind him and loped up the porch steps without waiting for her at all.

Natalie sighed, then grabbed Oskar and headed for the door. Her job as family caretaker was highly overrated and very underappreciated. But somebody had to do it.

She let herself into the house, locking the stained glass inlaid door behind her. Aubie had long since disappeared up the stairs, without Natalie even being able to tell him that Newland was in the room Aubie normally slept in.

She shook her head. He'd figure it out soon enough.

"I'm glad to see you made it back okay."

She spun around, pressing a hand over her wildly beating heart. "Newland! You scared me."

"Definitely not my intention."

"Then why are you lurking about out here in the foyer?"

"Well, first, I wasn't in the foyer, I was in the parlor, and second, I was waiting on you to come home. There was no lurking involved."

"Why are you waiting for me?"

"I know that Turtle Creek is small, but crime happens everywhere. I just wanted to make sure you got home safely."

Natalie was not going to let herself be touched by the gesture. He was just trying to get in her good graces so she would spill some other family dirt. Then he would have the story he needed to get himself back on top in the journalism world. Though for him back on top might mean a desk job with *The Enquirer*.

She pushed away that mean thought. "I'm touched, really." She was, but she made sure her voice did not reflect it. "But you can go to bed now. I'm sure you have a long day of ghost hunting ahead of you tomorrow."

She moved to go past him, but he stepped in front of her, effectively blocking her escape.

"Why is it that you're always trying to run away from me? Are you scared of me or something?"

Natalie scoffed. "Of course not. Why would I be scared of you?"

His eyes darkened to a shade akin to black, their depth bottomless as he stared at her. "That's what I'm trying to figure out myself."

Something in the room seemed to change. If Natalie believed in the ghost, she might've said his

65

spirit had walked in. She had read about spirits making the room colder and scarier, but this was something else entirely. She felt flushed and warm. Again like a magnet drawing her to Newland Tran.

How had she gotten so close to him? Had she taken a step forward? Or had he?

If she had thought he was tall before, he seemed doubly so now. She had to crane her neck back to stare at him as he moved nearer still.

"You don't need to be afraid of me. I wouldn't hurt you." His voice was nothing but a whisper.

Natalie nodded mutely. She wasn't afraid of him, just this. This way that he made her feel. Like she was special, like warn chocolate sauce, like she never been kissed before. "I need to go to bed."

Whoa, too intimate a thing to say.

Heat rose into her cheeks. Natalie knew that she had turned an uncomfortable shade of red, yet she couldn't move past him, couldn't look away, could only manage to stare at him and wait to see what happened next.

"Yeah, we should go to bed."

"We?" The one word was nothing but a rush of air from her lips.

"You…we…" He seemed as confused as she was.

"Okay." Though she had no idea what she was agreeing to. That she needed to go to bed? That they needed to go to bed together? What was wrong with her?

Somehow she managed to move past him, brushing against him as she took the first stair. But like that magnet, he somehow turned her around so she was facing him once again. This time they were on a more even plane as she was standing on the step ahead of him. It would be just so easy to lean in... Closer... And touch her lips to his and finally see...what all this was about... This pull...

Maybe she wasn't the only one drawn like a magnet. He moved closer and closer still until she could count every dark lash on those exotic eyes.

Before she could protest—not that she wanted to—he kissed her.

Natalie sighed and leaned into him, thankful for his strong presence to hold her up right. As his mouth moved over hers there was something sweet and thrilling and somehow forbidden in that wonderful kiss. Forbidden... Not because he was a tabloid reporter, not because he was a Yankee, but she was almost engaged.

The thought swirled around in her head like the stars in that famous painting, but she couldn't quite grasp its meaning. Almost engaged wasn't engaged. And she wanted to experiment just a smidge. Just to see why every time she got close to Newland Tran her heart knocked in her chest like the trill of a woodpecker.

Almost engaged. Somehow she grabbed hold of the thought and realized this was wrong. She was kissing another man when she was nearly engaged to Gerald Davenport, the man of her dreams.

She used her hands to push Newland away. How had they gotten to his chest to begin with? Hadn't they been at her sides just moments before?

"No." Her voice was a breathless whisper as threadbare as the rugs in the hallway.

Despite the insubstantial word, he took a step back.

She swayed in place, and he reached out to steady her.

"I'm sorry," she said, though she wasn't sure for what or to whom she was apologizing. Him for stopping their kiss? Herself for enjoying it? Or for Gerald because he wasn't standing there?

She shook her head.

"I'm not."

Her eyes flew open and she studied his expression. He didn't look sorry at all. In fact he looked quite satisfied with himself.

"That can never happen again."

"Why, because you're engaged to a stuffed shirt?"

"Gerald is not a stuffed shirt."

"Oh yeah, and I forgot. You're not exactly engaged, now are you?"

Her palm itched to slap his face, but even as she wanted to, she knew he spoke the truth. She wasn't engaged to Gerald. Not yet. But she would be and that in itself would put her life in brilliant order. Just the way she liked it.

"It's only a matter of time," she said.

He nodded, but she could tell from the smirk twitching at the corners of his mouth that he didn't believe it, not for a second.

"Uh-huh," he said. Then he shoved his hands in his pockets and walked away whistling as he went, leaving Natalie staring behind him, her lips still throbbing with his kiss.

CHAPTER SIX

Natalie was exhausted by the time she pulled up in front of her aunt's house the next evening. She had gotten up before everyone that morning and was out of the house before they even knew she was gone. And that was just how she wanted it. She called the school later just to make sure Aubie had made it to his classes.

But it wasn't her brother who had her lingering in the car. Nope, it was him, the last person she wanted to see. Newland Tran.

She sat in her car for another moment under the shade of that big sycamore, with Oskar next to her whining a bit, wondering why they were inactive.

She reached over and scratched the pup behind his ears, effectively stanching his worry. "I know, boy. It's not the best situation, hmmm?"

That was an understatement.

Despite her sleepless night she still hadn't figured out what to do about that kiss. That bad night coupled with the busy day she had was the reason she hadn't figured out what to do. Or at least that was what she was telling herself. There was more to it than that. Much more.

Her day had been busy, including a lunch with Gerald. That hadn't been as busy as it had been uncomfortable. She couldn't help but think of kissing Newland as she sat across the table from her almost fiancé. But it was only a kiss.

A kiss that curled toes and melted plastic.

"But that's not important, right?" She looked to her dog for answers.

Oskar simply wagged his tail and gave her that sweet look she loved so much.

"If only men were as easy to get along with as you, my baby."

She grabbed her purse and her dog and got out of the car. No sense putting this off any longer than she had to.

So she had kissed Newland. That didn't mean anything. It was simply a kiss, and an unwelcome one at that.

Liar!

She pushed that word away. So what? She might've kissed Newland Tran, but that didn't change anything. She was still almost engaged to the most handsome and influential man in Turtle Creek. In all of Alcorn County perhaps. And that was not something that could easily be changed. Not that she wanted it to.

Once she married Gerald, her life would smooth out and the chaos that currently reigned wouldn't be an issue anymore. Somehow she knew. They would be a wonderful, loving couple doing good work for the community and all of its citizens. The thought made her warm inside.

"Aunt Bitty," she called as she entered the house. "I'm home." She expected to walk in and find no one, except maybe Bitty in the parlor. Instead she found Newland painting the foyer. "What are you doing?"

He looked down at his paint-splattered clothes to the brush he held in his hand then to the wall. Apparently he had just slapped on a wet coat of Mint Dream semi-gloss. "I'm painting."

Natalie shook her head. "*Why* are you painting?"

"Your aunt asked me to."

And that was the power of Bitty Duncan. Somehow she could charm the birds out of the trees and sell ice to Eskimos. It had always been that way, and it would be that way until she went to meet her maker.

"Just because my aunt wants you to paint, don't think you have to."

Newland turned back to the work at hand. He had done well for a day's work—almost the entire foyer had a fresh coat of paint. "It wasn't like I have a lot of other things to do. I spent the morning at the library, then came back to this."

"What exactly is 'this'?"

He glanced at her over one shoulder before dipping his paintbrush in the pan. "When I got back here, the tarp was out, the paint was ready, and the brush was in the hands of your aunt." He shook his head as if to say, *What's a guy supposed to?*

He was a gentleman. That was for sure. And he wouldn't let an eighty-six-year-old woman paint a room in her house. Regardless of the fact that it didn't need paint or, at the very least, her aunt had enough money to hire it done.

"Next time let me know. I'll hire painters if she wants something painted."

Newland turned to look at her, his brown eyes so intent Natalie shifted in her nude-colored pumps. "Is that what you do? Just go around like some sexy fairy godmother making everybody's wishes come true?"

Natalie scoffed. "No." She wasn't making everybody's wishes come true. Her job was to make things run smoothly. Just the way she liked them.

Wait. Had he just called her sexy?

Newland continued to study her for several long seconds until it felt like it stretched into an hour.

"Did Aubie come home?" She had to change the subject and fast. Something in Newland's look was wholly unsettling. Somehow it brought back that kiss from the night before, and that was something she didn't want to experience again. Not in the least.

"He's in the parlor reading a magazine. He said something about a project due tomorrow."

Natalie closed her eyes. "The science fair."

Her brother had put off to the last minute what should've been done months ago. Now this biology grade was dependent on his interpretation of the dissection of a bullfrog.

"And my aunt?"

"She's in the kitchen baking some mini quiches for tonight...?" His voice turned up on the end as if he wasn't sure he should tell her that part.

"Of course, chick card night."

Newland nodded. "She said something about that."

That was the last thing Natalie needed. She had to make sure that Aubie got the rest of his science fair project done—which pretty much meant *all* of his science fair project done. Now Newland was painting the foyer, and Aunt Bitty was getting ready for card night. When would things slow down?

When you marry Gerald.

She sighed at the thought. That was just one more reason to keep that kiss between her and Newland to herself. No sense getting Gerald all up in arms about something that meant nothing. Though there was no reason not to tell him if it didn't mean anything to her, right?

She shook her head as her thoughts went around in a circle.

"Okay, quiches first, then the science project." She nodded as if to confirm her decision, then started toward the back of the house.

Newland spoke before she set even one foot out of the foyer. "If you need some help, just let me know. I'll be done in a bit."

****

Newland watched her go and hoped his mouth wasn't hanging open. Didn't she see? No, she couldn't. She was too involved. But Natalie Coleman went around sprinkling fairy-dust magic everywhere she went to make sure everyone's life was smooth and bump-free. So much so that her life was one chaotic rollercoaster ride of making sure everybody else was happy.

He shook his head and loaded up his paintbrush once again. The last thing he thought he'd be doing when he came to Mississippi was painting the foyer of an antebellum home. But he had time to kill and he liked Bitty Duncan.

There had to be something more to this whole ghost story than was meeting the eye. What kind of ghost only showed up on the last Thursday of the month? And where had all that extra dirt come from in the cemetery?

He shook his head. Painting helped clear his thoughts. He had done a little of that back in the day. Not a lot, just working part-time as he was trying to get through college and earn his degree in journalism. He had fallen short by ten credits and decided that embellishing stories a little bit was much more fun than telling the exact truth. Plus, who wanted to write about car wrecks when they could write about alien visitations and Elvis impersonators from Japan? He knew there were people who thought his job was beneath "real writing." But he sat down every day to a real computer and wrote on real files and got paid real money for doing it. Well, he *had*.

With his thoughts clearer since he had been painting, he still had more questions than ever. Like the dirt and that glass car knocked off from the bookcase. He'd tried all day to ask Bitty about anything else weird that had happened besides the stove and the refrigerator door left open, but she had flitted about like a bird not landing on any one topic long enough to get any real information.

He hated to admit it, but he almost agreed with Natalie that some of these occurrences could be just an old lady losing track of what she'd been doing. Hell, he lost track of things himself and he was less than half her age.

Still he could understand Natalie's concern. No one in their right mind would want to see someone as marvelous as Bitty Duncan hurt in a home accident that could've been prevented.

But even with as many times as he tried to pin her with questions about other occurrences, anything else that might have been broken, any odd happenings, he hadn't been able to get her to focus long enough to tell him. He was hoping tonight that he might sit in and listen to the old ladies talk. There was certainly information to be had observing four longtime friends chatting about the neighborhood. Some secrets would have to be released. And he was going to sit back and absorb them all.

****

He tried to make himself as unobtrusive as furniture. He had helped Bitty set up the card table and pull the mismatched wooden chairs from all over the house to go around the rickety aluminum table. In the true form of a southern gentlewoman Bitty had covered it with a fine linen cloth and set everyone's place with a saucer and silverware—the real kind—and the finest china she owned.

At six o'clock on the dot the doorbell rang. Newland turned to her. Her eyes alight like a child at Christmas, Bitty clapped her hands. "Goody! It's time to play."

She all but ran to the door and flung it open to reveal two of the strangest ladies that Newland had ever seen. One looked as if she had just stepped out of a 1960s fashion magazine. She wore a leopard day coat—even though it was no less than eighty degrees outside—along with black leggings, zebra flats, and a red beret. Extra-large Jackie Onassis sunglasses hid her eyes, and bright red lipstick, perfectly applied, graced her pouting mouth.

"Darling," she said, sweeping into the room in front of her companion. She clasped Bitty's hands in her own and kissed the air near each cheek.

Newland bit back a smile.

Next in was a little old lady wearing a large, floppy straw hat and overalls. The shirt underneath was long-sleeved and plaid, but at least it wasn't flannel. Her pant legs were rolled up revealing purple Crocs that looked as if they had been rinsed off for the occasion, but not quite cleaned.

"Myrtle," Bitty greeted, taking the woman's hand into her own and pulling her farther into the house.

The door shut behind her, and Myrtle sniffed the air.

"Why does it smell like paint in here?" Myrtle sounded like she had smoked for forty years, maybe fifty. Her voice rasped with each word and reminded Newland of what a badger would sound like if it talked. She had two silk daisies tucked into the brim of her hat, one yellow one red. They too, like the Crocs, had seen better days.

"Because my man here has been painting," Bitty said.

Her man? Newland couldn't stop a smile at the moniker. Today he was Bitty Duncan's man.

The lady in the red beret approached. "You must be the reporter. Selma Loveland-Pierce. It's a pleasure to meet you." She held out one hand, her jewel-laden fingers twinkling. Did she expect him to kiss it?

He guessed so. She smiled at him, revealing pearly dentures. At least he thought they were dentures. They were so perfect it was doubtful they were real teeth.

"And this is Myrtle Meeks," Bitty explained, motioning to the woman in overalls.

Myrtle Meeks from Turtle Creek? Newland shook his head.

"Where's Josephine?" Bitty asked.

According to Natalie, Josephine was the voice of reason for the ladies. He also found out today that they had been dubbed the Fab Four by the women's auxiliary for the Jaycees club, though none of them were actually members.

"You know her and those boyfriends," Myrtle said with a frown.

"That Josephine." Bitty shook her head. "I don't know about you, but I don't need a man underfoot. Unless he's painting." She winked at Newland.

"Well," Selma said in that cultured voice of hers. "Josephine's not as used to being widowed as we are. Especially you, Bitty."

Bitty gave a solemn nod. "That's true. I lost my husband fifty years ago it is now." She shook her head as the other women murmured things like "tragic" and "just so sad."

"So how long has Josephine been widowed?" The reporter in Newland couldn't allow the question to go unanswered.

Selma tapped one perfectly manicured fingernail against her wrinkled cheek. "Let me see now... I suppose it's been... What? Twenty-five years?" She looked to the others for confirmation.

Newland choked. The other two women nodded.

"About twenty-five, yes," Bitty said.

Newland supposed that twenty-five years was short term when compared to fifty years, but twenty-five years was still an eternity to be widowed and alone.

"So she's not coming tonight?" Bitty looked to each of them again for their nods of agreement.

"What should we do?" Myrtle asked.

"You don't suppose Natalie..." Selma asked, but she didn't finish the sentence as Bitty shook her head.

"She's got to work with Aubie on something for school. We probably won't see her for the rest of the evening."

As if in unison the three women turned to look at him.

Newland resisted the urge to glance behind him to see if there was someone else lurking, maybe even the ghost. But he knew that he was the only one in there.

His mind scrambled around trying to find a legitimate excuse as to why he couldn't play bridge with three little old ladies. The first being that he didn't play bridge. And the second ending with he really didn't want to. He needed to use this time to find out more about the neighborhood. The other women lived so close. Had they seen the ghost? Did they see it on any other night than the last Thursday of the month? Maybe one of them had seen something dealing with the dirt that had been dumped in the cemetery.

"I don't play bridge," Newland said, hoping that would nip this in the bud.

"That's fine, dear," Bitty said with a smile. "We play poker."

How could Newland say no to that? He vowed to go easy on them as they settled down at the table.

Selma picked up the cards and split the deck in two and executed the shuffle with all the precision and skill of a Vegas dealer. "Okay, ladies," she said. "The game is seven card stud, eights or better to open, trips or better to win. Nothing wild. Ante up."

****

Being taken to the cleaners was a mild way to put it. He hadn't won a hand all night. Well, maybe he'd won a couple. But not good ones. He'd like to say that he blamed it on the fact that he was trying to gain information about the ghost and other items and details for his article. But the truth of the matter was these women were tough. Whether it was the wrinkles, the sunglasses, or that bright red lipstick, their poker faces were a study of perfection.

Maybe it was their age. Maybe because they'd had a longer life, they'd had longer to perfect that deadpan look that gave nothing away.

Or maybe they were just sharks.

Sharks and flowered dresses, red berets, and overalls. He shook his head. "So, anybody know anything about that dirt in the cemetery?"

"Why, there's dirt all over there," Selma said.

"There's a big mound of dirt sitting on the other side of that oak."

Bitty shook her head. "I don't know why there would be any dirt in the cemetery. I mean, not in a pile, anyway. Nothing's been buried there for a hundred years at least."

"But there is dirt there," Newland tried again.

"I don't think it's been a hundred years," Myrtle said. "Maybe eighty."

"It's half covered with a tarp."

"I think that Danny Carstairs was buried there in 1960," Selma said.

Bitty shook her head. "I don't think so. No wait, Danny was buried there because his father had bought a plot from his grandfather back in 1920-something."

"How do you know that?" Myrtle grumped. "You weren't even born in 1920-something."

"I listen to people," Bitty said. "You should try it."

"Are you in?" Selma asked looking from Bitty to Newland.

He pushed his nickels across the table. What was that saying? In for a penny in for a pound. As of right now he was in for a nickel in for a dollar. *And* he'd lost twenty dollars already. Good thing they weren't playing for anything more than pocket change.

"I wondered if anybody has seen anything lately. Maybe a bulldozer or some kind of earthmoving equipment?" In a town the size of Turtle Creek surely a big bulldozer or excavator would draw attention.

But the women simply shook their heads.

"Not that I know of. Of course they could come in the middle of the night and I would never know it," Myrtle said.

"I don't sleep as good these days. So the doctor prescribed me some medication," Selma said.

Myrtle shook her head. "All you need is a good shot of moonshine and that'll knock you out."

Bitty spread her cards on the table in front of her. "Read 'em and weep, ladies. Full house kings over fives." She scraped the kitty toward her growing pile.

"Moonshine?" Newland asked. Moonshine was big business still, but these women drinking moonshine…it just didn't seem quite right.

"I got some jars in the cellar," Bitty said. "You want me to get you some?"

Newland shook his head. The last thing he needed to do was get his mind out of the game by drinking contraband liquor. No, thank you.

"I don't get it out much anymore because I can't go down the steps to the cellar. It's too steep for me now." The other ladies nodded as if their cellar stairs were in the same condition as Bitty's.

"So have any of you ladies seen the ghost?"

"This town is full of ghosts," Myrtle said.

Selma nodded in agreement.

Bitty shook her head. "Don't listen to Selma. She doesn't know. She wasn't even born here, *and* she's practically a Yankee."

"How can one be practically a Yankee?" He hoped he didn't regret asking that.

Selma frowned at her two friends. "I *was* a Yankee. Though it doesn't seem to matter that I moved here in 1964. They will always and forever consider me a Yankee."

"Do you know the difference between a Yankee and a damn Yankee?" Bitty asked. Myrtle smiled but tried to hide it behind her hand.

"What?" Newland asked.

"A Yankee comes to the South to visit. A damn Yankee stays."

Myrtle and Bitty collapsed into fits of girlish giggles.

Selma pretended that she didn't hear them or perhaps pretended to be a little annoyed, but Newland could see the sparkle of humor in her eyes as she gathered up the cards. "Then I guess I'm a damn Yankee."

Newland chuckled, realizing that if he stayed any longer than two weeks he would be in the same boat with Selma Loveland-Pierce.

CHAPTER SEVEN

"Can I talk to you for a minute?" Natalie let the screen door slam behind her as she stepped onto the porch. Whether it was her presence or the bang of the door she didn't know, but Newland jumped, startled out of his own thoughts.

"Oh. Yeah. Sure." He pulled his long legs in, closer to the chair so that she could walk by. She sat down next to him. Her aunt had always had wooden rockers on the front porch, a small table in between. It was the perfect setup for coming outside and drinking iced tea or mint juleps or whatever happened to be the beverage of the day.

But the day was practically over and Natalie was just now getting around to bringing up last night.

"I need to talk to you about the kiss." Well, it was a start. "I'm going to marry Gerald Davenport and that was just a big mistake. You kissing me, that is." She chanced a look at him though she couldn't see much of his expression on the dim porch. Why hadn't she turned the light on before she came out here? There was a lamppost in the yard that cast some illumination and the light coming in from the windows, but it wasn't enough to know what was going on behind those exotic brown eyes.

"I see. And does Gerald Davenport know the two of you are going to get married?"

Natalie blustered. "Of course." How absurd. Of course Gerald knew they were getting married. "I'll have you know that we have been dating exclusively for the entire year."

"Like an entire calendar year or since January?"

Natalie tossed her head, not liking the direction this was going. "I hardly see why it would matter to you. I just wanted to be sure you understood. That won't happen again."

"It might."

She wished she could see his face. Was he teasing? Was he being serious? Was he trying to ruin her life? "I thought I needed to be open with you. I don't want you to get the wrong idea."

He turned in his seat, his gaze raking over her. She didn't need any illumination to know the heat behind that gaze. "I don't think I have the wrong idea at all."

Natalie jumped to her feet. "What is that supposed to mean?"

Newland shrugged. "Let's just say I've seen it before."

"Seen what?" She was growing weary of this game.

"A bright and funny girl like yourself, spunky and beautiful, thinks she's in love with someone completely wrong for her."

Natalie crossed her arms and leveled her gaze on him. She hoped even with the darkness he could see the venom she flashed his way. "You think Gerald's completely wrong for me?"

"Yeah. I do." He stretched out his long legs, once again effectively blocking any escape she might've made. Or maybe she didn't want to escape. No, that couldn't be it.

"And whatever gives you that idea? You've only known me for a day and a half and you think you know what kind of man I need?"

He nodded but didn't say anything. His silence just infuriated her more. "So tell me, oh wise one, just what sort of man do I need?"

He unfolded himself from the chair and she wished she hadn't asked. He towered over her, so close, smelling so good, and just being...him.

"You need someone who can handle you. Someone who can give you as good as you give. Not someone who's a puppet to the system, who caves at propriety, and wouldn't know how to have a good time if it came up and bit them on the—"

"I'll have you know—" Natalie sputtered to a stop. She had no argument for Newland's description of Gerald. He did follow propriety, and he didn't seek out good times just for the sake of a good time. But what was wrong with that? So their dates consisted of benefit dinners and benefit auctions and benefit meetings. That didn't mean he didn't know how to have a regular good time. They were just busy people. And as for being a puppet to the system, the system made the world go round. "That is exactly why he's perfect for me."

To her amazement Newland started to chuckle. "Have you looked at your life lately?"

Why was he standing so close to her? They had the entire wraparound porch at their disposal yet he seemed to be determined to stand directly in her space. She took a step sideways hoping to gain a little room and a whole lot of fresh air. Air that wasn't filled with him. "What's wrong with my life?"

"Sugar, if you haven't noticed by now, your life is utter chaos."

She sniffed. "Which is exactly why I need someone like Gerald." She'd spent her life making sure that things went smoothly. She'd practically taken on all financial responsibility for the family at age seventeen. Once her parents knew that she had an affinity for numbers and finances, they'd headed out to Grand Cayman.

They stopped in every so often, mostly in between their stays in tropical regions. As long as they had her to monitor the family fortune, their presence wasn't needed.

"Do you know that I just had to talk your aunt and her two elderly friends out of drinking moonshine?"

Natalie rolled her eyes. "Dear God, I thought I had gotten rid of all that."

"You better check the cellar. She swears there are jars down there." He looked around as if he could find the underground room in the pitch-black night. "Where is it anyway?"

"Around back. There's a door. It looks like it might be a basement, but it leads down into a cold cellar."

"Well, they didn't go in it because the stairs are too steep, and I refused to go down there and get it for them. You're welcome."

Natalie sighed. Okay, if she was being honest with herself, her life was chaos. But that was her job: making it not chaos. Once she had Gerald Davenport on her side, she would have double the power to make the not-chaos spread throughout the Coleman-Duncan clan.

She made a mental note to get into the cellar and get out the moonshine. If her aunt could manage in one day to get Newland painting the foyer then after a week of this, she would probably have him taking dancing lessons with her. New stairs for the cellar wouldn't be a challenge at all. That was Aunt Bitty, she could charm the socks off a monkey.

Natalie brushed past Newland and headed back to the door. She paused there, turning to shoot him her best "I've got this" smile. "So about that kiss. I hope you understand." And with that she reentered the house, once again letting the screen door bang shut behind her.

****

Newland watched her go, somehow managing to keep the chuckle from falling from his lips. She was something else. But even more than that, she was clueless.

She was smart. He'd figured that out long ago. But there was something about Natalie Coleman that seemed surprisingly naïve. Like she really thought she could control her genius brother and her eccentric aunt. The two of them would keep her busy until Jesus came back.

He shook his head at his own thoughts. He had been in the South two days, and he had already been there too long. He was already starting to sound like them. "Them" being the three ladies who'd skinned him playing poker. Somehow this place was getting under his skin.

Then there was Natalie. The kiss last night had been amazing. If he was truly being honest with himself it was the best kiss he'd had in a long time.

He knew what he was talking about when he told Natalie that she needed somebody with more spunk than she had. Gerald Davenport was not that person. But thinking about spunky women and stuffed-shirt men brought thoughts of Roxanne and Malcolm back to mind.

Newland hadn't gone to the wedding. He should have, just to get some closure on the whole situation. There had been a time once, when he had fancied himself in love with her. But the truth was he wanted to take the pain from her eyes, give her back some of the joy that he knew she'd had once upon a time.

What was a guy to do? Propose marriage, follow her to Tennessee, and make an utter fool of himself. But that was over.

Tennessee was behind him now. And if he happened to be in the state of Mississippi for much longer, he wasn't about to make a fool of himself over another woman. Not even Natalie Coleman with her silky brown hair and sky-blue eyes. She was not the girl for him. Though he wouldn't mind stealing another kiss sometime soon.

****

Newland made his way downstairs about the same time Thursday morning as he had the day before.

Natalie was seated at the breakfast table sharing biscuits and jelly with her aunt and her brother. Yesterday morning he had been disappointed to find Natalie already gone by the time he came downstairs. But he'd enjoyed himself, talking with Bitty about the town and other things, problems with the school board, Josephine's boyfriend, and Myrtle's mortgage payment.

"Good morning," he said to the room at large. He stopped off at the buffet and poured himself a cup of coffee, then settled down on the other side of Natalie.

She shot him a look that said *this means nothing*. What was it about her that had her so jumpy around him? So he was sitting by her at breakfast. Did that really matter? Something was up with her.

Maybe she could feel the pull that existed between them. She wanted to ignore it because she was set to marry a stuffed shirt. But Newland didn't see a ring on her finger. Still, he had other reasons to disregard the attraction. The last thing he wanted to do was get involved with a southern belle.

"Good morning," Bitty sing-songed. Natalie and Aubie echoed something that sounded like "morning," but Newland wasn't keeping score.

He reached for the butter, and said in an offhand manner, "Glad I got here in time." He nodded toward the two lone biscuits he'd snagged from the plate. There were a couple of pieces of bacon left and a little bit of sliced cantaloupe.

"I'm sorry, dear. I thought you might want to sleep in today."

"Yeah?" He scraped the last of the jelly from the jar. It was only enough to coat one half of one biscuit. "And why is that?"

"Natalie told me you weren't feeling good last night and that you were going up to bed. She thought you would probably need some extra sleep today."

"She did, did she?" He somehow managed to keep his tone neutral. He wasn't sure whether he should yell or laugh.

He cut his eyes in her direction. Her face had turned a shade of pink not much different than the rose print on the sofa in the parlor.

"Isn't that what you said last night?" Natalie's voice had lost its usual confidence.

"I don't recall anything of that nature." Let her squirm on that.

"Dear me," Aunt Bitty said. "You need some more jelly. Aubie, would you run down to the cellar and get him some more jelly?"

"Uh-huh." Aubie had done nothing but stare at his lap since Newland had sat down. The boy's lap couldn't be that interesting so it had to be whatever was on his cellphone that was commanding his attention.

"I'll go down." Newland pushed himself back from the table, just as Natalie did the same.

"I'll help," she said.

Newland launched one eyebrow in silent question and eyed her, testing her motive.

"I hardly think it appropriate for a guest to run to someone's cellar and start digging around for jelly."

"But you'll get your dress all dirty," Bitty protested.

Natalie looked down at herself and Newland found himself doing the same. She looked beautiful today. As she always did. But he'd noticed that about her. She dressed to the nines every day—perfect hair, perfect makeup, perfect jewelry. Today's ensemble was a coral dress that hugged her figure perfectly. Imagine that. It molded to each curve and dip, showing off every aspect of her assets. It ended just below her knees, revealing shapely calves made even more so by the black and white printed pumps she wore. He had been out with enough women to know that they had cost a pretty penny. It seemed that there was no end to the Coleman funds.

"You can't go down like that." He'd almost managed to get those words out in a normal tone, but his voice cracked a little on the end.

"I'll show you the way." She sashayed ahead of him.

Yeah, you will.

He followed her out of the house and around the back side of the porch. Just around the corner was a set of double doors. They were bigger than he'd expected, almost the size of regular doors. They were slanted as if they had been stuck awkwardly into the ground. Once upon a time they had been painted blue, though the weather and the rain had taken their toll. They were faded and had little rust spots, especially around the corners.

"There they are." She pointed to the handles. "The shelves are on the right. That's where you'll find the jelly."

"Where's the moonshine?" Newland reached for the doors, chuckling all the while.

"Bring up two or three jars," she said, ignoring him. "That way we don't have to come down again in a day or two."

Newland stopped. "How much jelly do you guys eat?"

She shot him that dazzling smile. "Quite a bit. This is the South after all."

Newland shook his head and started down into the dark cellar. Bitty was right, the steps were narrow. He couldn't imagine her trying to navigate them. He had trouble, even with the rustic handrail nailed to the wall. He had almost reached the bottom when Natalie called from above.

"If you feel around a little bit, there should be a light toward the left."

"There's a switch on the wall?" The walls looked like they were part of the ground. He couldn't imagine any electrical wires coming out of that.

"Don't be ridiculous. There's a shelf with a flashlight on it."

"Got it."

He felt around for the flashlight. It wasn't hard to find. But when he hit the switch it didn't come on. He called back up the stairs. "Batteries are dead."

She said something, but he couldn't quite make out what it was. He figured it was unladylike, and she had planned it that way.

"Never fear, I have my cellphone." He turned on his flashlight app and let his illumination spill over the wall. There were jars of all sorts of things—pickles and eggs and things he didn't recognize. Sometimes Southerners were a strange bunch. Rows and rows of jellies of all sorts. And then jars of clear liquid that he supposed was the moonshine Bitty had been talking about. Over in one corner several crates were stacked four high. They looked like they had hay on the inside, most probably for cushion. He couldn't imagine what she had stored down there, but that wasn't his mission. He grabbed two jars of strawberry and one dark jar that said "purple hull" in red marker across the top of the metal lid. Then he headed back up the steps.

He shoved his cellphone and the dead flashlight in his back pockets and grabbed the rail. As he got near, he handed the jars of jelly to Natalie before hoisting himself out of the cellar.

"You weren't joking, that's one steep incline."

"I keep asking—" She stopped and shook her head. "I really want to have the steps made a little elder-friendlier, but it keeps getting pushed to the bottom of the list."

Newland looked down at the steps where they disappeared from view. "I could fix that." He said the words wondering who Natalie kept asking. But he knew. And he couldn't imagine Gerald Davenport in his Armani suit and silk shirt building steps leading into a cold cellar.

"I couldn't possibly ask you to do that."

Newland shook his head. "You didn't ask. I offered."

"I could pay you."

"Does it always come down to money?"

She shot him a rueful smile. "Usually."

"Not this time." Newland said. "I'll do it, but not for money. Only for Bitty."

"And?"

What in his tone had tipped her off? "A date." They were his stipulations and yet they still amazed him. Why in the world would he want to go on a date with sassy Miss Perfection? He wasn't sure about the answer to that. But he did. Something to do. Because he still had a week before the ghost would show up.

"A date?" Her eyebrows shot so high he thought they would get caught in her hair. "Why do you want to go out with me?"

"Why not?"

"I told you; I'm almost engaged." Finally her eyebrows returned to their normal position.

"Almost. So not officially." He looked down at the bare finger of her left hand. She had other rings on, funky little rings that created a juxtaposition with her sleek dress and designer shoes. There was more to Natalie Coleman than met the eye. For some reason he wanted to find out what it was.

She sniffed. "No. Not officially. Not yet."

"Will he care if I take you out on a date?"

She closed her eyes for just a moment, then opened them again and leveled that blue gaze on him. "Of course he will."

"But you're still willing to go out with me?"

"One date," she finally said. "And you fix the stairs leading into the cellar."

Newland smiled. "Deal." He held out a hand to her.

She balanced the jelly jars in her arms and managed to give it a shake.

But he had an ulterior motive. He used his grip to pull her closer and plant a sweet smacking kiss on her lips.

Well, that had been his intent. But once his lips touched hers, the whole world seemed to spin a little differently.

He expected to take her off guard. Surprise her. Deliver his kiss, back away, and watch the emotions chase across her face. But instead she melted into him.

Newland accepted her warm weight, somehow managing to keep his hold on the jars as she leaned into him. Her lips were soft, responsive, and eager for his. And like their first kiss this one was explosive. A hundred thoughts, feelings, emotions raced through him. Past, present, future. All of it seemed rolled up into that one kiss.

He deepened the kiss, his tongue pushing past the barrier of her teeth to explore the sweetness that was all Natalie.

She gave a little mew, like a satisfied kitten, and edged closer to him.

He slid his arms around her and hauled her to him, pressing all of his aching parts against all of her warm ones.

Amy Lillard

She wrenched herself from his one-armed embrace and pressed trembling fingers to her mouth. Her blue eyes were wide and filled with the surprise that he had wanted. But he had a feeling that his own expression reflected hers. Just what had happened here?

"Did you find the jelly?" Bitty's voice floated to them from the other side of the porch. He hadn't heard the screen door open, but maybe Natalie had and that was what had caused her flight from his arms. Still, from where they stood no one in the house could see them. But Newland knew. This was life altering.

Natalie smoothed her free hand down her dress and fanned her face, he was sure, to get the redness in her cheeks back to normal. "Y – yes," she said, her voice as trembly as her fingers. "We found the jelly. We'll be right in."

"You didn't happen to get any of that moonshine while you were down there, did you?"

He wasn't sure, but he thought he heard Bitty laugh.

The words seemed to serve as an anchor for Natalie. She straightened her shoulders before rolling her eyes and calling out, "No, Aunt Bitty, you don't need any moonshine."

"Who said anything about needing it?"

Newland watched as Natalie turned on one spiky little heel and marched back to the house.

He needed to remain right where he was for a few minutes. He could shove his hands into his pockets, but he wasn't sure it would convincingly hide the evidence of their kiss.

Think of something boring, he told himself. Bank statements, spreadsheets, board meetings. But those things just brought Natalie to mind and made his hard-on worse.

Damn!

"Newland?" Bitty called. "Are you coming in or not?"

Newland shook his head. "I'll be right there." He walked slowly back to the house, tugging on his shirt hem as he went.

****

Newland spent the rest of the morning at the hardware store which was a cross between an old-fashioned general store and a true hardware store with a soda fountain in one end. Who even had those anymore? Groceries were in the middle with a section for the do-it-yourselfer on the other side. He'd promised to fix Bitty's steps, and he would. He knew the Colemans had more money than God, but he wasn't about to ask for any to complete the project. Any extra expense at this point strained his already so-thin-he-could-see-through-it budget, and these days he didn't have a company credit card to fall back on. So there he stood looking through the stacks of remnants. If he was clever, and he usually was, he could find enough in the scraps to build her a decent set of steps going down into her cellar. Then again, he wondered if that was such a good idea, if she kept all her moonshine down there. She might go down after one nip too many and break her leg.

He shook his head. That wasn't his responsibility. But as it was now, the poor lady couldn't even get jelly, and as far as he was concerned, that was unacceptable.

He continued to pilfer through the lumber, measuring off pieces and going through the design in his head. That was one thing about being poor and raised by an uncle who couldn't care less. Newland had learned a lot with a plethora of odd jobs under his belt. He could paint. He could build things. He could re-shingle a house if necessary. He had a host of small talents to get him through the hard times. Some people called that a jack of all trades, but he preferred Renaissance man. It sounded so much nicer.

He placed his lumber into a shopping cart, trying not to shake his head at it all. What kind of lumber store had shopping baskets anyway? *The kind that are conjoined with grocery stores.*

There was no one behind the cash register in the lumber-slash-hardware part of the store and, considering the thick layer of dust on the counter, nobody had been there for quite some time.

He grabbed some nails, thinking surely that Bitty would have a hammer stashed somewhere, and took his finds back through the grocery store. It was busy enough for a Thursday afternoon. He was third in line, which had to make this the rush of the day in Turtle Creek. In front of him was a middle-aged lady with a box of unmentionables and a can of ravioli. In front of her, a young mom with a baby on her hip juggled a bag of diapers, a can of formula, and other miscellaneous baby things. The poor child squalled as she tried her best to soothe his cries.

Newland took a deep breath. If there was one thing he couldn't stand, it was a baby crying. Not that it made him irritable, but he hated that one so young could be so unhappy. He had spent so much of his childhood sad and missing his parents. If he knew what to do for the child, he would do it right away just to stop that flow of tears.

In front of the poor mother stood Gilbert Hughes. Or was it Darrell? The twins were nearly identical, big hulking mountains of men who didn't look like they had the good sense to get out of the rain. He shook his head at his thoughts. He really had been hanging out here too long if he was even thinking things like that. Or maybe those Southern sayings were just too easy to pick up. After all he'd only spent about a week in the South his whole life put together.

"Is that all for you?" the cashier asked. She looked no more than fifteen, but he supposed that if she wasn't in school at this hour she had to be older than that.

She had her dark hair pulled back in a ponytail, big hoop earrings dangling from each ear, and a wad of chewing gum the size of Texas in her mouth. She blew a bubble and waited for Gilbert/Darrell to fish out his money.

"Did you get my special order in?" Gilbert/Darrell asked.

She gave him a look, smacked her gum one more time, then went to the microphone on the other side of her cash register. She turned it on and her magnified voice floated over their heads. "Bob, you got that order for Gilbert?"

"Darrell," the twin corrected.

"Darrell, I mean."

From somewhere on the other side of the store Newland heard the man yell, "Gimme a sec!"

She put Darrell's purchases in a sack, one by one. There were huge cartons of strawberries and blackberries along with what looked to be five large bottles of Karo syrup. Who needed that much syrup?

Was it Southerners in general that seemed to be insane or just the good people of Turtle Creek?

"You'll have to wait over there, sugar." Cash Register Girl waved him away.

Newland checked her nametag. Naomi.

Darrell looked about to protest but took his sack in one beefy hand and stood aside so Naomi could ring up the poor mother with the bawling baby.

Newland could say one thing about Naomi though: she was quick. And in no time at all, even before Bob got Darrell's special order to the front of the store, it was Newland's turn.

"Is that all for you, sugar?" The girl smacked her gum and blinked at Newland.

"Yeah, that'll do it."

"That'll be twenty-four fifty," she said with a smile.

He handed her his money, and she punched in the appropriate keys hardly taking her eyes from him as she put his money in the drawer. "You're new around here, huh?"

"I'm a reporter."

"I bet you seen a lot of things."

"You could say that."

"You going to work for the *Gazette*?"

The *Turtle Creek Gazette*? "No, I'm staying with Bitty Duncan."

"That Bitty." Naomi shook her head, her ponytail swinging from side to side. "She's a piece of work."

"Why is that?" Newland asked.

The girl shrugged one shoulder as if doing both was too much of an effort. "I don't know. Some say she's a little batty. She stays holed up in her house so much these days it's hard to say. Of course she goes out with her friends when she wants to and everything." She was talking in circles, and Newland couldn't figure out the meaning of anything that she was telling him. This was his one good opportunity to get an outside opinion of Bitty Duncan, and yet he couldn't even seem to do that. "But she's nice enough I suppose." Naomi finished.

"She is at that." Newland grabbed up his wood and started toward the door. He was halfway there before Naomi called out. "Hey, shug, you forgot your nails."

He backtracked to get the box of nails just in time to see Bob—or rather he assumed it was Bob—wheel in a huge pallet from the back.

"This ought to set you up for a while." Bob dusted his hands as he dropped the load next to Darrell's feet.

Newland couldn't see everything that was on it, but it looked to be mostly Mason jars and sugar.

He remembered a documentary he had seen once a long time ago about NASCAR racing and how it got its origins in moonshine running. Of course in order to talk about moonshine running, the narrator talked a lot about moonshine.

There was only one reason Newland could think of for somebody to need that much sugar and that many Mason jars. And it didn't have anything to do with pie.

CHAPTER EIGHT

Natalie let herself in the front door at her aunt's house, ready to relax and just enjoy a little bit of downtime. But as she entered, that was the last thing it seemed was in store for her that evening.

A loud yowl rang through the foyer followed by several sharp barks. The next thing she knew, Oskar came scrambling down the hallway, his toenails scraping against the wood floor. Behind him, in a rage, was the fluffy Mr. Piddles, running full speed. Well, it was fast for an overweight, extremely stocky cat.

Fortunately, Oskar could out run Mr. Piddles. The pooch flew straight toward her and jumped into her arms just in time. Just in time for him, anyway, but Natalie wasn't so lucky. Mr. Piddles tried to stop himself and instead slid into Natalie. He anchored himself with his claws.

"Ow!" she cried. "Aunt Bitty! Get your cat, please!" Her leg stung like the dickens, but she couldn't stop to look at it. She had her hands full of trembling, scared-witless Oskar.

"Aunt Bitty?" Where was her aunt now? It was Thursday, not a day she typically went out. But that didn't mean anything in the world of Bitty Duncan. The woman figured that since she was eighty-six she could do whatever the hell she wanted to and whenever the hell she wanted to do it. And nothing could stop her either way. Case in point...

"Did you call?"

Tran stood at the doorway to the kitchen. He had on a toolbelt, hammer slung in the side of it, and little pouches bulging with nails and who knew what else a guy thought he needed when he built something. "I need somebody to get Mr. Piddles. And to make sure I don't have any claws still stuck in my leg."

Newland hurried over to her, scooping up the cat who promptly started to purr. It seemed that Mr. Piddles completely forgot about terrorizing Oskar whenever Newland was within ten feet of them.

"That looks bad. Come on. I'll help you get it disinfected."

"It's fine," Natalie said, though she could feel blood trickling into her shoe. She needed to do something quick before it ruined them.

"Quit being so stubborn and let me help you. He took Mr. Piddles into the parlor and shut the door behind him. Then he turned back to Natalie and took Oskar from her. Wrapping one hand around the dog and one around her arm, he steered her up the stairs.

Newland set Oskar down on the second-floor landing and steered her into the bathroom.

It wasn't the largest bathroom in the house. She should've protested, but going into Aunt Bitty's master suite wasn't exactly an option either. Somehow it felt like trespassing, though Natalie could never figure out why.

He lifted her up before she could protest and plopped her down on the edge of the cabinet. With gentle hands, he picked up her leg and braced it against his thigh, slipping off her shoe and wincing as he noticed the blood inside. "You want to take care of that?"

She nodded, and he handed her a cotton ball and some peroxide. "What's this for?"

He shrugged. "I worked at a vet's office for a while. If you use peroxide, it'll get the blood out without any problems."

"A vet's office?"

Newland nodded. "Yeah, sometime after journalism school and before I went to work at *I Spy*."

"Why would you go to work at a vet's office after you finished journalism school?"

He took his sweet time in answering, using his own cotton ball to dab at the smears of blood across her leg.

Natalie sucked in a sharp breath. "Yeow," she said.

He dabbed again, and she felt his cool breath against her leg as he blew it dry. "Better?" He looked up at her, and Natalie was lost.

Why, oh why, did he have the ability to do that? Just look at her and make her insides melt? It was disturbing on many levels. First of all, she didn't want to feel that way. And second of all, she was practically engaged to the most handsome man in the entire county, and third of all she... Well, she really didn't have another reason. Weren't the first two enough?

"Who said I finished journalism school?" His brown eyes twinkled as he spoke, and she wondered if he was teasing her. She made a mental note to check it out on the computer.

Why should she?

He seemed to be on the level. If he wanted to murder them in their sleep or steal all the family heirlooms, he could have done that long ago without offering to fix Aunt Bitty's cellar stairs or paint the foyer.

"I see." Just how many jobs had this man had?

Natalie did her best to ignore his soft hands and gentle touch as he lightly rubbed the area with the dab of antibiotic cream. Then he covered the worst of the cuts with bandages.

"There you go." He smiled that smile that made everything tilt on its head. Maybe she just needed some alone time with Gerald.

When was the last time they had any time together alone? She thought back. The last time they were together was at the town meeting. Before that it was the board meeting for the historical society and before that it was a luncheon with the county sheriff and other law officials in the county.

She couldn't remember the last time she had just sat on the couch with him and watched TV. Okay, so they never did that. Gerald Davenport wasn't the type to sit around and watch TV, or go to the movies, or something else equally blue-collar. And there weren't a lot of highbrow things to do in Turtle Creek, Mississippi.

"T–thank you," she stammered.

Before she knew what happened, he swung her to the ground. Like she couldn't get off the cabinet by herself. She could have, but she had sat there, dumbly watching him as he put away all of the medical supplies.

"I'm going to head out to the cemetery tonight. You want to go with me?"

"Sure," Natalie said before she could stop herself. The last thing she wanted to do was go out to the cemetery at night. Again. Especially not with a man who made her feel so… tremble-ly. "Why don't we go in the daytime? Wouldn't it be easier to see things?"

"Your aunt says the ghost always comes at night. I figure if I'm going to get a chance to look at him, then I need to go at night… tonight. He does come on Thursdays, correct?"

Natalie shook her head. She wasn't going to fall for this. "There is no ghost."

"I thought we had an agreement. Now do you want to go with me or not?"

"I already said I would."

"Put on some good shoes and let's head over there after dinner. We can maybe get a look at the place a little better before night falls."

"I suppose." She stopped. "You don't really think whatever's causing the ghost is going to be there tonight, do you?"

"Anything is possible. Maybe Bitty thinks the ghost only comes on one night because that's the only time she looks out the window."

Natalie shook her head. "Whatever." She started toward the door trying to ignore the tingle in her legs and on her arms where he had touched her just moments before. Surely that would fade in a bit. She didn't know how much longer she could take it.

"After dinner then?" he asked.

"Yeah." She nodded.

"And Natalie?"

She turned to face him.

"This does not count as our date."

****

"Are you sure this is a good idea?"

Newland looked at Natalie and smiled. He had to give her kudos for dressing a little more comfortably tonight than she had the time before. At least she had on walking shoes without a designer label and a pair of jeans that had seen better days. And a T-shirt from the Turtle Creek Snappers.

He shook his head. Some people just didn't know a good mascot when they saw one.

"I never said it was a good idea at all." He went back to crawling on his hands and knees through the tall grass of the cemetery. She walked behind him careful not to step on him as she inched along.

"Then why are you doing it?"

"There may be something we're missing." He felt around in the grass, confident there was something about the cemetery that was special.

"Tell me again about the Confederate soldiers." He shifted his weight and sat, folding his legs crisscross style. They still had another forty-five minutes before the sun went down, that was forty-five minutes that he could study the lay of the cemetery, talk to her more about its history, and try to figure out why there was one lone ghost in the cemetery full of departed souls.

"There's not much to tell. I guess you could go to the library and look at the old reports.

He nodded. "I already have."

"I don't remember the exact date. I wasn't even born then, but I hear people talk about it. The federal government decided to go ahead and rebury all the Confederate soldiers that they could find in the national cemeteries."

"So they came and exhumed the bodies and took them away, right?" He couldn't quite wrap his mind around that. There was something there. Like why some of the graves were sunken in and some of them weren't. Did that mean that all didn't have Confederate bodies? It was apparent that some didn't. Were those the ones that were level with the ground? It just didn't make sense. Seemed like there was something more going on here than sunken Confederate graves.

And then there was that large pile of dirt. It hadn't dropped down from the sky. Somebody had brought it in. Though no one on Bitty's street had ever heard large equipment in the middle of the night. Or in the day for that matter. The dead end about where the dirt came from was like a rock wall. Did the dirt have anything to do with the ghost? He had no idea.

"I have a confession to make," he told Natalie as he sat there on the ground. She had plopped down next to him, one knee almost touching his as she gazed out over the overgrown cemetery. "What is that?"

"I don't think this ghost is a ghost at all."

"Well, hallelujah! Will the wonders of this world never cease?"

"You know, sarcasm does not become you."

She had the audacity to chuckle. "And what was your first clue?"

"Well," he started, "the first one is the fact that the Confederate graves have all been dug up and yet he still haunts a grave site where he's not even buried."

"You think that matters?" she asked.

He made no comment as she rolled her eyes at his statement.

"There was this lady in Montana. She had a cowboy ghost that came to her house every third week. No one knew why he picked every three weeks, but that was pretty much his time to arrive. He stayed for three days and then disappeared."

"Why is that so odd?"

"Because she lived in downtown Billings in an apartment complex."

"Oh."

"We did some investigation and found out that the apartment complex was built on land were a saloon used to be. The cowboys would come in from the range every three weeks or so. They would buy a drink, stay a couple of days, and then head on back to the ranch."

"What does that have to do with our ghost?"

"The cowboy ghost came back to that spot because that's where he died. It wasn't where he lived and it wasn't where he was buried. So there has to be some kind of connection to pull a ghost to a place, don't you think?"

Natalie shook her head. "No, I don't think. I don't usually think about ghosts at all."

"That's because you're too busy thinking about numbers and things like that."

She shrugged. "That's what I do. That's my job."

He nodded but didn't comment further on the matter. "If the ghost keeps coming back here and his body isn't buried here, then maybe he died here. That could be his connection to this place, but other than that…" He trailed off. "If he didn't die here and he wasn't buried here, why is he haunting here?"

CHAPTER NINE

"I'm bored," Natalie said. "Is being a journalist always like this?"

He shrugged. "I don't know. I usually don't have to go looking for a story. I worked at a national magazine. Stories came to me."

"But now you're freelance."

"Yeah." He looked away as he said the words, and Natalie had a feeling he was hiding something.

"It was a girl." From the look on his face she'd hit the nail right on the head. "A coworker? A mark?"

He turned to her, disbelief written so plainly on his face even the fading light couldn't hide it. "A mark?"

She shook her head. "Whatever it is you call someone that you're going to interview and get a story from."

"You've been watching too much TV." He looked back over the graveyard, but she had a feeling it was just to keep him from looking at her. "What was she like?"

"I didn't say it was a girl."

Natalie smiled. "You didn't have to."

He sighed, but he didn't turn back to face her. "She was beautiful." He hesitated before he said that last word as if he was looking for one special description for this unique lady.

"Yeah?"

"Not like beauty pageant beautiful, but she had this beauty on the inside. Why are we talking about this?"

"You're the one that dragged me out here without anything fun to talk about. So if you're going to abandon me in the middle of the graveyard with nothing else to do, I'm going to start asking questions."

"A born reporter."

They laughed together. Then Natalie tried again. "Seriously? What was she like?"

"She was sad."

Something in his voice prevented her from asking any more questions about her. Had he loved this mystery woman? "What now?" she asked instead.

"We wait."

"For?"

"I don't—" He stopped as a large truck pulled up beside the graveyard gate. He pointed as the truck killed its lights. "That." He smiled. "Can you see who it is?"

"Not from this distance," she said. "And not at dark-thirty."

"Who would be coming to the cemetery this time of day?"

"Besides us?"

"Hush."

"I think that's…" Natalie squinted as if that would help improve her vision. "Darrell."

"Or Gilbert," Newland added.

"Yeah." The twins were so much alike it was hard to tell them apart unless they were standing by side by side. Across the overgrown cemetery at ten o'clock at night it was damn near impossible. It could be either one of them. "Maybe both."

The passenger door opened and another big hulking shadow got out. It could only be the other Hughes brother.

"What would they be doing here?" Newland asked.

"Maybe they have relatives buried?"

Natalie glanced around pointedly at the overgrown and neglected cemetery. "Really?"

"Right. If they haven't come to visit graves, then why are they here?"

"No idea."

"Can you see what they're doing?" Newland asked.

Natalie shook her head. "Whatever it is, I wish they would do it in the daytime when I can see better."

"You suppose it has something to do with our ghost?"

She decided not to point out that the ghost was in no way "theirs." "I have no idea. I mean, they've been in trouble before," she whispered. "But never anything big. Small-time vandalism, you know. Things like that."

"Are you saying that this is small-time? Whatever this is," Newland added.

Natalie shrugged. "Yeah, I suppose. Neither one of them is very smart."

"I noticed."

"So if it is something more than petty vandalism, then someone else is probably in charge."

They watched as the two men circled around the other side of the oak tree, messed with the tarp and the dirt, then got back into the truck and drove away.

"Maybe it's nothing," Newland said.

"Do you think they're responsible for the ghost?"

Newland shook his head. "No idea. But I do know this. Two grown men don't come in the cemetery after dark without a reason." He pushed himself to his feet, leaving Natalie to scramble behind him.

"Hey," she called, stumbling as she went after him. There might be a ghost or not; she didn't really know. But the last thing she wanted to do was be left behind.

She caught up with him and slipped her arm through his and matched her stride to his longer one. Or maybe he matched his to hers. Either way, together they made the dark trip over to the tarp.

Once again, Newland used the flashlight app on his phone to light the area.

What had the two men had been doing? From what she could see, there was nothing. The tarp wasn't pulled completely over the dirt, the tree didn't have a notch in it, and the grave looked undisturbed. Nothing. It was all the same.

"I just don't know…" He swung the flashlight one last time.

Something twinkled in the light just before he switched it off.

"Wait. There."

"What?" He turned on the light once again.

Natalie took it from him, swinging it in the same arcs that he had used just seconds before. There in the grass lay something shiny. And not something one would normally see in an overrun graveyard.

She held the light steady as he bent to retrieve the item.

He held it out in his palm under the light so she could look at it as well. "A gold cufflink?"

"It has a C on it," Newland said.

She could see that. But what did that mean? "Confederate?"

"Were gold cufflinks part of Confederate uniforms?"

It didn't seem likely, but it wasn't completely improbable.

"That's something we could find out at the library tomorrow," he said.

"Or maybe in Aunt Bitty's reading room," Natalie added.

Newland frowned in confusion.

"My Uncle Stan was something of a Civil War buff. He might've had a book on it. She's kept his possessions perfectly intact. Right down to his underwear drawer." She laughed as Newland made a face.

"Let's skip that part, okay?"

"You got it."

****

Newland took his cellphone back from Natalie and tucked it into his pocket along with the cufflink. He didn't know much about such things like when cufflinks were first used and if Confederate soldiers had cufflinks or if the designs had changed over the years.

"What about the ghost?" Natalie asked as they headed out of the cemetery.

"What about it?"

"Why would a ghost need a cufflink?"

Newland almost stopped in his tracks. Somehow he managed to keep walking down the sidewalk and around the corner with Natalie at his side. He was ready to get back and look up all the information he could about Confederate uniforms. But that gave him pause. "They wouldn't."

"Unless…" Natalie started.

He took three steps before he realized she wasn't at his side. He had to backtrack to get her. "What if the ghost is actually someone reenacting? There's a reenactment unit here in town. They go over to Corinth all the time and reenact the battle there."

"But why would someone dress up like a Confederate soldier in the middle of the cemetery on the last Thursday of the month?"

Natalie shook her head. "Beats me."

****

Natalie wasn't going to think about what a thrill it was to walk next to Newland all the way back to her aunt's house. Of course she had thought on the way there what a thrill it was to walk with him all the way to the graveyard, but somehow this was different.

They had found out something tonight. Something exciting. Though she didn't know what it was. Somehow she just knew that the cufflink in his pocket was important. It had to be. Why else would Darrell and Gilbert be looking for it?

Her excitement was something that couldn't be touched by board meetings and financial reports and all the other things that she found herself doing on a daily basis.

"You never did say how you did in the science fair," Newland said as they walked.

"I wasn't in the science fair. Aubie was."

"Uh-huh," Newland said.

A little bit of the thrill leached out of her. "What's that supposed to mean?"

"It means you go around doing everything for everybody, not caring one iota about the things that you do for yourself. Or even doing things for yourself. When was the last time you had a mani-pedi?"

"Last week," she volleyed back.

"Posh," he said, imitating Aunt Bitty spot on. "You only did that because you have to keep up appearances. When was the last time you had a mud bath?"

She shot him a dry look. "I have to say I was about ten."

"Okay," Newland said. "Something else then, something you find enjoyable. When was the last time you took yourself to get an ice cream? Watched a movie you wanted to watch? Or sat in that alcove in your aunt's house and read a book without anybody bothering you?"

She opened her mouth to speak, but he cut in before she could answer.

"Including Oskar."

"That's not fair. Oskar doesn't count."

"He sure does. Because you do everything for everybody and not one damn thing for yourself."

"Why do you care?" It was Natalie's job, albeit a job that she had been thrust into at a young age, but that's what she did. She took care of things. "What about tonight? I got nothing out of tonight."

They were almost to her aunt's house, and the sidewalk was starting to get uneven. She had to maneuver a little more carefully as she walked next to Newland.

He stopped and whirled around to face her. "Nothing, huh?" And then he swooped in.

She wished she could say that she didn't enjoy his kiss. But this was number three and each one seemed a little more spectacular than the one before. She wanted to push him away in case anyone was watching, melt into him in case no one was, and keep on kissing him just to see where it might go.

Somehow he knew just how to make everything hum. From the way he cupped her face, his thumbs cradling her cheeks, to the way his lips moved over hers, masterful yet soft, urging, the most remarkable thing ever.

She wanted that kiss to go on forever. And ever. And ever.

She sighed as he lifted his mouth from hers. Forever sure was a short time.

"Never say I didn't give you anything," he whispered, his voice lilting on a laugh.

Natalie's eyes snapped open. "What? You—" She wanted to smack the smug look off his face. He knew just how to push all her buttons. Never mind the humming part. He was just testing her to see if he could push her over the edge. This time he had.

She yanked herself out of his embrace, stumbling over a particularly jagged section of sidewalk, then hollering for him to let her go when he kept her from sprawling flat on her face.

"You are the most ungrateful person I've ever met in my life."

"I. Am. Not," she said succinctly. "I never asked for your kiss, I never asked for your help, and I never asked for you to come here."

"Why are you so threatened by my presence?"

Now that was the question she didn't want to answer. It brought up too many things that she didn't want to think about. "I'm not threatened by you at all."

"Then I should be able to kiss you again." He moved as if to just do that, but she put her hands up to stop him. She was so incredibly proud of herself. Though a little piece of her cried out in extreme disappointment. If the first kiss was great and the second kiss was spectacular and the third kiss was bone melting, what would his fourth kiss be like?

She shook her head. "I think we need to set some rules right now."

He folded his arms across his chest and gave her that unreadable look. She had a feeling he was about to make fun of her. But she didn't care. Mr. Chicago couldn't come buzzing in, kissing her and wooing her only to run out of sight a week later. She wasn't going to have it. She had her life perfectly lined out, and he wasn't going to step in and ruin it.

"One: no more kissing."

"I don't agree to that."

"You don't have that option."

"Yeah, I do."

Natalie closed her eyes and shook her head. "Two: you are not to make the people in this house love you. You cannot come into our lives and then walk back out again breaking everybody's heart."

"What about yours?"

"Impossible. I love Gerald."

"I doubt that very seriously."

"Nobody asked you."

"Maybe you should."

"Maybe I shouldn't."

"He's all wrong for you, you know."

"Again, no one asked you."

"Again, somebody should."

Natalie closed her eyes and rubbed her fingers against her temples. "This is getting us nowhere." Talking to Newland Tran was sort of like trying to herd cats. "Somehow I have become protector of this family. And as protector, I demand that you make sure everyone is just as you left them when you decide to fly on to your next freelance project."

"Who said I was leaving?"

Natalie couldn't stop the bark of derisive laughter. "You're going to stay here? In Turtle Creek, Mississippi?" She shook her head again. "I went to school with guys like you. You have 'vagabond travel' written all over you. You can't stay in one place for long and certainly not a place as boring as this."

"Who said I think this place is boring?"

"Don't start that again," Natalie begged, her voice stern. "Just do this for me, please."

He seemed to think about it a minute. "Okay, then. Whatever you want."

CHAPTER TEN

"Where are we going?" Natalie asked shortly after six the next afternoon. It was Friday and there weren't a lot of things to do on the weekend in Turtle Creek. Come the fall, there would be football games, but until then…

"On a date." Newland opened the front door and held it open for her to precede him out of the house.

"I know that. But you're not going to tell me where you're taking me for our date?"

"I will as soon as we get there."

Natalie followed him out to his car. She eyed the rattletrap and tried to keep her expression from looking completely horrified. "I've got an idea. You want to drive my car?"

He shot her that bone-melting smile. "Normally I would tell you no. That you shouldn't be such a snob and think you're too good to ride in my car. It may not be the prettiest car, but it's clean." His eyes twinkled. "But I would love to get behind the wheel of that Jag."

Natalie smiled to herself. Most guys would love to drive a car like hers. It was her one big luxury. The one thing she allowed herself to have. It was a beautiful car, and she loved it.

She held up the keys, and he palmed them, placing one hand at the small of her back as he led her toward the Jag.

Natalie ignored the warmth his palm spread through her as he helped her over the uneven sidewalk.

"Someone should fix this," he commented, then he gave a discreet cough. "You know the mayor. Why not have him come take a look at it?" He opened the door for her, and Natalie slid inside. It felt strange being on the passenger side, but she was looking forward to being able to enjoy the car without driving.

"You want the mayor to fix it, you tell him. I have to tell him when it's time to brush his teeth, when it's time to go to bed, when he needs to go to school, and to finish all of his homework. I don't really like telling him much else. That's quite enough for each day."

Newland walked around the front of the car and slid into the driver's seat beside her, sighing with pleasure. The thought made her happy. Which was ridiculous. Why should she be happy that he enjoyed her car? Six more days and he'd be gone.

He put the key in the ignition, started the car, and backed out at the driveway.

"You've really have broken the biggest date rule of all, you know that, right?" she said as they headed off to who knew where.

"And what is that?" He cocked his head toward her, the wind blowing through the strands of his blue-black hair. He really was the cutest. And the Least Likely To. That was the one thing she needed to remember.

"You always tell the girl where you're taking her. How am I supposed to know how to dress for a date when I don't even know our destination?"

Those exotic brown eyes slid over her, and Natalie shivered despite the ninety-plus degree weather. "You look just fine." The look and those words were more like a caress.

No, she wasn't thinking about that. She'd only promised him this date so she could get her aunt's stairs fixed in the cellar. And that was all. That's exactly what she would tell Gerald when the time came and he found out. *If* the time came. She could only hope...

She dressed as she usually did: dress, heels, matching jewelry, matching handbag, up-do, and makeup. It was a girl standard. Surely she couldn't go wrong with her slim-cut teal jersey knit and camel-colored pumps. Teal was a color for any occasion, wasn't it?

"Fine," she said, her voice husky. He wasn't going to tell her where they were going. So be it. She would find out soon enough.

Newland slowed the car for the one stoplight they had in town. It blinked yellow in one direction and red in the other. As a formality everyone stopped... just to be sure.

"Are we staying here in Turtle Creek?" She hadn't meant for the question to slip out; it just had. And now that it was loose, she wanted to know the answer to it.

There wasn't a whole lot to do in Turtle Creek. There was a movie theater over in Corinth, which wasn't very far. They could drive there for their date. That might even be better actually. No one there knew her that well. And they surely didn't know Newland Tran. The two of them could go have their date in Corinth, drive back, and she wouldn't have to worry about Gerald's reaction when—no, *if*—he found out.

"We could go to Corinth, you know," she said, hoping he got the hint.

"Uh-huh." He didn't bother to look at her as he put the car into motion once again. Pass the Billups Fill-ups, past the post office, past the police station, only to stop in front of the hardware store.

She looked at him. "You sure know how to treat a girl."

"Just relax, Natalie. And enjoy yourself. You might find that you like it."

Once again, he placed that big hand at the small of her back and escorted her into the general store. Well, into the grocery part of the store. It was an odd setup, she knew, but small towns couldn't support so many different stores. This one had kind of emerged out of necessity.

"Why are we here?" Surely this wasn't their date.

Newland nudged her toward the left, and Natalie followed his direction, unable to do much else. Maybe it was better this way. Gerald wouldn't expect them to be at the general store on a date.

They could walk up and down the aisles to their heart's content and no one would be the wiser that she had gone out with the handsome reporter from Chicago. It was perfect. He led her through the groceries and into the section that had, at one time, been the Rexall drugstore. But then a major chain had come in and the pharmacy had shut down. The soda fountain had remained open, and for that everyone in Turtle Creek was grateful.

"We're eating ice cream?" She tried not to sound horrified. She watched every bite she ate. Ice cream was definitely not on the list of approved sustenance.

"I told you last night you don't even take time for yourself. So tonight, that's what you need to do. And eat ice cream."

She shook her head. "No, I'm not." She had a reputation to maintain, a figure to maintain, a diet to maintain. She didn't go around willy-nilly eating ice cream with strange Yankee men. It wasn't proper.

"Come on," Newland said, leading her toward one of the small wrought iron tables with sweetheart-back chairs. The whole place looked something like an outdoor patio, without the outdoors. Oddly enough, there was barely a window in the place. And that one was in the front and up so high no one could see in.

Yes, this wasn't a bad idea. Aside from having to eat a billion calories and fat grams in a scoop of ice cream that was probably so delicious.

"Do you know what you want?"

Natalie shook her head. "Just a Diet Coke for me."

"Oh, no," Newland said. "We came to eat ice cream, and ice cream we're going to eat."

"You can have ice cream, I'm having a Diet Coke."

She expected him to argue, but instead he pinned her with a look as his mouth twisted into a serious slant. He didn't respond, just turned back to the counter and placed their order. "Are you really so uptight that you can't sit here with me and eat an ice cream?" he asked as he returned to their table.

Heat filled Natalie's cheeks and she knew that her current shade clashed terribly with the teal in her dress. "I am not uptight."

"You are so uptight you squeak when you walk."

She gasped. "I. Do. Not."

"Maybe not, but you are the most uptight person I know."

She scoffed. "Like that's saying much."

"Are appearances that important to you?" he asked.

Natalie didn't have time to answer; the young girl behind the counter came out bearing a tray containing two chocolate ice cream hot fudge sundaes.

Oh! She hadn't had chocolate in so long. And it looked so good.

Just one bite, she told herself. One surely wouldn't do harm. She would have one bite, then stir the rest of it around as it melted. He could eat all he wanted, then they would go home. It was a perfect plan.

She took her time scooping up a bite, making sure it had just the right ratio of chocolate ice cream to chocolate syrup to nuts and whipped cream. If she was going to eat just one bite of this beautiful concoction, then it was going to be a good one.

Newland didn't have such criteria. He scooped up a big bite and shoveled it in, then pointed his spoon at her. "You never did answer me."

"What's the question again?" she asked. She was still working on getting that bite to be the best bite of ice cream in the history of dairy products.

"You know full well what the question is."

"Appearances. Right." She pretended to think about it a second. She wasn't really thinking about the answer as much as she was thinking about the beautiful dessert in front of her. "I take it appearances aren't that important in your world." She tried to shoot a scathing look at today's concert T-shirt underneath his standard corduroy blazer. My Chemical Romance. She wondered if her brother knew their music. She had no idea.

He took another big bite and Natalie watched him eat, hoping the jealousy wasn't plastered all over her face for him to see. "You can clean me up and put me to the task, but I'm still a pencil jockey. And everyone knows it. I can dress up when I need to. I just don't have to dress up all the time." He shot her another pointed look.

"I enjoy dressing this way."

"I bet you sleep in matching pajamas, don't you?"

"What's wrong with that?"

"And your underwear probably matches." Before she could protest he continued. "And not only the other underwear pieces. I bet your panties and bra match your whole outfit." He looked at her again, as if analyzing what was underneath her dress. "What color do you have on right now? Baby blue, I bet. That would be pretty with that green dress."

She wasn't sure if she wanted to slap him or bust out laughing. "First of all, my dress is teal. And second of all, the color of my underwear is none of your business." Never mind that he'd hit too close to home. Yes, her underwear always matched, and yes, it usually matched her outfit as well. What was the point in having nice things, if she didn't do it tastefully?

"Right." He nodded. "They're probably a boring tan color like your shoes." His eyes held a mischievous twinkle as he devoured yet another mound of ice cream. But what she really hated was

124

the self-satisfied smirk that rose to his lips as she blushed.

"Bingo!" he singsong.

"You," Natalie sputtered.

"Am I right?" He grinned at her. Natalie wanted to ask what was so wrong with wearing nice clothes, having nice things, and matching. But the questions and answers sounded incriminating, so she didn't respond at all.

"Are you going to eat that?" He nodded toward her quickly melting ice cream.

She tried not to drool as she looked down at the sticky, gooey mess that had once been a chocolate-chocolate sundae. "It's not exactly on my diet."

Newland shook his head, then wiped the chocolate from his chin with a napkin. "See? That's the problem with you Type A's. You can't enjoy yourself. Not even a little. Because it might ruin whatever—the balance of the universe—so even ice cream is off limits because you might gain a pound or two. It'll be fine. I promise."

"You don't know anything about Type A's considering you're not one." She hated the harshness of her words. But it seemed like he had been doing nothing but picking on her since they'd started their evening. A girl could only take so much criticism before she fought back.

"I know enough about Type A's to know that I don't want to be one. I like ice cream too much." He scooped up another bite and shoveled it into his mouth. Natalie had a hard time not licking her lips in response. What would one bite of ice cream hurt? That's what she had said she would allow herself, one bite. But then they started talking and she rethought her decision. After all, one bite could lead to eating the whole sundae. Like she needed those calories.

"You don't think I know how to have a good time, do you?" She hadn't meant to ask; the question slipped out all on its own. And now that it was out there, there was no calling it back.

He sat back in his heart-shaped, wrought iron seat and leveled that brown gaze upon her. "No. I don't. And you've done nothing to make me think any differently."

His words dropped between them like a challenge. She knew how to have a good time. So she hadn't been voted Most Likely to Paint the Town Red in high school. She knew how to do it up when the time was right. Though tonight it seemed she needed to show Newland Tran just how good she was at having a good time.

She scooped up a glop of the ice cream, not even bothering to make sure that the ratio between chocolate syrup, ice cream, whipped cream, and nuts was a good balance. Instead she spooned it in, her gaze never leaving his.

She almost moaned her pleasure out loud. She closed her eyes, savoring the bite even as she knew it had to be the only one she took.

She'd taken one bite of ice cream. She had done something for herself. She had gone out with Newland Tran, and he couldn't say that she didn't know how to let loose.

Her eyes fluttered back open, and it was then that she realized that she had shut them in her pleasure. The ice cream might have become a runny sticky mess, but it tasted amazing.

He crossed his arms and eyed her dubiously. "One bite of ice cream does not a good time make."

She scooped up another bite and shoveled it in. The challenge had been uttered. The second bite was even better than the first.

Still he watched her, each blink of his eyes a gauntlet.

She took another bite and another, then another until a searing pain shot through her head behind the one eye. "Yeow!" she cried, gently rubbing the area, careful not to destroy any of her carefully applied makeup.

Newland chuckled. "Brain freeze," he said. "Just proof that you need to eat ice cream more. Then you wouldn't be so desperate to eat it that you make yourself sick."

Desperate? "Did you just call me desperate?"

He handed her a napkin across the table. "Yeah, desperate. I see it when you eat ice cream. I can feel it in your kiss."

"That. Is. Absurd." She had never heard a bigger bunch of bunk in her whole life. Who was he to come waltzing in here after two days, telling her what she needed to do?

He shook his head, a self-satisfied smirk on his lips. "Sure. Sure."

Natalie wanted to crawl across the table and kiss him silly, show him exactly what she—no, she wanted to slap him. Yeah, that was right. She wanted to smack him. Not kiss him.

"So tell me, Natty Nat, have Mr. Almost Fiancé and you... you know?" He raised his eyebrows as if to define the blank space in his speech.

"Are you asking…?" *Of all the nerve!* "I hardly think that's any of your business." She shook her head and crossed her arms. That was telling him.

"Yeah… I didn't think so."

Natalie fumed. "I'll have you know that Gerald and I have a mature and mutual relationship." She stopped as he started to laugh. "What's so funny?"

Newland wiped his eyes. "A mutual relationship? What the hell is that?"

"It's a relationship built on trust and caring."

"And no sex." It wasn't a question.

"Again, a complete inventory of my intimate doings with Gerald isn't any of your concern."

Newland shook his head. "That may be, but it seems like somebody needs to talk some sense into you."

****

And that someone might as well be him.

Newland got to his feet and reached out a hand to Natalie. "Are you ready to go?"

She nodded, and stood, but refused to take his hand.

He shrugged again. It was no skin off his nose if she didn't want to touch him. And he surely didn't care that she would rather touch a stuffed shirt like Gerald Davenport instead of him, a flesh and blood man. A man who didn't kid himself about things like the importance of his own existence. But who was he to say?

Maybe bringing her here was a mistake. He'd thought he would show her how to relax a little, but he just made the two of them more uptight.

He followed her out to the car, and they got in, each seemingly waiting on the other to say what was next.

"So?" she asked.

Newland shook his head, then put the key in the ignition. "I think this is a wash."

She buckled her seatbelt with more force than necessary, then pinned him with that sky-blue gaze. "So you think I'm a lost cause?"

"I didn't say that."

"You might as well have. You've already said that I don't know how to have a good time. And that I've denied myself too many pleasures in life and I'm too bossy with everybody. Of course a date with me would be a complete wash. Why would you expect anything else?"

Newland backed the car out of the space and kept his eyes on the road instead of on her. "I think it's best if we just call it a night. Cut our losses, embrace our differences. Life goes on."

"You're not getting off that easy. You promised me a good time tonight. And I haven't had a good time yet."

He remembered the way she had eaten the ice cream, like she was starving. She seemed to have a good enough time then, he thought, remembering how she had licked the spoon. He shifted in his seat, suddenly uncomfortable in his own jeans.

"Forget I said that."

"No, no, no. You're not going to say that now. You don't think I know how to have a good time. I'll show you."

"Natalie, I don't think that's a good—"

He broke off as she reached up and grabbed the wheel, wrenching it to the right. "Turn here," she said.

He had no choice but to comply.

"Now left," she said.

He held up a hand as she made a move to grab the steering wheel once again. "I got it this time." He executed the left and found himself driving down a tree-lined residential street. "Would you like to tell me where we're going?"

"Up there. Second house on the right."

"Whose house?" he asked as he pulled his car into the drive. On second glance he realized that it wasn't a house, but a duplex, one building with two entrances to separate apartments.

"Mine."

"What are we doing at your house?" He asked the question, but she was already out of the car and slamming the door behind her. "How about I follow you in?" he mumbled to no one in particular. He turned off the engine and pocketed the keys. "Are you going to tell me why we're here?"

She turned to him and held her hand out palm up. "Keys, please."

He fished out the keys and handed them to her, biding his time until she got the door open. It seemed that Natalie didn't want to tell him why they were there, but he figured he'd find out soon enough.

She stepped into the apartment and flipped on the light, setting her purse down in the chair by the door. He wanted to think that the apartment was a complete reflection of her personality, but on closer inspection he realized that it was a hybrid of her and Aubie. Pristine white sofa paired with a worn-in black gamer's chair. High def, seventy-two-inch flat screen, paired with every game console known to man. Original artwork hanging behind the sofa, polished wood floors, and one lone glass sitting on the coffee table without a coaster.

She made a noise of disgust, then crossed the room to pluck the glass from the coffee table. Shaking her head, she walked it out of the room—he presumed to the kitchen—and returned seconds later.

"Are you going to tell me why we're here?" Images of the two of them together, naked, flashed through his mind. It was very tempting. They were here, they were alone, and they had the chemistry necessary for such…ahem, activities. But he had a feeling she had something else in mind.

She plopped her hands on her hips and leveled her gaze on him. "The other day you asked me the last time I had watched a movie. Well, we're going watch a movie."

"O-kay," he said, "if that's what you want to do." Personally, he could think of a lot of other things to do that didn't involve movies, but he pushed those thoughts away. She fancied that she was going to marry the stuffed shirt and really it was no concern of his. He would be leaving in just a week. What difference did it make to him if she married somebody completely wrong for her?

"But," he continued, "no romantic comedies, no tearjerkers, and no animated."

"What do you have against animated movies?"

Newland shook his head. "Nothing, really. But the last thing I want to do is sit here and watch *My Little Pony*."

"I'll have you know, I don't even own *My Little Pony*." She sniffed and walked over to the shelves framing the wall on either side of the television. A vast array of items were placed there. Polished rocks, small figurines, mixed in with a few books and a ton of movies and games.

She pointed to a shelf at eye level to her. "This is mine."

"Are you asking for help choosing a movie?" Little Miss I Organize Everything for Everybody was going to give up the decision?

"I'm sure you don't want to watch the *Saw* series."

Newland made a face. "Horror's not really my thing." He took a step closer, his gaze traveling over the titles she had indicated as her own. There were some great movies there—a few classics and a few that would be one day. But one name kept appearing over and over. "Do you own everything Brad Pitt is in?"

If he wasn't mistaken a blush rose into her cheeks, but that didn't seem possible. "Maybe," she hedged.

"We could watch one of his I guess." He reached toward *The Curious Case of Benjamin Button*, but she shook her head.

"I don't watch that one."

Newland blinked a couple of times, trying to get his thoughts in order. "You own it, but you don't watch it?"

Natalie nodded. "That's right."

Damn, sometimes talking to her was like trying to pull teeth. "Why do you have it but don't watch it?"

"I suppose it's safe to say that he's my favorite actor."

Newland nodded encouragingly.

"But I don't like to watch the ones where he dies. He dies in that one."

Newland looked back to the title under his fingertips, trying to figure out why it mattered to her. He shook his head.

"Pick another title," she said.

He sorted through them, thinking back on the ones he had seen, the ones where Brad Pitt's character had died, but Natalie seemed to take the decision from his hands.

"This one." She handed him *Legends of the Fall*.

"Doesn't he die in this?" Newland asked.

Natalie shook her head. "Trust me. I know." She held the movie out to him.

"What do you want me to do with it?"

"You'll have to figure all this out," she said waving a hand toward the media set up. "This is Aubie's domain."

He looked to the movie and back to her. "Are you—?"

"Just play the movie." She walked over to the sofa, then perched on the edge.

He eyed her carefully. "Don't you want to change in to something more comfortable?"

"I am perfectly comfortable, thank you."

She looked like she was going to a board meeting. He might not be staying for another week, but he was determined that by the time he left she would not be a stuffed shirt to match that of her almost fiancé.

It took four and a half minutes, but he managed to get the movie playing. Then he settled onto the couch next to her, laying his arm across the back and crossing one ankle over his knee. Natalie sat on the edge of the couch, perched there like a bird about to take flight. Why was she so nervous in her own home?

"You don't have to be afraid of me," he said as the opening sequence played. The Native American narrator told the story of Captain Ludlow and how he came to be in Montana.

"Whatever gave you that idea?" She scoffed.

He waved a hand toward her. "No reason."

She seemed to realize the distance she had placed between them and eased back onto the sofa. Her rigid spine finally touched the back rest, but she held herself ramrod straight as the young Tristan went seeking the bear.

Newland ran his hand closer toward her, entwining his fingers in the back of her hair. As usual it was pulled back into a sexy librarian bun.

She jumped as if she'd been stuck with a cattle prod.

"Relax," he urged in a sweet whisper. "It's a date; you're supposed to be enjoying yourself."

"Are you saying that I don't know how to enjoy myself on a date?" She half turned toward him, movie forgotten.

Newland sighed. "I didn't say that. I said relax. You're supposed to be having a good time."

She nodded sternly. "I am." The words sounded almost like a threat.

"You are not. You're as stiff as a board, tied up in knots, acting like I'm going to jump on you any second."

Natalie was on her feet in an instant. "Maybe this was a bad idea."

He stood as well, waiting for her to make the next move.

"You want to tell me what's wrong?" he asked.

She shook her head. "Maybe we should go back to my aunt's house."

"If that's what you want to do. But I have a feeling it's not."

She scoffed again. "Don't be ridiculous."

She moved around the coffee table and across the expanse of wood floor to stand by the front door. "Can you turn off the TV and stuff?" She waved an expressive hand toward the media center.

"Of course," he said, not mentioning the fact that her fingers trembled as they hung in the air.

He moved behind her, stopping at the television cabinet to turn everything off. He ejected the movie, put it back in its case, and set everything to rights. Then he walked over to where she waited.

"Are you sure this is what you want?" he asked.

Natalie nodded, but he had a feeling she couldn't find the words.

"What if I think you're lying to me again?"

"Don't be ridiculous." She moved to open the door but stopped, sucked in a deep breath. Then she whirled around, both hands clutching the knob behind her.

"What's the matter?"

She shook her head but made no move to get out from in front of the door.

"Natalie?"

She stared at him for a moment, her eyes conflicted and stormy. She dragged her bottom lip through her teeth, the action so sexy he almost groaned out loud.

What was wrong with her? He had a feeling he would find out, in her time. How long they stood there just looking at one another Newland couldn't say. What could have been seconds or maybe two lifetimes passed, then she pushed herself off the door, her eyes never leaving his. Each step was slow and sexy, one foot in front of the other until she was standing just inches away.

He inhaled sharply, getting a big gulp of pure Natalie. That alluring smell that belonged just to her. That odd blend of roses, baby powder, and dry-cleaning fluid.

Another lifetime passed as she stood there in front of him, trembling. Or was she merely vibrating with the same need as him? It was crazy, this attraction that he had for this uptight southerner. But it was there all the same. She was always in control, always so perfect. He wanted to muss her hair and smear her lipstick and... He wondered what she looked like with mascara smudged under her eyes and chipped fingernail polish.

He never thought something as mundane as messy hair to be particularly erotic, but somehow with Little Miss Perfect Natalie Coleman, it would be.

He wanted to reach out and haul her toward him and find out just how great her lipstick looked smeared, but he had promised he wouldn't kiss her. Just last night.

Last night? That was insanity. Had it only been last night that she had laid down her ultimatum and her ground rules on how they were to behave?

He had made his promise. He wasn't going to kiss her. He might not think she belonged with a fuddy-duddy like Gerald Davenport, but that didn't give him the right to go messing around with her emotions and desires. So he stood there, just breathing in her scent, humming with the need to pull her into his arms and kiss her like there was no tomorrow.

Even eye contact with her was almost too much. He tore his gaze from hers and cast a downward glance. Like that was any better. It fell immediately to her breasts rising and falling with her rapid breathing. But then his gaze centered on the small stain on her otherwise perfect dress. It had to be from her earlier chocolate ice cream binge. A stain on her dress should not be so... Irresistible.

This time his groan was audible. But he had made his promise and he was going to keep it, even if it killed him.

He raised his gaze to hers. The light in her eyes relayed that she knew his every thought. Was he that transparent? Could she see how badly he wanted her? Did she even understand how ridiculous it all was?

"Natalie," he breathed, her name somewhere between a plea and a prayer.

"Newland," she said in return and took one more step. Her body brushed against his, and he felt as if he'd been touched with wildfire. He took a step backwards out of sheer survival. How could he manage if she burned them up?

But for every step he took back, she took one forward until he felt the couch behind him. It cut him off at the knees, and he sat down hard. With Natalie on top.

CHAPTER ELEVEN

"What are you doing?"

Natalie sighed as she leaned in and pressed her lips to Newland's. "I'm pretty sure I'm kissing you."

Somehow they had sprawled across the sofa, Newland underneath her. Every curve she had molded to his hard planes. It was exquisite. Never in her life had she felt like this. So out of control, so in control, so scared, so confident. She loved it, and she hated it all in the same moment. But more than anything, she couldn't resist it. She wanted to go on kissing him and kissing him. Until the dawn came. Or eternity. Whichever.

She mumbled her protest as he slid his fingers into her hair on either side of her face and pulled her lips away from his. "What about the ground rules? You know, no kissing."

"Screw the ground rules." This was what she had been waiting for since she'd first laid eyes on him. Even the first time she saw him, she knew. He was the one who would make her lose control. And she relished it as much as she despised it.

But what harm is there? the voice inside her whispered. It wasn't like he was staying forever. Another week and he would be gone. Out of her life forever, taking with it the only chance she had at letting go.

She resisted his hold, doing her best to kiss him once again. He laughed and braced his elbows, effectively holding her away from him. "You mean that?" he asked.

Did he have to ask? Could he not tell? "Yep."

That was all it took. She yelped as she found their positions reversed. One minute she was on top of Newland and the next minute she was underneath.

His weight was wonderful, exquisite and warm as he took over their embrace.

So accustomed to being in charge and running everything, Natalie found this switch in positions to be refreshing. She closed her eyes and allowed him his way, following his lead instead of battling for control.

Except for one thing. She bucked against him, urging him on. With Newland she felt renewed, wild, and able to abandon the façade she donned every day.

He moved one hand between them to press her hips into the sofa. And she nearly cried out, bereft when he lifted his mouth from hers.

"Slow down." His words were breathless. "If we don't take this easy, I'm not sure I'll be able to stop."

"That was sort of the idea, yes." She snagged his gaze with her own. His brown eyes were nearly black with passion. And she loved that she had done that to him. Those high cheekbones held a tinge of pink, and he was breathing as heavily as she.

"You don't mean that." His voice rose on the end making it almost a question, but not quite.

"Yes, I do." She lifted one knee, effectively dropping him between her thighs. Her dress had ridden up. And the rough fabric of his jeans was a thrill all its own.

"Natalie."

"Newland," she mocked his tone.

"You can't—"

She effectively cut him off placing one finger over his lips. "Yes. I can."

"What about—"

She shook her head. "For a guy who is about to get lucky, you sure do protest a lot."

"I just don't think—"

"Then don't. What's the harm in just feeling?"

He closed his eyes, and she could tell he was tottering. "I'm not going to beg."

Once again he pinned her with that dark, exotic gaze. "But if you did…" His expression was pained, and she knew she had taken him to the edge of his limit.

For some reason he was trying his hardest to resist her. But where was the benefit in that? She could see none. He wanted her. She wanted him. It was as simple as that. Why shouldn't they enjoy themselves? Hadn't he'd been fussing for days that she didn't know how to have a good time? This was the best time she'd had in a long while.

"Newland," she started her voice breaking at the end. "Please."

His breath hitched. "Please what?" he whispered.

"Please make love to me."

The dam broke. One moment she could feel his resolve between them, then it was gone, and only sweet warmth lingered in its place.

She bucked against him again, and nearly came as he ground against her.

"Never in my life," she rasped.

"I know," he said. He lowered his head, his teeth scraping against one pebbled nipple.

When had this happened? When had he unhooked her bra? When had he pulled her dress aside? Pushed her bra up, revealing her straining breasts to him?

Why did it matter?

He trailed the line of kisses from one side to the other, cool air brushing against the wet trail he left. She was on fire, out of control, and she needed this burning in her to be extinguished. Now.

She reached for his waistband, fumbling with the button and trembling so badly she could barely work his zipper down. But she had to have him. Had to have him now.

She tugged at the fabric of his jeans and he sprang free. Success! She palmed him in one hand, feeling more powerful than she ever had as he sucked in a breath. She wanted this to last forever. She needed this to happen now. All the conflicts raging through her competed for top billing with her overwhelming desire to have him. They weren't even undressed!

She didn't care. It needed to happen and it needed to happen now.

She squeezed him, that silky skin over hard steel jerking in her hand as she applied the sweet pressure.

"Natalie," he groaned.

"I want you," she breathed.

He worked his way back up to her mouth, kissing her deeply as she toyed with him, running fingers along his length, testing, measuring, teasing.

"We have to slow down."

She shook her head. "No. We need to go faster."

Couldn't he tell? Couldn't he understand how important this was? How they couldn't lose this momentum? She'd never felt this way in her life. And she had to grab it with both hands before it disappeared forever.

"A minute," he beseeched. "Condom."

She stopped just briefly. "Do you have one?" She hadn't thought about that. Did she have one? She couldn't remember. Of course it was hard to hold any thought in her head when his warm weight was pressing her into the sofa cushions.

Did Aubie have one? He better not. She'd kill him if he did. Or maybe she would kill him if he didn't. She couldn't decide.

"Just give me a minute," Newland said.

He shifted, his weight moving from one side to the other as he dug out his wallet.

She laughed as he retrieved the little foil packet and tossed his wallet to the floor. Some things just weren't important right then.

"Give it." She took it from him, opening the package as he buried his face in the crook of her neck. She reached between them, finding him with ease, and rolled the condom down him as he nibbled and kissed his way from her shoulder to her lips.

She held him in her hands, directing him where he needed to go, so ready to have him inside her.

"Your dress," he rasped.

She shook her head. "It's okay." With one hand between them she moved the tiny crotch of her panties aside and lifted her hips urging him where she needed him most.

He entered her, strong and full up to the hilt. She gasped. This. This was what she had been waiting for. Maybe even her whole life.

He stopped, his body trembling with the effort.

"Newland?" she whispered, the one word a question and a plea at the same time. She needed to know why he wasn't moving. She needed him to take up that old rhythm.

"Just give me a minute." He shifted, driving deeper and nearly taking her breath away. His elbows braced on either side of her head. He stopped, allowing her breathing to return to an almost normal pattern. Then he pulled back and slammed into her again, driving her closer to the arm of the couch with each thrust. It was insane. It was insanity. It was exquisite.

She wrapped her legs around his hips holding him as close to her as she could. Over and over. Deeper and deeper until she thought she would scream from the pleasure of it all.

"Just one," he gritted, shifting his weight again to work one hand under her. He ran one finger from her tailbone, following that sweet crease until he touched where their bodies were joined. Then he dragged his thumb across that sweet spot, and Natalie shattered into a billion pieces. But even that was not to be enough for Newland. He drove into her hard, taking her breath. Then, wrapping one the arm around her waist, he switched their positions, pulling her above him.

The change drove him deeper and a strangled cry escaped her lips. He grasped her hips and lifted her, driving toward a place beyond comprehension. Again she felt herself rising, rising above, higher and higher until with one final thrust he sent them both over the edge.

She collapsed on top of him, their breathing erratic, heavy and audible.

What just happened here? This was so not like her. On so many levels.

She pushed herself off him, only then realizing that she hadn't bothered to take off her shoes.

"Natalie?"

She didn't respond as she pulled her dress back into place and started for the bathroom.

****

Newland pushed himself up from the couch and started after her, before realizing that he had another stop to make first.

With a frustrated growl, he glanced around the apartment, then headed off into the doorway Natalie had disappeared through earlier.

It was a kitchen as he had suspected. Feeling beyond weird standing—naked—in a strange kitchen that belonged to a woman he had just met and peeling off a used condom...

He shook his head and went in search of the trash can. He had to open two of the bottom counter doors before he found it tucked away under the sink. He disposed of the condom, washed his hands, then tucked himself back into his jeans.

It was almost embarrassing, this urgency to have her. But he knew she felt it too. Neither one of them had gotten remotely undressed, both still wore their shoes, nor had they made it off the couch. Where were the ground rules now?

He ran his hands through his hair and started after Natalie.

There were four doors down the hallway where she had disappeared. Two led to the bedrooms and were open. The one other led to what appeared to be a linen closet. That left only one.

He knocked lightly on the closed door. "Natalie?" No response. He knocked again. He had no idea what he was going to say. How do you say *Wow, thanks for the best sex of my life. That was great. I just hope you don't regret it as much as I do*? Hallmark didn't exactly make a card for that. But why did he regret it? Because he was leaving? Because it seemed so impulsive? Or because he thought she regretted it?

"Natalie?" He rapped again.

"Go away," came her muffled reply.

"You don't mean that." At least he hoped she didn't.

"Yes, I do."

"Well, too bad. Because I'm not going anywhere. At least not until we talk."

"I don't want to talk," she said.

"Too bad. Because I do."

He could hear her rustling around inside the bathroom, but she didn't come out. He heard water run, and what sounded like the flip of a towel ring when somebody stripped the hand towel from it. More water running, the toilet flush, and then nothing. He had a sinking suspicion that she had put down the lid on the toilet was just sitting there waiting for him to give up.

"I'm not leaving here, until we talk."

"Not leaving from in front of the bathroom? Or the apartment?"

"Either."

Tonight was a night of firsts. The first time he had ever had sex with his shoes on. The first time he had ever lost control. And the first time he'd stood outside a bathroom trying to talk to the woman he'd just made love with.

He shook his head. "Your aunt's going to wonder what happened if we don't come home tonight."

That worked. She wrenched open the door, and he was ecstatic to see that she hadn't been crying. He couldn't have handled tears.

"Take my car to go back to Aunt Bitty's. I'm staying here." She went to shut the door, but he stuck his foot in the way, effectively ending her efforts.

Well, mostly.

"Ow," he cried as she pressed the door against his foot.

"Get out of the way," she said.

"I just want to talk to you."

"I don't want to talk."

This was ridiculous. He shoved his shoulder against the door and popped it out of her grasp. "We're not sixteen," he said. "We should be able to talk about this. In fact, we *should* talk about this."

"There's nothing to talk about. We did everything right." Then a horrified look descended on her features. "The condom didn't break, did it?"

"Tell me that's all you care about, and I'll call you a liar."

She seemed to crumple in front of him. As he suspected, she had put down the lid on the toilet seat. She collapsed back there like a dejected marionette abandoned by his operator.

"Natalie?"

She shook her head again but didn't bother to raise her gaze to his. "That was a—"

"If you say mistake, I swear I'll—" He broke off as the sound came from the living room. He turned his attention back to her. "Does anybody else live here?"

A frown puckered her brow. "Just Aubie, but he should be at Aunt Bitty's." She jumped to her feet, smoothing her hands down her skirt. Since she'd been in the bathroom she'd had time to put everything back in the right place. And he had to say that it made him sad. He would like nothing more than a second chance at taking his time. But it seemed that was not in the cards tonight.

He walked back down the hallway, peeking around the corner in time to see Aubie let himself into the apartment. The mayor shut the door behind him, then turned around, noticing Newland for the first time.

"Yikes!" he screamed. "You scared me." Aubie shook his head, then narrowed his gaze. "What are you doing here?"

How to answer that... How to answer that... "Your sister and I came to watch a movie?" He hadn't meant for the explanation to come out as a question.

Aubie crossed his arms and looked around the apartment noting several things, Newland was sure. The indentions on the couch, the crooked lay of the cushions.

Or maybe Newland was just being paranoid. How would Aubie know if anything had been going on between Newland and his sister?

There was no way.

Newland released his breath slowly so it didn't come out as a sigh.

Aubie took two steps into the room and bent down to pick up something, holding it out to Newland between two fingers. "Sorry to interrupt."

Not knowing what else to do, Newland took the condom wrapper from Natalie's brother and managed to keep a straight face as the teenager pushed past him and made his way down the hall. A few minutes later, Newland heard the door to the bedroom shut, then what sounded suspiciously like gales of laughter.

"Tell me that wasn't my brother."

"Nope. That was Aubie."

She closed her eyes. "I told you to tell me it *wasn't* him."

"Not in the habit of lying," Newland said.

Natalie leveled her gaze on him as if to say, *You're a tabloid reporter, really?*

"There is one more thing," he started.

She looked at him with those so blue eyes and he reconsidered his stance on lying.

He stepped forward and took one of her hands into his. With the other he pressed the condom wrapper inside and folded her fingers over it.

She didn't have to see it to know. She closed her eyes again. He wasn't sure but he thought she might be praying.

"Great," she muttered. "Just great."

CHAPTER TWELVE

"Where are you going?"

Natalie didn't take time to answer. She grabbed her purse and headed for her car. She had to get out of there. And she had to get out now.

A sense of urgency rose in her gut. She'd messed up. She'd messed up big time. She got to her car then stopped. She couldn't leave Aubie at the apartment all by himself. He could barely get dressed in the morning without help. She turned around, nearly running over Newland as he stood directly behind her.

"Natalie! What's wrong?"

She shook her head and started back toward the apartment door, barely aware that Newland was behind her every step. She just kept on walking through the living room down the hall to Aubie's door.

"Aubie? Open up."

No answer.

"Aubie?" She rattled his doorknob, but it was locked. "I know you're in there. I'm leaving, but I expect you to be at Aunt Bitty's in no less than two hours. Don't turn on the stove and don't open any windows."

She turned on her heel and marched back through the apartment.

"Natalie?" Newland was right behind her, but she couldn't stop. He didn't understand. He wasn't the one who'd let everything go. He would never understand how she felt. "Where are you going?" Newland asked again.

"Home." She shook her head. "Aunt Bitty's. I can't let her stay there alone tonight with…you." Her voice got small on that last word. She shook her head again, trying to clear her thoughts. But it was no use. Aunt Bitty was in no danger from Newland Tran. Of that much she was certain.

She closed her eyes and crumpled against the front of her car. She wrapped her arms around herself, suddenly chilled in the warm southern air.

It was too much. It was all just too much. Her chin dropped to her chest and tears rolled down her cheeks.

"Hey." The voice was gentle, soft, and caring, but it only made her tears fall harder. "Hey," Newland said again. He hooked the fingers of one hand under her chin and lifted.

Reluctantly, she opened her eyes. Like it mattered now. He knew all her secrets. He knew more about her than anyone, and he didn't even know it.

"I—" Her voice caught on a sob.

He shushed her as her tears fell harder. His arms wound around her, and he held her close, his warmth giving her the strength and comfort. She leaned into him, needing as much of that strength as she could get.

"Are you going to tell me what this is about?" Again his voice was gentle, caring and soft. It only made her want to cry harder.

"It doesn't matter," she blubbered into the crook of his neck. "Nothing matters now." With his arms around her, Newland turned her. He leaned against the hood of her car, cradling her in his arms as he nestled her between his thighs.

"Really," he said. "There's no need. There's no need for tears."

"You don't understand. You didn't just—" She gestured wildly toward the apartment door, but the words stuck in her throat. He had been with her every step of the way, every heart-pounding, sexy inch they had gone. But what did it matter to him?

"I didn't just what?" His voice was once again gentle and caring.

"I don't—" She hiccupped. "I don't lose control."

He smiled, his eyes twinkling, but she was thankful that he didn't laugh at her. That was something she wouldn't have been able to stand. "Maybe it's time you did."

She shook her head. "I can't. Everyone depends on me. You don't understand. Everybody doesn't depend on you. And now Gerald—"

The twinkle in his eyes was quickly replaced with clouds. "Yeah, him."

Natalie shook her head. "I need him."

"But you don't love him."

"I need him," she said again, the emphasis even stronger. "He's everything I need."

"So because you need somebody to help you babysit your family, you're willing to marry a guy who's—"

"Careful," she warned.

"— too conservative for his own good."

"You don't understand. You don't have people depending on you."

His arms dropped back to his sides, and he nodded in her direction. "You're right about that. I don't have people depending on me. I can do whatever I want whenever I want to do it. And it sucks. You know that? It sucks." He spun away from her. Natalie was chilled as his warmth moved away.

"Where are you going?"

He shook his head. "Somewhere else."

"How will you get back to my aunt's house?" That wasn't what she should have said. She should've asked him to come back. Told him that she would take him to Aunt Bitty's. Apologize for creating that pain in his eyes. But it seemed it was her night for royally messing up.

He stalked across the dark parking lot, not even bothering to turn around as he waved a dismissive hand in her direction. "It's a small town. I'm sure I'll find a way."

****

As best he could figure, it was about five miles back to Bitty's. Turtle Creek wasn't that big, but he didn't want to go back to the house. He wanted to stay with Natalie, make love again, give it one more chance. Take his time, make her scream his name. She'd only *thought* she had lost control tonight. He wanted to truly see her lose control of it all. He grew hard at the thought.

It was ridiculous. What did he care if she kept her life in control? What did it matter to him? She had everything all in order, all planned out. All he needed was a story, and he was out of there. He would leave Little Miss Perfect, I'm-In-Control behind, and she could worry all she wanted about appearances and clothes and Harvey Johnson's hound dog.

It was getting late, he knew, but it was still Friday night in a small town. He heard the music before he saw it. Some little honky-tonk squatting between an insurance agency and the Dairy Queen. A log cabin stuck in the middle of town, lit with multi-colored Christmas lights. A flashing neon Bud Light sign declared they were open, as if the loud music spilling from the crack in the door wasn't enough.

Distraction. Just what he needed.

Newland pushed his way inside, immediately enveloped in the smells of beer, stale cigarette smoke, and Pine-Sol. It was a brutal combination, but he suspected after ten minutes and a shot of whiskey he wouldn't care.

He wound his way through the pool tables tossed at odd angles in the front section of the building, toward the back where tables only big enough for two or four people were scattered around. A bar ran the length of the room, with swivel top seats on the stools in front and rows of bottles reflected in the mirror behind.

He slid onto one of the stools, rapped his knuckles against the wood, and waited for the barkeep to notice him. Either way it didn't matter. He had gotten away from Natalie and her poison attitude about control.

Didn't she know she had no control over life? He'd had no control when his parents were killed. He had no control when his uncle had taken him in. And he had no control in the years that had followed. He'd just recently felt like he had any control over his life only to be smacked down by falling in love with the wrong woman.

"What'll it be?" the dark-haired bartender asked. He had a mean look like he'd just stepped out of an alley in New York City, and he seemed to be the antithesis of all things Turtle Creek.

"Dewars on the rocks." It wasn't something he drank all the time. But today was a special occasion. Or maybe he just needed it. "Make it a double."

The bartender gave him a quick nod then moved away to fill his request.

Newland couldn't say that he'd fallen in love with the wrong woman. Every day that came between then and now seem to add to his quick healing. He'd only thought himself in love with Roxanne. He just wanted to help her. Help her get over a bad divorce, a bad marriage, and all the other little things that seem to hang around her like streamers of tragedy. She had a good heart, a good soul, and she deserved better than how she came to him. Broken, vacant-eyed, determined to be everything that her family didn't want her to be.

Now she was happily married and living in Tennessee, no more than an hour from where he sat at this very moment. But she belonged to another.

A sense of well-being at Roxanne's happiness descended upon him.

The barkeep stopped a few stools down, poured his double, then slid the glass to him.

Newland caught it in one hand, then lifted it in salute to Roxanne.

To Roxanne and Malcolm. And the happiness they deserved.

He took a sip, enjoying the burn as the whiskey slid down his throat. Yes, they deserved happiness. But so did the woman he'd just left.

Natalie Coleman.

What a piece of work. So wrapped up in perfection that she couldn't even enjoy the life that she had.

You don't need to save her. He could tell himself that a million and one times. But something in him wanted him to save her, wanted to show her how to appreciate the things she had.

Not the money. Anybody could get money. Money could come and go just like a snap of the fingers. But her wonderful aunt who liked to play poker and drink moonshine. Her brother the mayor and all the other little eccentric players in this crazy town. That was what she needed to embrace. The people and the love around her. But she was so consumed with everything being perfect she couldn't see that she was missing out on the greatest life anybody could have.

He braced his elbows on the bar and took another sip.

Why did he care if Natalie was consumed with perfection? It was no skin off his nose the things that she did. And yet tonight...

Never. Never in his life had it been like that. He wasn't a player, but he wasn't a monk either. He'd had his fair share of women, good times, and great sex. But tonight was on a different level completely. Just remembering her cries of passion made him shift uncomfortably in his seat. She had so much passion inside, pushed way down deep so it couldn't ever see the light of day. Because passion meant lack of control, and lack of control for Natalie Coleman was detrimental to her peace of mind. But lack of control is what she needed to experience most. She needed to lose control of her life now and then. See what was right in front of her.

Stay out of it, he told himself. *It's none of your concern*. He took another sip, movement down the bar catching his attention.

It took him a minute through the haze and smoke to recognize the two men talking to the bartender. Gilbert and Darrell Hughes, resident mountains and sneakers into the cemeteries after dark. What were they doing here?

He shook his head. This whole place was making him paranoid. It wasn't like it was Friday night in what was most likely the only honky-tonk in the area. Where else would they go to let off steam on the weekend?

He turned away, but his eyes kept straying back to that corner of the bar where the three men stood. They seemed to be discussing something in great earnest, and Newland had the feeling it wasn't how the Braves were doing this year. Not that he kept up with baseball, but he knew enough to know that their season was tanking out. No, this was something much more important.

Like it mattered. Small-town drama was not his style. And he had already experienced way too much of it since being in Turtle Creek. Right now he just needed to count down the days till next Thursday when he could check on this ghost of Bitty Duncan's and head out of town. Hopefully with a great story under his belt. And if not, he still had enough information that he could make up the rest of the details and sell the story to somebody. It might not make a fortune, but it would help him make rent this month.

The three men seemed to have reached some sort of agreement. At least they were all nodding their heads and shaking hands. An envelope appeared out of nowhere. Gilbert went to tuck it in his pocket, but Darrell took it away. Or was that the other way around? It didn't matter. It was sealed and no one opened it.

Newland's reporter instincts kicked into high gear. An envelope like that could only contain money. A payoff?

The guy next to him sighed. "Women."

Newland nodded in commiseration. "Ain't that the truth?"

The man stuck his hand out for Newland to shake. "Jack Russell."

"Like the d— never mind. Newland Tran," he said in return.

"Hey, aren't you that reporter who's supposed to check on Bitty's ghost?"

Newland laughed. The town really was too small for words. He gave a quick nod. "That would be me."

Jack shook his head. "It's the damnedest thing. She swears that it only comes on the last Thursday of the month. But I tell you there's something else going on there."

Thankfully Newland had limited himself to one double whiskey. His ears perked up. "You know about the ghost then?"

"Yeah, not much. I'm not even sure there is one. But there's definitely something weird going on in that cemetery come the end of the month."

"Like what?"

"All sorts of moving around, noises, big trucks coming in and out."

"How do you know all this?"

"I live across the street. Not on Bitty's block, but on the other side. Across the street from the gate."

Newland almost gave himself a V-8 smack on the head. He talked to everyone on Bitty's block but hadn't even thought about asking the homeowner across the street from the cemetery.

"Big trucks, you say?"

"Like clockwork."

"What about those two?" He nodded his head toward Darrell and Gilbert as they disappeared into the back room behind the bartender.

After all, Newland had seen them out in the cemetery looking for something just before he and Natalie had discovered the cufflink with the C on it. One trip to the library had told him that it wasn't an old cufflink. But who in this town with the initial C had enough money to wear French cuffs?

Jack looked toward the darkened doorway. "Awh, they're practically harmless. Small timers, you know."

"No. Small-time what?"

"Bootleggers." He said the one word as if it was so apparently obvious, and that he was surprised Newland hadn't known it before he hit the town limits.

"You don't say? Moonshine, right?"

"Yeah. They have a pretty good product here." He slid his glass closer to Newland. The clear liquid seemed innocent enough, almost like water.

Newland pointed to the drink. "That's moonshine?"

"Some of the best this county has to offer."

Newland looked from the drink back to Jack again. "And those two guys made it?"

"Yup."

"Darrell and Gilbert Hughes made the moonshine in that glass right there?" He knew people made moonshine. He just wasn't prepared to run into the bootleggers at the bar.

Jack nodded. "Go on, get a snort of it. But just a little one. That stuff is lethal."

Newman lifted the glass, taking a cautious sniff before raising it to his lips. It was smooth, with a hint of fruit and a damaging burn. If he went bald anytime in the near future he would blame that glass of moonshine right there.

"Whoa," he said. "That's got some bite."

Jack nodded. "Yeah, it does. One more sip and you won't care."

Newland was sure that what Jack said was right. But he didn't plan on drinking any more of that stuff. Not tonight. "So Gilbert and Darrell make this and then they bring it here to sell to the bartender?" He was reeling from the discovery. "What's the sheriff have to say about that?"

Jack laughed. "He's their best customer."

****

Natalie paced across the freshly painted foyer, waiting for Newland to return. She should've never let him walk away from her in the parking lot of her duplex, but she had. She hadn't been in the right state of mind to realize how many of her secrets he now carried with him. Secrets she didn't want anyone to know.

Strangely enough, there was the comfort in Newland knowing that about her. How she liked to be in control. That everyone depended on her. It was a burden she carried, every day, and sometimes it grew so heavy it was impossible to carry by herself.

Still, she didn't want him going around town blabbing about it to every Tom, Dick, and Harry he came in contact with.

159

Who was she trying to kid? She didn't worry about him spilling her secrets to anybody. She just wanted him back. He didn't seem to care that she lost control with him, that she stopped being perfect and for a few moments was just herself. In his arms, all her defenses had been down, her facade evaporated, and for the first time in a long time she felt exposed, but wondrous. She didn't have time to think about that, or maybe it was just too uncomfortable.

She whirled around as the door opened. She was all prepared to lay into him, fussing at him about running around after dark in a strange town. Turtle Creek might appear innocent enough, but crime happened everywhere. He could be in just as much danger here as he was on the streets of Chicago. She refused to call bullshit on her own comment.

But she wasn't able to read him the riot act. It was Aubie who let himself in. He grinned at her. She narrowed her eyes in return.

"Have a good time tonight, sis?"

"Don't. Start."

Aubie grinned. "I think I'll get my stuff and head on back to the apartment. Unless you'd rather I call Gerald."

Panic shot through her. She'd messed up, and she knew it. But she didn't need her baby brother rubbing her nose in it. "Get upstairs, Aubie, and get in bed."

He shook his head with a laugh. "It's not a school night, Mom," he taunted. "Though I do have some reports to review before the town meeting next week."

With that he turned on his heel and headed up the staircase. Natalie managed to hold her spine straight as he disappeared from view. Then she resisted the urge to crumple into a broken heap on the floor.

Her whole life was falling apart. And it seemed there was nothing she could do to stop it. She took a deep breath, one of those breathing exercises she had learned about at the doctor's office.

There. She admitted it. She had seen a therapist. Just to make sure that she was doing right by Aubie. That was the only reason. And then it just morphed into other things. It was just another of her dirty little secrets that she managed to hide from everybody.

But knowing she held so many secrets buried deep inside only made her stomach hurt. She'd probably have to go to the doctor for that next.

The door opened, but she didn't turn. She knew it was Newland this time. Her whole body seemed to be in tune to him, answering a call that his made as he walked into the room.

Dear Lord, what have I gotten myself into?

"Awh... Natty Nat. You waited up for me."

"Where have you been?"

"At the Last Call Saloon." He swayed a little on his feet, though his grin never wavered.

"You're drunk." She tried not to sound as indignant as she felt, but she'd been pacing the floor worried about him while he had been out drinking.

"I didn't start out that way." Those exotic brown eyes turned suddenly serious. "Just went in for a minute, you know. And then I met Jack and we drank moonshine. Gilbert and Darrell were there."

Natalie had seen and heard enough. As much as she wanted to be angry with Newland, she just couldn't muster the emotion. In fact, she felt a little sorry for anyone who encountered some of the local hooch.

"How much did you drink?" She looped her arm through his and steered him toward the stairs. He stumbled a bit but managed to catch himself. Natalie was grateful. He was too big for her to lug up the stairs alone. And after this evening, there was no way she was asking for Aubie's help.

"Just a couple. Five, maybe six." He nodded solemnly. "Seven, I think."

"Please tell me you're talking seven *drinks*." And not jars. *Pint* jars. Surely not. He would still be on the floor of the bar right now instead of staggering up an antebellum staircase.

"Yeah, I think… I mean, yeah."

Natalie pointed him toward the stairs and said a little prayer that he would make it up without falling and breaking his neck. "Have you got this?" she asked.

He studied the stairs, swaying a bit like a flagpole in a breeze. Then he nodded his head. "Yeah, I can do it." She hoped so. She needed to get him into bed and get some sleep herself. Tomorrow was Saturday, but she still had a lot on her plate.

She lined herself up behind Newland as he centered himself on the stairwell. "Are you ready?" she asked, hoping he said yes. She didn't know any other way she could get them up the stairs except on his own accord.

Newland nodded.

"Okay," she said. "Here we go."

It was tough. Newland seemed to get confused about every step and a half and decided to go down instead of up. Thankfully he only took one complete step down which left a half a step of progress with each two steps he took.

I'll take it, she thought. Any advance was better than none.

Three steps from the top, he stopped and slung one arm across her shoulders. They almost fell backwards, but somehow she managed to save them both by wrapping one arm around the closest newel post and hanging on for dear life.

"You're a good girl, Natty Nat." He patted her shoulder, his weight resting against her. Natalie managed to get them safely on the landing and steered him toward his room. It was at the end of the hallway. Never before had the hallway seemed quite this long.

"Come on," she said. "Just a few more steps, and you can rest for a while. How does that sound?"

He pulled away slightly and frowned at her. "I'm drunk, not a preschooler."

"I know." She wasn't going to argue with him. She had caused that pain in his eyes, which had caused him to walk away, which had him ending up at the town dive drinking his problems away. This was all her fault, and she had to do everything she could to make it right.

He bumped into her, she bumped into the railing. And on down the hallway they went. Finally, she opened the door to his room and helped him inside. He stumbled over to the bed, somehow managing to turn as he fell, flipping himself so he was staring at the ceiling. Well, he would've been had his eyes not been closed.

"What a night, huh?" he said.

Natalie didn't reply. She just grunted as she pulled off his shoes. But the simple act made her think of earlier when they hadn't remembered to remove their shoes, and that was something best forgotten.

"Did you know that Gilbert and Darrell make moonshine?"

Natalie dropped one shoe to the floor and went to work on the other. "Everyone knows that."

"But it made me think. They were at the cemetery. Maybe they…" His words trailed off into nothing.

Natalie sighed. Whatever he had been about to say was lost to the moonshine. Her gaze ran over him. She should loosen his clothes, maybe take off his jeans or his jacket. But again those sexy memories from earlier resurfaced.

She shook her head and turned away, only to be pulled back as his hand snaked around her wrist.

A strangled yelp escaped her as he pulled her to the bed. She tumbled down on top of him, breathless from the fall and the closeness to him. How could a man be three sheets to the wind and still smell like a million sexy things?

"Don't go," he murmured, tucking her close to him as he rolled toward the center of the bed.

Natalie was trapped, pinned by his arms and one leg, paralyzed with the need to be close to him.

But he would never know. She could sneak away when his grip slacked and head to her room, and no one would be the wiser.

With that thought lingering in her mind, Natalie relaxed and allowed sleep to take over.

CHAPTER THIRTEEN

Newland wished that every day he could wake up like this. Except for the headache. It was dull, throbbing behind his eyes though he had no idea where it came from. Maybe he been drinking the night before. Had he been drinking the night before?

He couldn't remember. Or maybe he didn't want to remember when his arms were full of sweet smelling... Natalie.

He inhaled that soft, familiar scent. Except the dry-cleaning fluid had been replaced with fabric softener. He buried his face in the crook of her neck, her soft sigh almost his undoing. How did they manage this?

Did he really care? She was in his arms, in his bed, and he really didn't care how she got there. The main thing was she was there. And as long as he moved slowly, that dull throbbing kept to a minimum. Or maybe the other sensations he was experiencing trumped any pain from the night before.

He allowed one hand to run the length of her from her shoulder across her breasts, her flat stomach, to the curve of her hip, and then back up again. Yet, she was real. And irresistible. He planted little nipping kisses along her collarbone, up her neck, across her jaw. She sighed again, and he was certain he'd never heard a sweeter sound. He'd been waiting for this for a long, long time. He just hadn't known it. Or maybe he had been blind by other desires, false desires. This... This was the real thing.

He continued his exploring kisses, wanting to make up for their haste the night before. Their lovemaking had been urgent, frantic, borderline crazy with intensity. But this was different. He wanted to take his time. He had her in his bed, all warmth and satin pajamas. He didn't take time to think about anything except how good she felt. She turned toward him, her lips meeting his. He opened his eyes just a peek to see that hers were still closed, and he wondered if she was more asleep than awake.

"Newland," she whispered when he lifted away from her. At least she knew who he was, and she wasn't dreaming he was Brad Pitt or something.

He pushed one hand under the thin sleep shirt she wore, brushing his fingers against the underside of her breasts. "I want you," he whispered. He planted teasing kisses all around her parted lips. She smiled in expectation, but her eyes were still closed.

"Yes," she said.

He wasn't sure if she was agreeing with the fact that he wanted her or she was saying she wanted him in return. Until she cried foul, he was plunging ahead.

He slid his hand to the crest of one breast, the nipple pebbling at his touch. He hadn't taken his time yesterday, but this morning was all about going slow. What was it the Southerners said? Slower than molasses in January? Yeah, that slow. He wanted to savor each taste, each sigh, each texture until they both died from the pleasure of it all.

A knock sounded at the door. Newland jumped from the unexpected intrusion, his head splitting open as he moved too fast.

"Mr. Newland," Bitty Duncan called, opening the door just a crack. "Are you in there?"

He didn't have a chance to reply as Natalie came fully to her senses, gasped at the situation she found herself in, and in her haste to get to her feet, rolled off the bed and hit the floor with a heavy thump.

Newland groaned cradling his head in his hands. Sparks of red and white shot from behind his eyes like crazed fireworks. "I'll take that as a yes," Bitty said. "Have you seen Natalie? She's not in her room this morning. Usually she's up by now and... Well, I'm a little worried."

He wasn't sure how to answer. As soon as the fireworks stopped, he gingerly released his head, peering over the edge of the bed to where Natalie sprawled, tangled up in the sheet and her robe that she had not taken off last night.

Suddenly, everything came back to him. He and Natalie in her apartment, admitting to her that his life was a mess and he wished he had someone to care about him as much as she cared about the people around her, walking to the Last Call Saloon, meeting up with some guy—he thought his name was Jack—and drinking a whole bunch of moonshine. From there everything got really fuzzy until this morning when he woke up with her spooned against him, smelling so sweet that he almost cried.

He looked to Natalie again. She shook her head, holding one finger over her lips to silence him. He knew what she wanted. "I'm sure she's around somewhere," he said to Bitty. "But I'm not decent. Can you give me a minute, please?"

"I'm sorry." She pulled the door shut, though she continued to talk through the wood. "I'm sorry. It's just not like her."

Newland looked down at himself. He was still wearing last night's clothes, except for his shoes, and he felt like an army of barbarians had taken up residence in his brain. That added to his raging hard on and it could be said that he wasn't decent at the moment. And Natalie was around somewhere. More specifically on the other side of his bed on the floor. But Bitty didn't need to know that.

"I'll tell you what," he started. "Let me get on some clothes, and I'll help you find her. Sound like a plan?"

He could almost hear her sigh of relief. "That would be great. Thank you, dear. Sorry to have bothered you."

"It's all right," he said, even though he had to close his eyes. He ran his fingers through his hair to hold his head onto his shoulders while he did his best to get the world to stay still for a minute. He wasn't sure how he would help her find Natalie. He wasn't even sure he could make his way down the stairs. Good thing Natalie was right there and not lost after all.

She managed to untangle herself from the sheet and stood.

He chanced a look in her direction, braving the glaring sunlight streaming through the bedroom windows to get a look at her. He wasn't disappointed. Her cheeks were flushed, her hair messed up, and her clothes all wrinkled. She had never looked more beautiful. Except maybe last night when she came apart in his arms. She had looked fine then for sure.

"Thank you." She ran her hands through her hair in what he assumed was an attempt to straighten it. All she did was muss it further. He liked her hair like that, framing her face and spilling down her back instead of being skinned back into a prim bun. "I brought you up here last night, but you wouldn't let me go. Sorry." She started toward the door in what he supposed was a quick escape.

"Thank you."

She stopped, one hand on the doorknob yet the door still shut on her hasty retreat. "For what?"

"For taking care of me last night. You didn't have to do that."

"I felt a little responsible for you if you want to know the truth."

The last thing he wanted her to feel for him was responsibility. That lumped him with everyone else in her life and as ridiculous as it seemed, he wanted to stand out from the others. He wanted to be someone special to her. More than a responsibility, more than another thing to check off on her to-do list.

He'd have to examine that when his head wasn't splitting in two.

"I wish you'd felt more of responsibility for me last night when I walked into that bar."

She shook her head. "That was all up to you."

She let herself out of the room, and Newland fell back on the bed, wincing as his head was jarred again. He'd have to find something to cure this hangover. The moonshine went down smooth, but the next day it came knocking again.

****

The knowing smirk on Aubie's face was almost more than Natalie could take. Still, she managed to sit across from him and keep her own expression as neutral as Switzerland. Even more so. That was the only way she could gain back control. And that was the one thing she badly needed. Control of her life, control of her emotions, and definitely control of her hormones whenever Newland was within fifteen feet of her.

She took up the bowl of scrambled eggs and scooped some onto her plate, just as he stumbled into the dining room.

Speak of the devil…

He walked slowly, as if he moved too fast he would puke. She supposed drinking contraband moonshine would do that to a man.

He eased forward, dark sunglasses hiding his exotic eyes from view. Other than that, he was the same old Newland. Concert T-shirt blue jeans and Converse. Today's offering was Green Day American Idiot. A prophecy if she had ever seen one.

"Newland," Aunt Bitty said, as he took his seat at the table. "Are you okay?"

He cleared his throat and gave a small nod. "I see you found Natalie." It was a poor attempt at changing the subject if she had ever heard one.

"Yes." Aunt Bitty took up the butter knife and slathered her biscuit. "I guess I just missed her. It seems she was upstairs the whole time."

The flush of heat that rose into her cheeks was hot enough to fry eggs. But as long as she didn't think about where she had been and what she'd been doing… *almost* doing when Aunt Bitty had come knocking on Newland's door, then surely it would fade in an hour or two.

"So did you have a good time last night, sis?"

Natalie switched her attention back to her brother. "A great time, yes. How about you?"

Aubie smirked. "Do anything special? Something maybe you haven't done in a long time?"

She kicked him under the table, and though she knew she hit her mark, his grin grew wider. Brothers were nothing but trouble.

"Nothing special," she said.

Newland ahemed from his end of the table.

"What about you?" Aubie turned his snarky gaze to Newland.

Unlike her, the reporter didn't flush red or kick Aubie. He just gave a one-armed shrug and took a sip of his coffee. "Everything I do in this town is new."

Natalie didn't know what to make of that. Was he talking about going to the Last Call Saloon or their wild encounter on her couch?

"Newland, dear, why don't you have a biscuit? Or some sausage?" Aunt Bitty lifted the plate covered with the fried meats.

Newland looked at them, his expression pained. "No, thank you. I'm not much of a breakfast eater."

"You ate four biscuits yesterday," Aubie said.

Natalie had been thinking the same thing, but she wasn't about to call Newland out on his lie.

"I'm not much for breakfast today," Newland qualified.

"It seems Mr. Tran has had a run in with our local hooch."

Aunt Bitty immediately perked up. "Did you go down to the cellar and find the moonshine?"

Newland almost shook his head. Almost. "I had a couple of drinks at the Last Call."

A couple of drinks to the tune of about seven. Two of moonshine was enough to put anybody in a stupor. But seven? He was lucky he could move today. That didn't take into account his strength last night. Or maybe it was her weakness?

"You drink moonshine?" Aubie asked his eyes wide. "Cool!"

Natalie shot her brother a look. "Not cool." That stuff would eat someone's liver out, and she wanted to make sure Aubie didn't have any part of it. It wasn't like he had to show his license and prove he was underage to the bootleggers. Darrell and Gilbert knew how old Aubie was, but that wouldn't stop them from giving him some. They had been raised on the stuff.

"It's good, huh?" Aunt Bitty's eyes sparkled. "I knew we should have brought some up the other night. Maybe you wouldn't have such an intolerance this morning."

To Newland's credit he flushed of pink but only continued to sip his coffee.

"Aunt Bitty, you have moonshine in the cellar?" Aubie asked.

Her aunt scoffed. "Of course I do. What kind Southern household would I be running if I didn't have a couple quarts of moonshine stashed somewhere?"

Natalie wasn't sure how to answer that. A legal household maybe?

"Can I have some?" Aubie asked.

"No," Natalie said emphatically. "Aside from the fact that you're underage, and it's illegal, I'm going to go with you're the mayor and the mayor doesn't need to be snockered."

"Awh." Aubie's disappointment was palpable.

"Snockered?" Newland asked.

"It means drunk," Aunt Bitty helpfully supplied with a knowing nod.

Something had to be done about this. And soon. Maybe she should talk to Gerald about getting with the sheriff and county commissioners and talking about the best way to clean up this illegal activity. Turtle Creek was a nice little town, the last thing they needed was the smear on their reputation from bootleggers. But before that, she needed to clean out her aunt's stash. It'd been safe enough in the cellar when Aunt Bitty couldn't make it down the stairs, but now that Newland had repaired them, it wouldn't be quite so easy to keep that moonshine from her table.

Natalie dabbed her mouth, took one last drink of coffee, then stood. She turned to Newland. "Can I see you in the kitchen for a moment?"

He looked as if he was about to tell her no, then gave a careful nod and gingerly pushed to his feet.

Natalie turned back to her family. "If you'll excuse us…" She turned on her heel and made her way to the kitchen, all too aware of Newland Tran right behind her.

****

The barbarians had turned into evil leprechauns. They had multiplied by the thousands and were trying to tear his eyeballs out using dull spoons. Or something like that.

Newland put one foot in front of the other, cautious to hold himself steady as he walked behind Natalie to the kitchen. He didn't know what she wanted to see him about, but at this point, with his head hurting this badly, there was no denying her anything.

"We need to do something about this moonshine."

Damn straight, he thought. But it was a little too late now. He had already downed the stuff.

"I can't have my underage brother thinking it's cool that he can get moonshine in our county." She shook her head, and Newland grabbed hold of the countertop edge to keep from falling. Wait, he hadn't moved. But her motion was enough to make him dizzy.

Damn that stuff was rough. If only he'd known last night what he knew this morning.

He squeezed his eyes shut for a brief moment trying to block out the light and the lingering smells of today's breakfast. He didn't think he'd ever eat again. He hadn't actually gotten stick, but he was feeling bad enough that it didn't matter. He didn't want anything to do with moonshine anytime soon.

"Are you okay?"

"No. I've got a hangover like a son of a bitch, and I would like nothing more than to go back to bed."

She gave him a dry look. "So go."

There was no way he could go back to bed; he had things to do. He still had yet to figure out about Bitty's ghost, and he was wondering more and more if there was a story in all this bootlegging going on. The sheriff was in on it, and the bars were serving it. It had to be some sort of record, even for the South.

"Hold on a sec." Natalie turned around so fast that Newland clutched the countertop again. He knew it was only a matter of time before his body settled down. But he needed to lie down in order to make things go away. He had too much to do to feel like this. This was the most hungover he'd ever been in his life. Including college. And that was saying a lot.

But if he thought her turning around was bad, the rest of her actions nearly sent him to the ground. She bent down to retrieve the blender from under the cabinet, went to the refrigerator, and started pulling out things. Hot sauce, eggs, and a can of tomato juice, celery, olives, and something else he couldn't see. Then without a word she started dumping everything into the blender. Before he knew it she set a glass of thick red liquid in front of him.

"Here."

"What is that?" He wasn't about to just drink it. Most of what she had put in it was disgusting.

"It's a sure headache/hangover cure."

Newland eyed it skeptically. "What does it do? Make me throw up so much that I don't care any longer that I'm hungover?"

Natalie shook her head. "This may come as quite a surprise to you, but my mother and father lead a very active social life. I learned to make these when I was still in high school. Now drink up. It'll take care of it."

Newland wasn't sure what was worse, the throbbing in his head or the fact that she had learned a hangover cure in high school that wasn't even for her.

On the outside it seemed she had the perfect life—sweet sports car, beautiful clothes, the charming job of telling everybody in her life what to do, but in the last couple of days he'd come to realize that there were more ghosts than she let on. The glass in front of her was proof enough of that. And these ghosts didn't just show up every last Thursday of the month.

"Would you drink it, please?" Her tone turned soft and beseeching. "I need your help. And I know you can't help me with the way your head's hurting now."

He reached for it and took a tentative sip. But she shook her head. "Drink it. All down in one gulp, maybe two but no more."

Still he hesitated.

"Just drink it."

Newland was starting to give credit to his throwing up idea but decided that since she'd taken the time to make him this cure, he was at least going to try it. He picked up the glass and fought the urge to plug his nose with the other hand and started to drink. He managed to get it down in three big gulps. Though he wasn't sure how long it was going to stay there. It seemed to have enough hot sauce in it to kill him, but the heat wasn't his biggest concern. He looked back at the counter where two eggshells lay empty and broken, their contents no doubt added to the drink he'd just consumed.

No, he wasn't going to throw up. He could do this. He could. He'd done tougher things in his life, had been through more. He could handle a spicy cup of tomato juice with raw eggs. It wasn't a big deal. All he had to do was sit there and not think about it.

Do not think about it, do not think about—

"My head…"

"What about it?"

Newland blinked a couple of times then pushed his sunglasses to the top of his head. "It… It doesn't hurt anymore."

She chuckled. "I told you. Now can you help me?"

He moved his jaw from side to side and tilted his head, testing the scope of her hangover cure. "That's just a miracle. You should sell it."

Natalie shook her head.

"We wouldn't need it if we didn't have moonshine, now would we? And that's what I want you to do. Help me get the moonshine out of Aunt Bitty's cellar."

"You having a party or something?"

Natalie shot him a look. "She's eighty-six years old. She does not need to be drinking moonshine."

"If you ask me, eighty-six's the perfect age to drink moonshine. Eighty-six is the perfect age to do whatever the hell you want to do."

"I'm going to pretend you didn't say that. I've got enough to do without you adding fuel to the fire."

He chuckled in spite of himself, but her look remained serious. "Why do you want to do that? Why take it away from her?"

"Now that the stairs are fixed, I'm afraid that she'll get down there and start nipping at it. Then the next thing I know, she's got a broken hip and a life flight to Memphis."

"Do they life flight you for a broken hip?"

"Newland! Pay attention. Will you help or not?"

It really wasn't any of his business. It wasn't any of his business to help Natalie, and it wasn't any of his business whether or not Bitty Duncan had moonshine in her cellar. But he supposed that if he moved it from the cellar up into the kitchen, that would save Bitty from falling down the stairs.

"Okay."

Her features softened. "Thank you." She turned on her heel, evidently expecting him to follow as she made her way toward the back of the house.

Thankful that each step was not excruciatingly painful, Newland followed behind her to the screened-in porch, out onto the regular porch, then into the yard. They rounded the house to the cellar doors lying crookedly on the ground.

He looked back at Natalie, taking in her outfit before giving a small shake of his head. It was Saturday, but she still wore matching jewelry, a form-hugging dress, and four-inch heels.

If you dress like this every day, what do you do for an encore? But that question brought to mind those satiny pajamas she'd worn last night and that short robe of baby pink that made her skin glow like new milk and her eyes shine like the sky after a cleansing rain.

He shook his head. What was wrong with him? He didn't need these kinds of thoughts. She was the antithesis of everything he stood for. She caved to "the man," she did what she was supposed to do, and then she made everybody else around her do what they were supposed to do. He was a free spirit, and he wasn't buying her upper crust rules. It didn't matter how pretty she looked in baby pink.

"Why don't you come down a couple of steps, and I'll hand it up to you?"

"I'm perfectly fine going down the stairs."

He eyed her skeptically. "Okay, but you go down first. That way if you fall, you won't knock me the rest the way down too."

"Hardy-har." She opened the doors to the cellar, and he explained the changes that he had made to the stairs.

"It's more like a ladder now," he said. "Turn around and go down with your face toward the stairs and your hands on the handrails."

She did as he asked, and then he realized another benefit of having her go down first. It gave him quite an impressive view down the front of her dress.

Pervert, he chastised himself. Though if that was the case, he was a pervert who would very much like to get her in bed for the rest of the afternoon.

Yesterday had been spectacular and this morning showed that it was not a one-time deal. The two of them together had something explosive. Phenomenal. Outright special. And he wanted to experience it again. And maybe another time. And with any luck a couple more times before Thursday's ghost appeared.

But she thought she was marrying stuffed-shirt Gerald Davenport. Though he hadn't asked her to marry him yet. And she had no ring. And Gerald was completely wrong for her.

"Are you coming?"

He cut his gaze back down into the cellar to see if Natalie had made it to the bottom. "Be right there." He started down the steps the same way he'd instructed her.

From just the other side of the dark he heard her ask, "Is the flashlight still down here?"

"Watch this," he said, as his feet touched the cellar floor. He turned around and slung one arm through the air searching for the pull string. It took only a couple of seconds, then he jerked it down, flooding the basement with light.

Natalie shielded her eyes from the glare. He had to admit it was quite bright down there now. Not

179

at all like it had been when all they had was a single-beam flashlight.

"How did you do that?"

Newland smiled. "I spent some time with the Amish a while back. Long story. Don't ask. But I learned how to wire up a light to a battery." He pointed to the corner edge of the shelf where a car battery sat. The light was wired to it using cables which in turn were attached to the ceiling allowing the bulb to hang above them. "Now when your aunt comes down here, she can get inside a little easier because she's got the new ladder, but she's also got light to see her favorite jellies."

"And her moonshine," Natalie muttered. She walked over to the shelves lining the wall pointing to a couple of jars that appeared to be filled with nothing but water. "How do I get these back upstairs?"

"You aren't really going to make her throw it out, are you?"

Natalie plopped her hands on her hips. "I suppose I should just let my aunt get drunker than Cooter Brown all by herself?"

"What about card night? Maybe if she were to drink with her girlfriends." He stopped his explanation as Natalie begin to shake her head.

"They're worse than she is."

Newland had no argument for that.

"It's better this way," she said. But he realized then that was her solution for everything. Her way was the best way. She meant well. She had the best intentions to help everyone in her life. But was it really helping?

"Why don't you come over on card night and then you can have a drink with them?" Newland's words finished on a slightly higher note. It was almost a question. But not quite.

"Are you saying you know what's better for me and my aunt than I do?"

"Don't start getting defensive. You should spend a little more time enjoying yourself instead of making sure everybody toes the line."

He hadn't meant to disrespect her efforts, but he felt it was his duty to show her the error of her ways. She was young and beautiful and had her whole life ahead of her. If she would let loose just a tad, life would be so much more fun.

Who was he to say what she should do to enjoy herself?

"Whatever," he said. "She's your aunt." Which was the truth. As much as he wished that Natalie would loosen her white-knuckled grip on every aspect of her life, it really wasn't his concern. This was her family, her life, her choice.

Her lips parted at just the right angle for kissing, or maybe she was going to agree with him. But she stopped. She pointed to the corner of the cellar where crate upon crate was stacked on top of the other. "What's that?"

Newland shrugged. "How am I supposed to know? It's not my cellar."

"But those weren't here the last time we were down. Were they?"

"There were a few of them," he said.

"But?" Natalie prompted.

"But I don't remember there being so many of them. There was maybe two or three at the most. But now there has to be…" He trailed off and started to count. "Eight, nine, ten… There's at least a dozen now."

"And they were here when you fixed the light and the steps?" Natalie asked.

Newland shook his head. "I don't remember. I mean, there weren't that many, but I don't remember if there was the same number as before."

"You didn't bring them down here?"

He snorted, but otherwise didn't answer.

"Right," she said with a nod.

"So if I didn't bring them down here and you didn't bring them down here…"

She shook her head.

"Do you think Aubie did it?" He stopped. "He's sixteen. Stupid question."

"Maybe we just didn't see them because it was dark."

"Maybe," he said, but he wasn't convinced.

"What's in them?"

He shrugged. "No idea."

She looked at him, then at the stacks of crates. "Don't you think we should look and see?"

Newland grabbed the two jars of moonshine off the shelf to this left, then started for the ladder. "No, I don't. I don't see how it's any of my business." But he wasn't convinced about that either.

Natalie seemed on the verge of saying something else, but she shook her head again. "All this talk of ghosts is making me paranoid. Aunt Bitty stored some stuff down here. Simple as that."

"Yeah, I suppose. But I'm going to ask her about it just in case."

CHAPTER FOURTEEN

"Can I talk to you about something for a minute?" Natalie tapped on Newland's door and pushed it open a crack. He was sitting on his bed typing something into his laptop. She hated to bother him. But she knew that was just her reluctance to say what needed to be said.

"Sure." He gave a small nod and pushed his laptop to the side, motioning for her to come in and sit on the edge of his bed.

She eased into the room but ignored his invitation. "About last night," she started. She almost laughed at the cliché of it all. "That can't happen again. That's not me. I don't know what happened. It just can't happen again." Had she said that already?

Newland didn't say anything at all. He just stared at her as if she was a two-headed pig at the county fair. "You think I judged you for that?" he finally asked.

Judge her? Of course he judged her. Everybody judged everybody else. It was the way of life. She knew he had already made up his mind about her. So what did it matter what he thought? He was going to be gone in just a few days.

"It can't happen again," Natalie said.

"I believe you said that already." His eyes were unreadable, his expression a blank canvas.

Natalie stood there a moment just looking at him, unsure of what to say next. She wanted him to agree with her, tell her that it couldn't happen again.

Admit that it was a mistake. But he didn't. So she stood there, just waiting.

"Is that what you came to tell me?" Newland asked.

Natalie nodded.

"I see," Newland said. He rose to his feet and came slowly toward her.

Natalie refused to take a step back despite the fact she wanted to. Self-preservation and all. She needed to be as far away from Newland Tran as she could be.

He stopped just inches from her, their bodies not touching but that magnetic pull still there.

"You keep telling yourself that, sweetheart, and maybe you'll start to believe it. But deep down you know this: I can have you in three seconds flat. One kiss is all it would take."

Natalie was speechless. She stared at him, her mind running over a half a dozen possible comebacks but not landing on any one. What could she say to that? Anything she said would just be thrown back at her.

He moved closer still, and she thought for a moment he might kiss her just to prove his point. Instead, he raised a hand, almost touched her face, then turned and went back to sit on the bed.

Natalie almost collapsed with relief. Or was it regret?

"Okay then," she said. "Now that it's settled." Saying goodbye sounded odd so she turned on her heel and walked out of the room. She had too much to do today to give Newland Tran a second thought.

****

A knock sounded on Newland's door. He saved his document before calling, "Come in."

The door creaked open, and Bitty poked her purple head inside. "The girls have come over for tea. Would you like to join us?"

He stretched again, working out the kinks in his back. Typing while sitting on a bed wasn't an optimal situation, but he didn't have a desk in this room. It didn't help that he'd been sitting there for two straight hours, emerging himself in the story he was writing and doing his best to forget about Natalie and her little "that was a mistake" speech she had given him that morning.

"I'd love to." He smiled. He hadn't eaten anything for breakfast, and it was almost two o'clock.

Bitty smiled. "That's what we were hoping you would say." She disappeared out the doorway again, and Newland had a strange suspicion this would be the most different kind of tea he'd ever attended.

He turned off his laptop and made his way down the stairs. "The girls," as Bitty referred to them, had gathered in the parlor around the oval-shaped coffee table. They were laughing and talking as he came into the room, then they all stopped and smiled.

"My goodness," a lady he didn't know said as he walked in. She was a beautiful woman, with glowing mocha skin and snow-white hair cropped close to her head. She wore a bright red shirt, a long, tie-dyed Gypsy skirt and more than her fair share of jewelry, including earrings made of wooden disks that clicked together like a wind chime every time she moved.

"That's right. You weren't here last week, Josephine," Bitty said. She stood and took Newland by the elbow and dragged him farther into the room. "This is Newland Tran. He's the reporter who's come to help me with my ghost. "This is Josephine Waters. She lives across the street."

He remembered now. Josephine was the one with the boyfriend, the one who skipped out last week and left him playing poker with three geriatric cardsharps.

Newland stuck out his hand. "It's a pleasure."

She shook his hand in a surprisingly firm grip, and he immediately liked Josephine. There was just something about the sassy woman, that spark of life in her eyes, the mischievous slant of her smile. She was the perfect complement to the other three, and Newland could see why they had been dubbed the Fab Four. They truly were amazing.

He settled himself down in the armchair opposite Bitty. Before him on the coffee table was a spread worthy of high tea in any society parlor. Tiny little finger sandwiches, scones, cookies, and an antique silver pot with a puff of steam coming out the spout.

Bitty came around the coffee table and poured him a cup of tea. "Here you go, dear." She served his plate as well, but before she returned to her seat, she pulled a small flask from somewhere inside the bodice of her dress.

Newland tried not to look shocked as Bitty winked at him. "Would you like a snort?"

After this morning's hangover he was about to say no when she poured a large dollop into his tea.

"There you go." Newland stirred it around like she advised as she headed back to her own seat.

Maybe it'd been a mistake for him to bring that moonshine up from the cellar.

Bitty tucked her flask away in its secret place and picked up her own saucer. "Now, where were we?"

He listened as they talked about the troubles with the barking dog down the street, the lawn service they were convinced was out to scalp them, and Josephine's new boyfriend. He was amazed that no one mentioned the buckled sidewalk out front of Bitty's house. It seemed that was just part of the neighborhood.

"Bitty," Newland started. "Did you store anything down in the cellar?"

The women all turned to look at him, and he realized he had spoken out of turn. They had been discussing whether a peach cobbler should be baked at 400° or 350 when he blurted out his question. Still, it had been bothering him all day. Why was there stuff stored down there if no one in the house had stored it?

"Of course not, dear," Bitty said. "How am I supposed to get down into the cellar?"

That was just what he had been thinking too. So if she didn't put the crates down there that only left Aubie or the part-time housekeeper. Aubie seemed least likely to lug something to the cellar if he could find somebody else to do it for him, and Newland couldn't imagine the housekeeper dropping anything into the cellar without Bitty's prior approval. So how did those crates get down there?

He nibbled on his cookie, sipped his hooch-laced tea, and let their scattered conversation wash over him. He needed to get down there and check it out. Find out what was in those crates. But the last thing he wanted to do was alarm Bitty.

Maybe it was just a mistake. Maybe it would end up being nothing. Maybe he just hadn't seen them in the dim light the other night. He mentally shook his head. That didn't seem right somehow.

After an hour of listening to girl talk, Newland managed to excuse himself with promises that he would join them for church the next morning. He hadn't been to church in… Well, he couldn't remember how long it had been since he'd been to church, but he understood that it was a southern tradition with these ladies and somehow he just couldn't tell them no.

He made his way through the house, out onto the back porch, and around the side of the house to the doors to the cellar. He just couldn't get those crates out of his mind.

He eased down the steps and into the cellar, searching blindly around until he found the string connected to the lightbulb he'd rigged. One swift pull and the place was filled with light.

And there they were, the mysterious crates. Suddenly his mouth went dry, and his hands got a little sweaty. Which was ridiculous. Why was he so anxious? They were just crates. But they were unknown crates that couldn't be accounted for. How did they get there? Who brought them? And what did they contain?

That was one question he could answer. He picked his way across the cellar floor and hoisted one of the crates off the top of a stack. The stacks were only four or five high. They were solid-looking crates, wooden and sturdy. He set it on the ground at his feet, wishing he'd brought a crowbar or something down to pry off the lid. It was nailed tight. He looked around in the dark corners of the cellar, looking for something that might possibly help him get the lid off, but he didn't see anything.

"What are you doing down there?"

Newland peered up at the entrance to the cellar to find Natalie standing there. She looked just as good as she had earlier when she marched into his room and told them what they had done was a mistake. And he wanted to kiss her as badly now as he had then.

He pushed those thoughts away. "Can you give me a crowbar or something? I want to open this up."

She frowned, then gave a short nod. "Okay." She returned a few minutes later with a hammer. Not exactly what he had asked for, but it would do.

"Toss it here," he called, but she was already on her way down the steps.

It was ridiculously humorous, her standing there in a purple silk dress and her nude-colored heels. She looked so utterly beautiful and so utterly out of place that he wanted to laugh and kiss her at the same time.

She handed over the hammer. "Have you talked to my aunt about opening these?"

"Nope." He wedged the backend of the hammer under the top board of the crates and pulled, use leverage to pop it off.

"Don't you think you should? What if there's something she wants hidden?"

Newland didn't bother to stop as he replied. "She said she didn't put anything down here and neither did the housekeeper. I know Aubie didn't come down here, and you said you didn't. I didn't and that only leaves one alternative."

"If you say ghost…" She plopped her hands on her hips and eyed him coolly.

The lid gave away with a small groan. "No, not a ghost, but maybe somebody pretending."

"You're not making any sense."

Newland removed the lid. As he suspected, the crate was filled with straw, but he knew it was there for cushioning. He dragged the crate a little closer to the light so he could see inside. Then he started to gently feel through the hay to find whatever treasure was hidden inside. He had dreams of priceless urns and vases from decades long past, but what he pulled out was the last thing he expected.

He held the Mason jar up to the light, frowning as he stared at it.

"Moonshine?"

Natalie shook her head. "What is my aunt doing with so much moonshine?"

Newland felt around inside the crate. There had to be at least a dozen jars in this one alone. Multiplied by all the crates, there was quite a bit of money sitting here in Bitty Duncan's cellar.

"Your aunt doesn't know this is here."

"Then how did it get here?"

Newland pushed to his feet, brushing his hands off as he stood. "I'm not sure, but I think Gilbert and Darrell have something to do with it."

Natalie frowned. "Gilbert and Darrell? Why would they put moonshine in my aunt's cellar?"

"I think this might be like a halfway point for the moonshine. I don't really know; I've never bootlegged before. But it seems to me that they stored this here because they know no one comes down to the cellar with any regularity."

"That doesn't make any sense." Natalie said.

Newland picked up the lid and started hammering it back into place. "Of course it does. They bring the moonshine here, hide it out for a while, and then take it someplace else."

She seemed to think about it a minute. "So if it belongs to Darrell and Gilbert, then when do they come get it?"

Newland thought for a moment about how many more crates could be added between now and the pickup date. He shook his head. "I'm not sure, but I'm guessing the last Thursday of the month."

CHAPTER FIFTEEN

Natalie sputtered. "You mean you think the ghost has something to do with this moonshine?"

"That's exactly what I mean."

Natalie shook her head. "I don't understand."

"I'm not sure I do either, but it seems too much of a coincidence not to hold some merit."

"But—" she started but broke off. There wasn't much else to say. In a town the size of Turtle Creek job opportunities were slim. As hard as Aubie and the city council worked to keep businesses alive and thriving in the small town, the lure of the larger cities pulled young people away. Those with degrees and college credits to their name left to seek other opportunities in places that had more to offer. Left behind were the people who had learned how to scrape out a living from practically nothing.

She had been one of the lucky ones. Her family had been well off from long ago and didn't rely on the economy of Turtle Creek to support them. But she knew there were others...

Darrell and Gilbert to be sure. They had made a living out of making a living. They picked up cans, recycled wires and tires, and would haul off anything for the right to keep it, but would they bring moonshine into her aunt's cellar? She shook her head.

"You don't agree?"

It's just..." She looked at the many crates stacked there. This was a small-town operation that didn't appear so small-town. Not with days still left to go before the "ghost" appeared. Days left to cart more and more crates of contraband into the cellar.

"It seems like we're reaching."

Newland shook his head. "I know you love this town. I know you love these people. Something is going on here. You can't deny that."

He was right. She didn't want anyone in her town to be running an illegal moonshine ring. But the evidence was sitting there, stacked neatly in crates in her aunt's cellar. "Is it really that much moonshine?"

"Maybe not now." He turned in a half circle. "But look at all the room they have to store crates between now and the end of the month."

Natalie couldn't believe it. "I'll need to see that myself."

"That's not enough evidence." Newland pointed to the crates stacked against the wall.

As naïve as Natalie felt she was being, she didn't know what constituted a large haul of alcohol and she certainly didn't feel good stepping on someone's livelihood—illegal or not. Not for a few measly crates of liquor. Not when Gilbert and Darrell were just trying to make a living in a hard economy in a small town in Mississippi. Illegal or not, the southern girl in her just couldn't do it.

"We'll just have to see if they bring more," Newland said.

"And how do you suppose we do that?"

"Come down here tomorrow and see."

****

Newland waited until after dark before slipping into his darkest jeans and a black David Allen Coe T-shirt and making his way downstairs. He'd thought of nothing else during the afternoon but watching that cellar to see who came and put stuff in it. Somebody was using it as a halfway point for their moonshine business, and he intended to find out who it was. He still had a nagging feeling it had something to do with Bitty's ghost. He wasn't sure how, but the coincidence was too strong to ignore.

The southern night air was warm but not too thick as he made his way across the backyard. Katydids trilled and frogs chirped as he took up the position he had decided on earlier in the day. He could sit out of sight on the backside of the carriage house and still watch the cellar doors. And that's what he planned on doing. Even if he had to stay awake all night. It was Saturday night, the end of the month was coming, and surely there would be more moonshine to deposit in the bootleggers' little hidey-hole. He just wished he had an infrared camera set up so he could catch any activity whether he was awake or not. But for now he'd have to settle for cellphone video and staying awake to see who came. He rounded the corner of the carriage house and bumped into something soft and sweet-smelling. "Natalie?"

"What are you doing out here?" she asked.

"I think I should be asking you that."

She jerked away from his grasp and crossed her arms. "I don't think so."

"I came out into watch for whoever is putting moonshine into your aunt's cellar."

She gave a swift nod. "Me too."

Newland shook his head. "Go on back to bed, Natty Nat. I've got this."

But she stubbornly refused to move. "Are you going to run the camera all night long? There's no way."

"You think you can do better?"

She smiled and he felt a little bit of his heart melt. "We can do better."

The last thing he wanted to do was team up with Natalie on anything not sex-related, but he found himself nodding in agreement. "Okay, we do this as a team."

****

Sometime around two a.m. the wind turned a little cold and Natalie found herself snuggled up against Newland. He hadn't moved in forever. She wasn't sure if he was asleep or merely one of those people who could sit still for hours on end. If he was asleep, she didn't want to take the chance to wake him, so she kept her mouth shut and just scooted a little bit closer to gain more of his warmth for her own.

He growled low and under his breath. "If you move any closer, I'll be forced to forget all about my promise."

Natalie jumped at the sound of his voice but didn't move away. "What promise was that?"

"To keep my hands to myself."

Her heart jumped in her chest. Her mouth went dry. "I see."

He rolled his head over to stare at her, though she couldn't read his expression in the dark. "I don't think you do. Or else you would've moved by now."

"Oh." Natalie moved back away from him, suddenly cold since he was no longer pressed to her side. "Do you think anyone is coming?"

"I don't know. I thought they would have been here by now."

"Shhh…"

Just then the cellar door opened and a shadowy figure stepped out into the night.

"You're seeing this too, right?" Newland asked.

Natalie nodded. "How did he get it there?" she asked as another shadow moved across the yard pushing what looked to be wheelbarrow.

"What kind of ghost uses a wheelbarrow?" Newland asked.

"That's no ghost," Natalie whispered. "That looks like…the Hughes brothers."

"Gilbert and Darrell?"

"Turtle Creek is small, but there aren't any more Hughes brothers than Gilbert and Darrell."

"How can you tell it's them?" he asked. "I can't see two feet in front of my face out here."

"You've been to the town meeting. Did you see anybody else that large in this town?"

"Good point."

"What do we do?" Natalie asked. Adrenaline flooded her. These men that she had known since she was in grade school were using her aunt's cellar as storage for their bootleg business.

"Nothing."

Natalie gasped. "Are you kidding? You dragged me out here to do nothing?"

"First of all, I didn't drag you anywhere. You came out here of your own accord. And second of all, those guys are enormous. I can't take them on. They'd kill me."

"Good point."

****

Newland started to protest, his male ego suffering with her ready agreement. But those guys were big, and he wasn't about to be pounded tonight.

"Why aren't they coming back out?" he asked.

"Did we miss them?"

Newland shook his head. "Couldn't have. I haven't taken my eyes off that spot since they went inside." Except for the times when he was sucked up into her presence.

"So we just wait for them to come back out?"

How long could they sit there and wait for the two mountainous men to climb out of the cellar? Then again, was it safe to walk back across the yard and into the house?

"We have to wait a little while longer." He had no idea what the Hughes twins would do if they caught Newland and Natalie watching them.

"Fine." She settled back next to him, and Newland was glad for her warmth. Only because it was cool sitting in the shadows watching for small-time criminals to exit their makeshift contraband storage facility.

But the longer he waited, the longer he realized they weren't coming back out. But why? They couldn't stay in the cellar all night and the next day. They had to come out sometime.

As Newland watched nothing, Natalie relaxed against him. Her breaths became long and even, and he knew she had fallen asleep. He wrapped one arm around her to give her neck a little more support. Poor thing. Bossing everyone around must really take it out of a person. But in sleep, she lost that frown she wore during the day. Her features softened, and she was even more beautiful.

Not that it mattered to him. So they'd had one fantastic encounter. He couldn't even say they'd had a night together. She had already told him it was a mistake. And though his ego wanted to show her just

197

how much it was *not* a mistake, that in itself would be a mistake.

He shook his head as his thoughts went around in circles. Now she had him doing it. He leaned his head back against the side of the carriage house still keeping an eye open for the Hughes brothers. But he had the strangest feeling they were already gone.

****

She was dreaming. And it was a wonderful dream. She was floating along without a care in the world snuggled up against the man that she loved on a hot southern night. It was a dream she did not want to wake from.

"Natalie." The voice was soft and caring, but she didn't want to wake up. Not yet. Not while the dream was still so sweet.

She shifted to get more comfortable, her head sliding down his hard chest to rest in his lap. But that was all part of the dream. It wasn't like she really had her head in his lap. She was just sleeping. It was her pillow. The night was warm, and she was comfortable. And so very sleepy.

A firm hand gripped her shoulder. "Natalie?" He shook her lightly. "You need to get up. It's morning."

Morning? She didn't want to get up. Morning meant responsibility. Running everything, keeping everything in check, making sure her Aunt Bitty didn't have strange people staying at her house, making sure Aubie got to school, making sure her parents had enough money to put fuel in the yacht. She was so very tired of those responsibilities. She just wanted to stay here snuggled up in this pretend lap and dream just a little while longer.

"Okay," she mumbled, hoping the voice and that firm hand would go away. Despite their caring nature, they wanted to pull her into responsibility, and she needed a little time to herself. She rubbed her cheek against the fabric of her pillow. Strange, it felt more like denim than Egyptian cotton. She needed to make a note to buy Aunt Bitty some new sheets. These were terrible.

A groan sounded from above her. She sighed as she snuggled down again. "You have to stop that. And you have to get up. Now."

What was he so grumpy about? Why did he care if she got up? She braced her hands on either side of her head. Just then, it dawned on her that the pillowcase didn't just *feel* like denim. It *was* denim and her hands weren't on the pillow or even a mattress, but one was on a hard thigh and the other was on a hard abdomen. And her face had been…

She pushed herself up quickly. Her cheeks filling with heat. "I'm up." She smoothed her hands down her borrowed jeans, trying to bring some semblance of order to her appearance, her morning.

Morning? It took a couple of seconds, but the night came back to her. Coming out here to see if she could discover who was sneaking into her aunt's cellar, running into Newland, then falling asleep on his shoulder. And this morning…

She turned back to him.

He stood, slowly stretching out his legs and adjusting his crotch.

My goodness! She'd had her face pressed against him. For how long she had no idea.

"I–I'm sorry." Her gaze flickered from his fly to his eyes. They twinkled with a mirth she didn't understand. "I don't see what's so funny about this."

"Who said it was funny?" he asked in return.

"You…" She shook her head. "I…" She started again. "Never mind." It was best to let the matter drop. There was no coming back from this one with her dignity intact. And the more she talked about it the worse it seemed to get.

"Did we sleep out here all night?"

"You did. I stayed awake."

"How long did they stay in there?" *That's a girl, Natalie. Keep him talking about something else so he forgets that you were —*

"They never came out."

Natalie's jaw dropped. "They're still in there?" She looked around. The day was dawning. The sun coming up in the east painted red and indigo streaks across the horizon. It had to be almost seven o'clock. How had they stayed in there so long? And what were they doing? "What are we going to do?"

Newland shook his head. "Go get the police?"

Natalie scoffed. "The sheriff's not going to do anything. They're moonshine buddies, remember?"

"Right."

She couldn't let them get away with this. They were storing moonshine in her aunt's cold cellar, potentially putting them all in danger. It just wasn't right.

She went around to the front of the carriage house and took the key from the planter next to the door.

"Really original," Newland commented.

She shot him a look and unlocked the door, lifting it in one heave-ho.

Newland whistled under his breath. "That's some car."

Natalie nodded. "That's my aunt's Packard. I believe they bought it off the showroom floor in 1956. It was the last year they made them."

He took a step forward and ran his hand over the dusty front fender. "I take it she doesn't drive much?"

Natalie shook her head and began searching along the wall. There had to be something in here she could use as a weapon. "Not so much these days, but she won't get rid of it. Sentimental reasons, you know." Ah-ha. Just what she was looking for.

She grabbed an ax handle out of one dusty corner and started out of the carriage house once again.

She brushed past Newland who was still staring at the car as if he had somehow won the lottery and started toward the cellar doors. "Shut the door behind you, okay?" She marched across the yard.

"Where are you going?"

She heard the door of the carriage house shut, but she didn't stop. "They're not going to get away with this."

The next thing she knew she was grabbed around the waist and pulled completely off her feet. "Put me down!"

"Not until you promise you're not going in there."

"I have to. They stayed in my aunt's cellar all night long. That is unacceptable."

Somehow he wrestled the ax handle from her grip. She supposed it wasn't too hard since he had her by about six inches and sixty pounds.

"They could have guns, Natalie. Never bring an ax handle to a gunfight."

She deflated in his embrace. "I can't allow this, Newland."

"I understand that, babe. But you can't go down there like this."

Had he just called her babe?

He set her on her feet.

Natalie tugged on her T-shirt. It was a little short and kept riding up. "What are you going to do?" she asked him.

He pressed his lips together. "I don't know, but you can't go down there."

She crossed her arms and felt the cool morning air across her midriff.

He gave her a tiny nod. "Nice outfit by the way. Doesn't seem like something you would own."

She smiled. "I don't. These are Aubie's."

****

"Of course they are." Newland shook his head. Just when he thought she was relaxing a bit, she had to drop a bombshell on him like that. "Okay here's the plan. I'm going to take this ax handle and go down there. I'll check things out, and you're going to stay up here. Do you understand?"

She nodded, but he didn't entirely trust her. What he would've given at that moment for a pair of handcuffs. He would handcuff her to the door handle where she couldn't follow him. And then later... He pushed that thought away.

He stood to one side of the cellar doors and cautiously pulled open the right-hand side. He took a step back as he waited for something to happen. What, he wasn't exactly sure, just something. But when no one came out guns blazing, rebel yelling, karate chopping, or any other lethal retaliation, he opened the other side much in the same manner.

Natalie snickered.

He glared at her. This wasn't the time. "I don't think they're down there," he said.

"So they left? I thought you said you stayed awake all night."

"I did." He'd taught himself a long time ago to survive on very little sleep. He could stay up for three days straight if necessary. Whatever it took to get the story.

"Then where did they go?"

"I don't know, but I'm going to have a look."

"I'm right behind you." He opened his mouth to protest, but she raised a hand, cutting him off before he could even start. "This is my aunt's house and my aunt's cellar, and I'm going with you."

Only because he was fairly certain that the Hughes brothers were nowhere near, he reluctantly nodded and started down the newly constructed ladder. He turned on the light while she climbed down next to him.

Just as he suspected, they were the only two in the cellar. Them and about twelve more cases of moonshine. Just where was it all coming from?

"How did they do that?" Natalie asked. "How did they come in but not come back out?"

Newland took a penlight from his pocket and shined it on the walls, starting over by the steps and slowly turning around. He carefully examined each wall as he went. "I don't know for sure, but I have a theory."

"And?" Impatience weighted her voice.

But Newland was more distracted looking for a way out than he was by her at that moment. "I read this article once about southern houses that had tunnels and secret passages that were used in the Underground Railroad."

Natalie gasped. "There have always been rumors, but…"

Newland continued to study the wall. So far nothing seemed out of the ordinary, just packed-dirt walls hardened to rock over years of wear. "Didn't you tell me that this house was built by a Yankee sympathizer?"

"Yeah, it was." Natalie's voice turned wispy with awe. "So the tunnels are real? You think the Yankee sympathizer put them in to help slaves escape?"

"It's the only theory I can come up with. Two men the size of mountains came down here last night and never came back up. That means there has to be a second way out."

"And that would explain how they got in last night without us noticing," Natalie added.

He took a step closer to the wall reaching out one hand and touching… Fabric. "Here!" he cried. He felt toward the right again until he found the edge of the cloth. It was as big as a sheet and had been painted to look just like the wall surrounding it. Had he not been that close to it and looking at it directly he might have never noticed. The dim light coupled with the lack of expectancy had fooled them into thinking it was just another piece of the wall. He pulled the painted curtain aside to reveal a gaping hole big enough to easily accommodate two large men.

CHAPTER SIXTEEN

"Is that what I think it is?" Natalie asked.

"Yeah, it is." Newland shook his head. It was like some bad *Hardy Boys* mystery. Moonshine stacked in the corner and secret tunnels.

"Where does it go?"

He shot her a look. "Like I know."

"Only one way to find out," she prodded.

"We are not going in there."

"We have to!"

Newland pulled the curtain back into place. To the casual jelly seeker it looked just like another section of wall. And that's just the way it would remain. "No, we don't. It's dangerous. And if we can't get the sheriff on our side then we're going to have to come up with a different way to figure out why the Hughes brothers are storing moonshine in your aunt's cellar." He shook his head. "We don't need to know why. They're evidently moving it through the tunnel."

"And that's exactly why we need to know where the tunnel lets out."

He shook his head again and grabbed her by one arm, pointing her toward the stairs leading out of the cellar. "It's too dangerous, I'm not going to let you do that."

She growled at him.

"Let it go, babe," he said. "You can get frustrated with lack of control all you want. But you are not in control of the situation. I am, and I say you're not going down there."

"But—"

"No buts," he said, then placed his hand on hers and pushed her toward the ladder once more.

Reluctantly, she did as he bade, but a part of him wondered if she did it to get away from his touch or if she truly was relinquishing control to him.

Fat chance.

****

Natalie fumed for most of the morning. Then she begged off spending any time with Newland and her aunt, citing she needed to go to her apartment and do some laundry. Most everything went to the cleaners except for the unmentionables and Aubie's school clothes. But she just had to get away. Of course her apartment wasn't any better, considering what had happened the last time she'd been there. She would never look at that couch the same way again. She'd probably have to get rid of it. And not just because it reminded her of Newland, but because it proved to her how quickly she could lose control. That was the last thing she needed. The one thing that she didn't want in her life was someone who could make her abandon all of her sensibilities.

But it felt good to feel free just that one time, a tiny voice inside her whispered.

She squashed the voice and flipped through the magazine again. Oskar whined at the sliding glass door off the kitchen. She let him out into the common yard. He usually took care of his business and came back in. Well, not without a little bit of incentive.

She poured herself a drink as she waited for him to come back, knowing what was next. He stood at the opened door and whined again.

"Come on in, baby," she crooned.

He whined louder.

Natalie sighed. "You want a piece of cheese?"

He barked enthusiastically and promptly pranced into the house. It was a bad habit they had gotten into. Now she couldn't get him to come in without the coercion. Wasn't that just the way of it? No one did anything out of the goodness of their heart anymore. Everybody had to have a reward.

Except for Gerald.

Normally the thought of him warmed the blood in her veins, but now she was just confused. How could she sleep with Newland if she was in love with Gerald Davenport?

It was just a matter of time before he declared his love for her and asked her to be his wife. Once that happened, everything would be perfect. Exactly the way she wanted it. And it wouldn't matter that her dog begged for cheese before he would come into the house or that her brother had to be constantly reminded to brush his teeth, or that her aunt drank moonshine and played poker on Thursday nights.

What about Newland?

She wasn't going to think about that. She had to look toward the future. And he was not part of that. Gerald was.

After Thursday night Newland Tran would be gone. Gerald would remain, steady as always by her side.

They just needed a date night. That's all it was. It'd been a long time since she'd gotten to spend any alone time with Gerald. They hadn't had a non-benefit dinner together in months. It seemed like everything on their social calendar involved a charity or a foundation. They needed a night to rekindle things. That was all. One night to set everything back to rights. One night and everything would be perfect again.

She grabbed her cellphone off the coffee table and punched through the directory until she found his name. She hit the little phone icon and waited for him to answer.

"Davenport." Not exactly the way she expected him to answer the phone, but he was a busy man. He probably hadn't checked the caller ID to know that it was her. Easy mistake to make.

"Gerald? It's Natalie."

His voice turned immediately soft and dreamy. "Natalie, so good to hear from you."

Natalie smiled even though she knew he couldn't see her. This was what she needed. Just some time with the man she was soon to marry. "I've missed you."

"I know, darling, it's been so hectic lately, but I promise things are going to slow down soon. Just wait and see."

"I know." Natalie played with the hem of Aubie's jeans. She should've changed right when she got home. But she was already wearing the clothes so she kept them on for now.

"Is there a reason for this call, Natalie?"

She stirred, sitting up a little straighter in her seat. "Yes. Of course. See, I was thinking that maybe the two of us should get together tonight."

"Tonight? Is there a charity dinner or something going on that I forgot to put in my calendar?" Had his voice turned urgent and just a little on the distracted side, or was she making things up?

"No dinner, I just thought maybe the two of us could get together and watch a movie." They had never simply sat in her apartment and watched a movie, spent time together, just the two of them. It seemed that they were always rushing around trying to help other people. Maybe it was time they helped themselves and their relationship get just a little bit closer.

"As much as that sounds like a great time, it's just not possible tonight, Natalie."

Papers rustled on his end of the line. Was he working on a Sunday afternoon? He was so dedicated to his job.

"Are you sure? I mean we hardly ever see each other anymore."

"I know it's been hard, but you have to trust me. It will all be worth it in the end."

"Of course," Natalie said. "I'm sure." She had no doubts that Gerald was working hard. She had no doubts that he would do anything in his power to spend the evening with her if he could. Tonight just wasn't a good night. She understood that. She would be the understanding girlfriend, which would turn into the understanding fiancée, which would eventually turn into the understanding wife. It was a role that she knew how to play well. "Any word on getting Aunt Bitty's house listed in the historical registry?"

She practically heard him shake his head. "No, they won't hear anything about it. I've been trying to convince them that historic means history, and Confederate is something completely different, but it seems the house has a few questionable attributes connected with it."

"Like what?" Why was he just telling her this now?

"Well, there's the matter of the fact that it was built by a Yankee sympathizer in the middle of the South. And then the rumors said the family helped slaves escape on the Underground Railroad."

"I would think that would make it all the more valuable," Natalie said. She didn't know a lot about history but it went both ways didn't it?

"You have a bunch of conservative old gentleman on this board, Natalie. You have to understand that. They don't turn loose of their traditions easily. And though we all know how wrong slavery was and is, a lot of these men lost their family fortune in the war. Bitterness runs deep when it comes to money."

"I suppose." But her aunt's house deserved to be on the historical registry. It just wasn't fair that her aunt's house seemed forgotten when so many around hers bore plaques at what role they had played in the war.

"Is that all?" he asked. "I really have some things that need to be done by this evening." She could almost see him check his watch across the phone line. She'd seen him do it so many times. The action was embedded in her brain like the blink of his eye or the gesture of his hand.

"Of course," she murmured. She wanted to say that she loved him before she said goodbye but the words stuck in her throat. "See you later then." She turned off the phone without waiting for his response.

****

Newland didn't know where the tunnel let out. But he had an idea. He jumped the back fence into the cemetery and started poking around. It seemed only natural that it let out somewhere around here. What better place than an abandoned cemetery where no one came any longer?

He walked past the graves, careful not to step in any of the sunken holes created there. It all seemed so terribly obvious now. Underground tunnel filled with moonshine and a Confederate ghost where no confederates were buried. It was like some bad Scooby Doo afternoon special.

Newland still couldn't figure out how Gilbert and Darrell played into the whole thing. Neither one of them were smart enough to concoct a ghost out of thin air or run a moonshine operation as big as Newland was beginning to suspect this one was. He couldn't see very far down into the tunnel, but he had seen down far enough to know that there were more crates stacked along the wall. And if there were crates stacked four high all the way to the opening… He shook his head. That was a lot of hooch.

He made his way over to the mound of dirt, knowing he wouldn't find anything in the daylight. But he wanted to see if it had been messed with, if it was bigger than it had been before, or if maybe the dirt had been added to or taken away from anything to signify there had been some change in the status quo since the last time he had been there. But it all appeared the same. Black tarp covering half of it, three sides pinned down allowing the fourth one to flap around. For a moment he wondered if maybe that oversight wasn't an oversight at all. What if it was just one more factor that set up a ghost in this abandoned cemetery?

He needed to get back to Aunt Bitty's house and find out exactly where she had seen the ghost. He had just assumed it had been over in this direction, though he had no idea why. The cemetery wasn't huge, but it was big enough, and it was important to know where the ghost had been seen. For some reason he had a feeling that would tell a lot.

"Newman, right?"

He turned as Jack Russell, the man from the bar, came striding through the cemetery toward him. The man seemed none the worse for wear after their evening together, but Newland had a feeling that Jack drank moonshine a lot more than he did.

"Actually, it's Newland. Good to see you again." He stuck out a hand to shake.

Jack took it with a smile. "Still looking for Bitty's ghost?"

"Yeah, I am. Have you seen anything out here lately?"

Jack shook his head. "I told you the ghost only comes the last Thursday of the month."

"So Bitty says as well," Newland murmured. He looked around as if he was expecting to see some old-fashioned projector set up somewhere, but there were only rows of overgrown graves all the way to the edge of the iron fence. "And you say you don't see anything else on these nights?" That seemed to be the only reason for a ghost he could think of. Well, at least a ghost that only showed up one night a month. It had to be some sort of distraction. Take people's focus from one place and turn it to another. He was certain they probably could move an elephant out of there as long as there was a ghost on the other side of the cemetery away from it.

"I ain't seen nothing."

"If you do…" Newland started.

Jack nodded. "Of course. I'll go find you at Bitty's house."

Newland nodded. He had a feeling he would never see Jack standing on Bitty's front porch, but it was good to know that the man was at least watching for something odd to happen. With Jack watching the front of the house and Newland watching the back, surely any nefarious undertakings would be apparently obvious.

"I meant what I said," Jack started. "Bitty Duncan's a nice old lady, and I would hate to think that someone was taking advantage of her. Or maybe putting her in danger."

"You think she's in danger?"

Jack shrugged. "I don't know. But something weird is going on here, and people seem to be investigating left and right. Soon as somebody hits on the truth…" He trailed off and shook his head. "It may be a small town, but there's some big money around here. I'm sure no one wants you to be messing with it."

The words stayed with Newland all the way back to the house. He took the long way around, walking down the block, checking the cemetery from all angles as if somehow that would give him a clue as to what was happening there. He also looked for places for the tunnel to let out which seemed almost ridiculous. The tunnel could let out halfway across town and he would never know it.

He let himself in the front door, and was immediately greeted by Mr. Piddles. The big feline seemed to have taken a liking to him. Newland picked him up and scratched him behind the ears as a low grumble came from deep inside the cat. He had never had a cat before, never even had a pet before. All this was new to him. But he decided that he liked having the creature like him. Somehow it made him feel that he wasn't all bad if the kitty cat could want his attention.

What if he got a cat when he went back to Chicago?

Why? So he could leave it for days on end as he went searching for the next big story that would get him back into the game?

He gave the kitty one last scratch, kissed the top of his head, and set him on the divan in the parlor. Bitty was there working the crossword puzzle but looked up and smiled as he walked in.

"Where is everybody?" He really meant Aubie. Natalie had gone to her house to do laundry. Though he felt it was just an excuse to get away from him.

Bitty pushed her glasses a little farther down her nose. "Aubie's up in his room. He said he had some issues to look over. They still haven't decided exactly what to do about the school uniforms."

"The school uniforms?" Newland asked. He settled down into the chair opposite her not surprised at all when Mr. Piddles jumped into his lap and demanded more attention.

"Not uniforms for school, but uniforms for the players and things. You know the basketball team and the cheerleaders. If they take the black off the uniforms then they'll need all new ones."

That would take a lot of money. Newland had no idea how much, but it seemed as if the Duncan-Coleman clan had more than enough of that. He was a little surprised that control freak Natalie didn't just donate what they needed to the school and be done with it.

"What are they going to do?"

"Aubie's looking at fundraiser ideas. But I don't see how selling candy bars is going to take care of this one." She picked up her paper again and started back with the crossword puzzle.

"I suppose not," Newland said. He wasn't sure exactly how many people were in Turtle Creek, or for that matter how many kids attended Turtle Creek schools. But he knew one thing: all new uniforms for every extracurricular activity would need quite a bit of money and the whole community to pitch in and help. He stood and deposited Mr. Piddles in the chair he'd just vacated.

"Where are you going?" Bitty asked.

"I've got an idea," Newland said and started for the stairs. He knocked lightly on Aubie's door and opened up the summons. "I hear you're looking for a fundraiser idea?"

The teen mayor pushed the papers on his bed aside and nodded. "Yeah, we need to raise money for new uniforms for the high school teams and the band, cheerleaders…"

"That's what Bitty said. I've got an idea about that," Newland said.

"Yeah?"

"Just hear me out, okay? It may sound a little strange at first but… Just hear me out."

"Okay." Aubie gave him a nod and a strange look then sat back as if prepared to listen to what Newland had to say. The boy might be scatterbrained at times and a little irresponsible when it came to day-to-day matters of hygiene and homework, but he seemed to genuinely care about the community. He might be as eccentric as the rest of his family, but he seemed to know when to listen.

"A benefit auction." He said the word on a gush of air, then went on to explain. "The Amish do it all the time. Members of the community donate items they don't want anymore to the auction. The community itself comes in and bids on these items. You can invite people from other communities to come in and bid or even donate."

"I see. Go on."

"People donate all sorts of items. Everything from pies to quilts to farm equipment, farm animals. Anything you can imagine can go up for sale and every penny that's earned goes to the cause. It's simple really, and it won't take much to organize and get together."

"This works for them?" Aubie asked, clearly intrigued with the idea.

Newland nodded. "They hold enough of them that it must. They even have a big one that benefits Haiti every year. Several communities hold those auctions. But this could just be one to raise money for the school teams to get new uniforms and get that black out of the school colors."

Aubie nodded. "It does sort of look drab. I think it brings down morale. We're not the biggest school out there nor are we the best, but I think we would certainly play better if we had a little pride in our mascot."

"About that—" Newland started.

Aubie laughed. "Don't ask. I've already tried. And everybody likes the Snappers. But if we can make them green and yellow instead of black maybe we could win a game come the new season."

Newland smiled. "That alone would be worth holding an auction for."

Aubie nodded and Newland started from the room. He put one hand on the knob to leave when the teen spoke again. "Newland? Thanks. That was a great idea. I'll put it to the town at the next meeting."

Newland nodded. "Glad to help." He stepped out into the hallway to find Natalie there. He quietly shut the door behind him and waited for her to speak.

"Why did you do that?" she asked. Her voice sounded strained.

"Because it's a good idea?"

Natalie shook her head. "Why do you care about this town? You're leaving in just a few days."

The thought made his heart give a funny pound in his chest. He was leaving in a few days, going back to Chicago, a place where he understood how things worked. But he would miss this tiny town with its weird school mascot and drab school colors, with tiny bars that served contraband moonshine and a sheriff who was the number one customer for the biggest bootlegger in the county.

And Natalie. He would definitely miss Natalie.

He straightened. "Yeah, but that doesn't mean that I can't help if it's needed." It didn't matter how badly he would miss Natalie. She was almost engaged to one of the most influential men in northern Mississippi. Gerald Davenport seemed to have everything that Newland didn't. He had a family, community standing, money, good looks, he was sure the man drove a car to rival that of Natalie's. Newland needed to face it. He was not in her league. Not even close.

He started to move past her, but she reached out a hand, stopping him. He looked down at her fingers against his sleeve and then back up into those sky-blue eyes.

"I really appreciate it."

He cleared his throat. "No problem." Then he pushed past her and skipped down the stairs.

****

By Monday afternoon it'd become painfully obvious to Natalie. Newland was avoiding her. She tried on three different occasions to talk to him about the cemetery and the tunnel in her aunt's cellar or whether or not he wanted jelly or honey on his toast. But no matter how hard she tried to engage him in conversation, it seemed he pulled away twice as hard.

The thought cut like a knife, though she wasn't sure why. Why did it matter what he thought? Why did it matter if he was distant with her now? So they'd had some great sex. It didn't mean anything to either of them. It was a chance encounter. And she needed to remember that. After all, she never wanted to repeat it. She couldn't go around losing control like that every day. It was detrimental to the wellbeing of the Coleman family as a whole. They needed her to remain in control. So why did she care if Newland was distant?

Because you thought it meant more.

Natalie shook her head. It shouldn't mean anything more than one night, great sex. But somehow it did. There was just this little side of her that wanted to know if it could happen again. Was it a fluke or a once-in-a-lifetime alignment of the stars that caused such chemistry between them on that Saturday night? If she went to kiss him now would it be like kissing her brother?

It. Didn't. Matter.

She was hoping soon that she could announce her engagement to Gerald. That was all that mattered. Not some fluky hot time with a man she barely knew. Still, heat rose into her cheeks as she thought of how she responded to the hunky reporter.

There was something about their encounter that made her feel so... alive. It was cliché and campy she knew, but it was true nonetheless. He had brought out something in her that she hadn't known existed. And she wanted to know if she truly owned that response or if it was a product of his touch alone.

If the ghost held true and showed up Thursday, then by Friday afternoon he would be gone and she might never know.

CHAPTER SEVENTEEN

Reluctantly, Newland made his way down the stairs at six o'clock Monday evening. He'd been listening for sounds that dinner was underway. His plan was simple: skip out on what everybody was eating, drive into town, find something to eat somewhere, talk to a few of the locals—maybe someone had seen something in the cemetery—and otherwise avoid Natalie at all cost.

His foot hit the bottom stair as a voice called out, "Newland? Is that you?" Bitty. How she'd heard him, he had no idea. For somebody pushing their eighty-seventh birthday the woman had ears of a hawk.

"Yes, Bitty," he called in return. "Just heading out to get something to eat."

"Out? Land sakes, dear, come in here and get yourself a home-cooked meal."

He winced as he heard her chair scraping the dining room floor. The next thing he knew she was standing in the hallway, motioning toward him to come. He couldn't very well dash out of the house and leave her standing there. She had opened her home to him after all. She had fed him and sheltered him in the past week, but he knew that Natalie was sitting there at that table. Aubie, too. Eating with the three of them just seemed so much like a family that it almost broke his heart. It was better if he started to distance himself now, before he got so used to having people who cared about him that he didn't know what to do without them once he left.

"Of course." What else could he say?

But when he made his way into the dining room, he found Gerald Davenport seated next to Natalie.

He nodded toward the man, the most gracious greeting he could muster, then went to sit next to Aubie. The position had him across from Natalie, and though he would love to sit close to her as he ate, it was probably better this way. At least he could not easily reach out and touch her as he so badly wanted to do.

She belongs to another.

Newland took his place and served his plate, smiling at the southern fare that was tonight's supper. Black-eyed peas that looked fresh, sliced tomatoes, fried okra, cornbread, and iced tea. It looked and smelled wonderful, and though he tended to be a meat and potatoes man, the meal was somehow comforting all the same.

He glanced up at Gerald, surprised to see the man had anything on his plate. He seemed to be more of a caviar-champagne sort of chap rather than the simple country fare that they were eating. Maybe there was more to him than Newland actually knew. He was Southern after all, but he didn't seem as comfortable as Newland might have thought. Gerald hardly looked at Natalie as they ate, never brushed up against her or acknowledged her presence in any way. It was as if she were his sister not his lover.

But she's not.

"So, Bitty," Gerald started, "have you given any thought to those papers I brought by a couple of days ago?"

Papers?

Newland didn't know about any papers. He squashed that thought. Why was he supposed to know about any business that Bitty was conducting? It was hardly any of his concern. Three more days and he was leaving. Yet he wanted to hear more.

"I read them over, yes." Bitty nodded. The light from the chandelier glinted off her lavender hair.

"And?" Gerald prodded.

"I don't see what my willing the house to Natalie has to do with getting on the historical registry. I thought that was our goal, dear."

"It is. Eventually." Gerald cleared his throat with a little cough. "I thought you should do this just as a safeguard. Then, in the event that something might happen to you before the registry goes through properly, Natalie will be able to take over."

Bitty shook her head. "I don't know. It would go to Babs, of course, as my next of kin. Wouldn't it? She is my niece, after all."

Natalie turned to Gerald, her blue eyes beseeching. "Maybe this isn't proper discussion for the dining room table, Gerald." Her voice was soft yet controlled. And Newland had the suspicion that she wasn't comfortable suggesting such a thing to her almost fiancé.

"I think it's a perfect time to discuss this." Gerald laid his napkin on his half-eaten food and steepled his fingers under his chin. "Important matters such as these shouldn't be put off until it's too late."

Natalie shifted in her seat, obviously uncomfortable with talking about the death of her favorite aunt. In fact, as far as Newland knew, Bitty Duncan was Natalie's only aunt.

"All right then," Natalie said, heaving a deep breath as she continued, "anything that Bitty owns would actually go to my mother as the next of kin. But then that power of attorney is transferred to me. So regardless, I would have control over whatever happens to the house at that point. Satisfied?"

Newland's head jerked up at the sharpness in her tone. He'd never heard her speak to Gerald that way. He'd never heard her speak to anyone except for him that way. And he smiled. The woman was getting some spunk.

"I think it's important is all," Gerald said. "I didn't mean to upset anyone."

Natalie visibly relaxed, and a small smile trembled on her lips. "You worry too much, Gerald. I made sure everything was taken care of long before my family headed off to Greece."

Newland smiled. Of course she did. That was his Natalie, in control of every little facet. Until it came to… His thoughts came to a screeching halt. She was not his Natalie. At least not in the sense that he wanted her to be.

****

Natalie looped her arm through Gerald's as she walked him to the front door. "Thanks for coming by tonight." She knew he was busy, but she was glad she had managed to talk him into coming to supper. They still had a lot to discuss about the historic registry of the house and why they were getting so much static over it being a northern built house. Just because the original owner had been a Yankee sympathizer didn't mean that the house didn't deserve to be on the historic tour. In fact, as far as she was concerned, it just deepened the rich history of Turtle Creek. But it seemed some people fought the war over and over again even a hundred and fifty years later.

"Of course."

It was the closest thing they'd had to a date in months, and Natalie wasn't ready to see it end. Most everything they did they were surrounded by others, and tonight was no different. She saw her opportunity to get Gerald by himself as she walked him out onto the porch.

"How about we have a glass of iced tea out here on the swing and talk for a while."

Gerald shook his head. "I've got a big meeting in the morning. I need to get home and look over the briefs. Sorry, this has to be an early night."

"Oh." Natalie did her best not to sound disappointed. And it wasn't just because she wanted to sit and spend more time alone with Gerald and make sure that he gave her that secret little thrill that she got when she sat next to Newland. It was so much more than that. But if she was being honest with herself, that was a big part of it. She needed to know, she needed that reassurance, that she and Gerald were going to be okay, that he could do the same things to her that Newland could, and that once Newland was gone her life would go back to normal.

"I'll see you at the town meeting tomorrow night." Gerald bent down and brushed his lips against her temple then started down the steps. He was halfway to his car before she realized that she hadn't told him about the tunnel they had discovered under the house.

"Well, that was cozy."

Natalie whirled around as Newland stepped out of the shadows. She clutched a hand over her heart. "What are you doing here?" she cried. "You scared the life out of me."

"I came out here for a little peace and quiet. I had no idea…" He trailed off.

"Yeah, well." She turned to head back into the house.

"Why don't you ask me?"

She stopped. "Ask you what?"

"Ask me to have a glass of iced tea on the porch with you. I have a feeling I won't turn you down."

That was something she should not do. She should just keep going into the house, go upstairs, and lock herself in her room. He had been avoiding her for days. She should thank her lucky stars that he had. Thursday he would be gone. And the quicker he was gone the quicker she could forget the passion she felt in his arms.

Still, she found herself turning to face him. "Would you like have a glass of iced tea with me?"

"I'd love nothing more."

To her surprise he insisted that she stay outside while he went in to fetch their tea.

Natalie used the heels of her feet to push the swing into a gentle motion as she waited for Newland to return. Nights here were so peaceful. There was something about this house on Sycamore Lane that was so special. She'd spent a great deal of her childhood here playing with Aunt Bitty. Eating sugar cookies and playing dress-up with the clothes from that big trunk up in the attic. She missed those days. Things were a lot less complicated then. She had known what she wanted out of life. Okay, so she had wanted to be a ballerina. What girl her age didn't? But she hadn't known then that she would be caretaker to her brother, have absentee parents, be running a foundation single-handedly, all the while keeping an eye on her eccentric aunt.

Oskar whined at the door, and she opened it to let him out. She went back to the swing and he jumped into her lap, happy to be sitting with his mistress.

A few minutes later Newland came out, carrying two tall glasses of cool iced tea.

"You know what's funny?" he asked as he handed her a glass. "No one here says sweet tea."

Natalie laughed. "That's because it's the way it should be served."

Newland raised his glass and clicked it against the edge of hers. "Hear, hear."

Natalie blinked at him in surprise. "You mean you don't want your tea unsweetened like the rest of the Yankees?"

"That was an unfair stereotype."

"True." Natalie smiled at him. The more she thought about it, the more it seemed that Newland Tran was settling into Southern life. She'd seen how he'd dug into the country fare that had been served at supper tonight. Gerald had hardly touched his peas and Newland had eaten two helpings. It seemed there was so much more to this man who sat beside her.

A thick silence fell between them. It wasn't quite uncomfortable, nor was it the silence of two old friends. It was strained, as if the words that needed to be said were pulling against both of them in their efforts to break free.

"Natalie," Newland said.

She shook her head. "Don't."

"You can't marry him."

"I have to."

"You don't. There's a whole world out there. A whole world beyond Turtle Creek and Gerald Davenport. He's after this house, Natalie. Surely you can see that."

"He's trying to look out for our best interests."

Newland let out a frustrated growl. "Okay, don't say I didn't warn you. But aside from the chemistry between us and his little business deal at the table, that should be enough for you to call off any almost engagement."

His words stabbed at her heart. She wanted to deny them—vehemently—but she knew somewhere, deep down inside, they were true. But what was she supposed to do about them?

****

By six o'clock the next afternoon, Natalie had managed to successfully avoid Newland for almost twenty-four hours. And she would make it too, just as soon as the town meeting was over. She pulled into the parking lot at the school, handing Aubie his portfolio briefcase full of notes and other documents that he needed for the meeting.

He took it from her and gave her a sad little smile. "You know I can get my briefcase myself, right?"

Her heart broke a little at his words. She was so used to taking care of him, giving him everything that he needed, and making sure that his life wasn't lacking due to his absentee parents. But to hear him say that he could do things on his own…

"Aubie, I—"

He surprised her by leaning in and giving her a quick kiss on the cheek. "I love you, sis," he said. "You're the best sister any guy could ever hope to have. But I'll tell you a little secret: the less you do for me, the more I have to do for myself."

On that cryptic note, Aubie got out of the car and shut the door. He walked toward the doors of the school without giving her a second look.

She shook her head as tears rose in her eyes. True, Aubie was growing up. And yes, it was more than likely time for her to give him more freedom. He was the mayor after all. But when he left, what was she going to have then?

Gerald's face came to mind, but it offered her no comfort. Maybe because on the heels of that image came Newland's words from the night before about how she couldn't marry Gerald Davenport, how the man didn't love her, and was only after her aunt's house.

But why? Why would Gerald want Aunt Bitty's house? And why was she trusting Newland Tran? She had barely known him a week— a *week*— and she'd practically fallen in love with the man.

The words clawed at her heart. She couldn't be in love with Newland. He was the antithesis of everything she wanted from life. He was disorganized and shaggy and a Northerner and… She scrambled around, trying to come up with any negative thing that she could think of about him. He wore concert T-shirts and tennis shoes. And he lived his life the way he wanted to and didn't allow other people to dictate to him and yet he did things for a woman he didn't know.

She shook her head. She couldn't be in love with Newland Tran. It was impossible. She loved Gerald, and he was going to ask her to marry him anytime now. Once they got married, they would be the best power couple in northern Mississippi.

Nothing could stop them. They would go around raising money and hosting benefits for charities and...

The thought filled her with dread. Was that all her life had to offer? Was the only thing she could think of concerning her marriage to Gerald future benefits and foundation dinners? Surely there would be more than that. Surely that passion would ignite. Wouldn't it?

She was so deep in thought that she jumped when someone rapped on the car window. Hand over her heart she looked up to see Newland standing there.

She shooed him away from the door and opened it, grabbing her purse before shutting the door and locking the car. "What are you doing here?"

"It's a town meeting, right?"

"It is, but you don't live here." Clouds formed in his exotic eyes, and Natalie immediately regretted her words. "Newland, I'm sorry, I—"

He shook his head. "No, I don't live here, but this seems to be the best entertainment going tonight." He turned on his heel and left, leaving Natalie to follow behind.

****

As far as town meetings went, this special session was not much different than any of the normal meetings. Complaints were heard about loose animals, loud radios, and various other small-town issues.

Natalie listened with half an ear tuned toward the council while she thumbed through her email messages. Her parents seemed to reach out to her at the oddest moments. She was constantly checking to make sure they hadn't emailed her concerning some tragedy, imagined or real.

But when Aubie stood and started talking about the fundraiser he was putting into place for the new school athletic and cheerleader uniforms, her heart constricted.

She turned to look for Newland. He had come into the gym in front of her, and had found his seat, not inviting her to sit with him. She had gone to the row behind him and sat a few seats away, not wanting to invade his personal space. It seemed that she had completely overstepped her bounds with him tonight.

Everyone who had anything to do with fundraisers knew about the Amish Haiti benefit auction. But most everyone else hadn't heard of it. But Newland Tran had. He'd said he'd spent time with the Amish. Which was why he had rigged up a light bulb with a car battery in the cellar. And that he had given that idea to Aubie…

It was more than that. It was more than just the idea handed from one mind to the other, it was that Newland had been thinking about the town and how to help. He'd come up with a solution where no one else had found one. That he cared about the town at all seemed to be a miracle in itself.

Natalie blinked back her confused tears as the council took a vote, setting a date for the auction that would allow the people of Turtle Creek to gather their items together and hold the auction in order to have the new school uniforms in by the time school came back into session in August.

Turtle Creek was growing, expanding and evolving, and for this particular project there was only one man to thank. A man who would be leaving in less than four days.

****

"I thought I'd find you here."

Newland jerked to attention as Natalie appeared out of the shadows, like the specter that Bitty talked about.

"What are you doing here?"

"I live here?"

Newland shook his head. "No, you live across town in an apartment with your brother. Bitty Duncan lives here."

He wasn't sure why he was being so mean, maybe because Natalie wanted to move Bitty out of the house and into a home. Gerald seemed to support the idea and wanted the house to belong to Natalie so he could get it when they got married, and Aubie was along for the ride. Nobody seemed to care what Bitty thought.

"Sorry. That was hateful." He said the words as she plopped down beside him. If she was sitting next to him, then she couldn't be too mad, right?

"You think I should live here with my aunt?"

"I wonder why you don't." He was sitting with his back against the carriage house once again waiting to see if Gilbert and Darrell came with any more crates of moonshine.

"I guess I felt like I needed some independence."

Newland snorted. "You need independence and yet you run everyone's life. Why don't you start there and see what happens?"

Natalie sighed. "I'm trying. I got a lecture from Aubie tonight about babying him."

"You do baby him."

"I just wanted to make up for our parents."

"What about them?" Newland was afraid he'd be sorry he asked. He had his own parent sob story. He wasn't sure if he could handle Natalie's on top of that.

She picked at the grass next to her legs, tearing blade by blade and tossing it away. "Nothing, really. As soon as they figured out that I could handle the financial end of things, they headed off to the Mediterranean."

"How old were you?"

"Seventeen." The one word dropped between them like a rock.

"You've been on your own since seventeen?"

Natalie nodded. "It's not been bad, you know. I had money to take care of things. I gained the power of attorney at eighteen. Until then I just made do and took care of things as they needed to be taken care of."

"And Aubie?"

"He was just starting first grade."

"So you stayed here and at eighteen raised a first grader all by yourself."

Natalie smiled, though the motion was sad. "I had Aunt Bitty's help."

Newland laughed. "I'm sure that was quite a relief."

"It was about the same as right now."

He wanted to tell her how sorry he was, but he didn't think that was what she needed to hear. Their conversation stalled, the only sounds were the katydids and the bobwhites calling back to each other in the night.

"My parents died when I was five." There. That wasn't so hard to say.

"Newland." The one word was almost a prayer. "I'm so sorry."

"It was a long time ago." It was his standard response.

It had been a long time ago. But he still missed them, wondered what his life would have been like if they had been a part of it. But then he also wondered if things hadn't been that way, would he be sitting here now with the most beautiful woman in the world watching for bootleggers to come store their contraband in her aunt's cellar? He wasn't sure he would trade back.

"What did you do?" she asked.

"I went to live with my uncle. Not the most maternal man you'd ever want to meet." He chuckled. "Nor was he particularly paternal either. I stayed with him till I was eighteen and then headed out on my own."

"Do you see him much these days?"

Newland shook his head. "You see your parents much?"

Natalie hesitated, throwing three more blades of grass to the wind before shaking her head. "No. They send a card on Aubie's birthday, but that's about it. It doesn't matter. We have everything we need."

Newland's heart broke for her. "What about love?" It was the one thing he missed the most about his parents. He'd never had that love, couldn't remember what it felt like to be held in his mother's arms and cradled at night. He couldn't remember throwing a ball with his dad or doing any of those things that he knew his friends had gotten to do over the years. His uncle had been too busy with his own pursuits to pay much attention to the young boy he had been saddled with. But the love? The love had always been missing.

"I think we did okay."

Newland shook his head. "Is that why you're willing to enter into a loveless marriage with a man who's all wrong for you? You think it's okay to live without love?"

"I don't know," she whispered. "I just don't know anymore. I had everything all planned out, then you showed up. Now nothing seems the same. I don't know whether I'm coming or going. What's real, what's not, what's important, what isn't." Her voice broke on that last word.

"You want to know what's real?" he asked. Even in the darkness of the shadows where they sat he saw her small nod. She swallowed hard. "This."

He reached out and, in one swift but deliberate motion, pulled her into his lap. She straddled him. He ran his fingers through the sides of her hair, tangling them in the long brown tresses. He gave her plenty of time to protest, plenty of time to tell him to stop. She didn't.

So he pulled her mouth to his.

****

She sighed as his lips touched hers and melted into him. He was warm and solid and real and kind. Very kind. If she hadn't already realized it this afternoon, it was so obvious now. She loved him.

She wasn't sure how it happened or even when. Sometime between watching him cart around her aunt's cat and come up with ideas to help the town survive, somewhere between all that, she discovered that he had a heart as big as the South and twice as sweet as the tea.

She protested as he used his grip on her head to pull her lips from his.

"Natalie," he started. His voice broke on the last syllable.

"Newland," she said in return. He might be stronger, but she had the advantage, perched on top of him like she was. And she used her higher position to her advantage.

She pressed her hips into his, showing him with the one move just how much she wanted him. She fought against his hold and won, taking over his earlier kiss. She deepened it, wanting more, needing more.

"I want you." She said the words even as she wanted to declare her true feelings for him. But what good would that do? He was leaving in a couple of days. This was all she could have of him. And this was what she would take. After he left she'd figure out what to do about Gerald. But right now, it wasn't something she wanted to think about. All she wanted was Newland, inside her, all around her, with her every step of the way.

"I want you too. But what about—"

"Doesn't matter," she said. Nothing mattered.

As they talked, they continued to place small kisses on the other's waiting lips. It was as if the conversation needed to take place but the kissing couldn't stop. She couldn't allow it to stop. It had to continue, on and on. But not like the last time. Not wild and out of control. But slow and deliberate. A different kind of control. Not dictatorial, but unhurried, each touch placed for maximum pleasure.

She ran her hands up his chest, sliding them under today's concert T-shirt to smooth over the hard ridges of his abdomen and pecs. She wanted to touch every inch of him, be with him again, yet not like before. She wanted kiss after kiss, caress after caress, until neither one of them could take anymore.

He wrenched his mouth from hers, his breathing heavy. "Natalie." He chuckled as she fought against his hold to kiss him once again. "We can't do this here. We're outside. In your aunt's yard."

Natalie won the struggle and kissed him again, showing him just what he'd be missing if they stopped. "Sure we can. It's dark. Who's around to see?"

Emotions and indecision chased across his face. Then he gave a small bark of laughter. "You're crazy, you know that?"

"I've never been told that before." It felt good to have someone say something besides dependable Natalie, conservative Natalie, always in control Natalie. She smiled. She'd take crazy over that any day. Especially when it came to Newland.

She grabbed the edge of her borrowed T-shirt and pulled it over her head. The warm Southern breeze caressed her skin as Newland sucked in a deep breath. She hadn't been wearing a bra. And he seemed surprised by that.

Heck, she'd even surprised herself by coming out here like that. But it felt good, a little on the decadent side to feel the brush of the fabric against her nipples as she searched for him.

If she were being truly honest with herself, she'd come out here for this. Though she had needed him to start. And now that he had, she would see it through to the end.

"Oh, God," he said his voice pained. "I must've been really good in a past life."

Natalie chuckled, then sucked in her own breath as his hands eased around to cup her breasts in his palms. His touch was exquisite, unlike anything she'd ever known before. Or maybe it had just been too long.

She shook her head. She wasn't going to think about that now. She had a wonderful man, open and willing, and she was taking advantage of it. To hell with tomorrow. She had him tonight.

"I need you," she admitted.

He pulled her closer, ducking his head to take one rigid nipple into his mouth. Natalie gasped, the tension in her building, and yet they were both mostly dressed. How could this be? How could he drive her so close to the edge with just a simple touch? Never before had it been this way. It was the most wonderful feeling in the world. And she never wanted it to end.

"Are you sure about this?" he asked.

"I wish you would stop asking me that."

He ran his fingers around the edge of the waistband of her sweatpants. "I just want to make sure. I don't want you to regret this."

"Stop." She grabbed his face in her hands and stared deep into those exotic, brown eyes. "I'll have no regrets."

He studied her features for what seemed like an eternity, but could've only been a few seconds, then he pulled her mouth to his once again.

This time he took over the kiss, nipping and biting, licking and otherwise making her mad with wanting him.

Somehow he worked a hand between the two of them, inside her baggy sweatpants.

She almost fell apart in his arms as he traced a finger along her cleft. She was ready for him. So ready and if he didn't touch her soon…

She gasped as he pushed one finger inside. She was more than ready. She was beyond ready, and she needed this more than she needed air to breathe.

She rose up on her knees, then ground against him needing that sweet friction but unable to achieve it. She pushed against him again, and he chuckled. "Slow down, we have all night."

She stilled in his arms. They had all night. All night to be in each other's arms, all night to explore, to kiss, to taste, to touch. That's what she wanted: all night.

But first she needed him now. Somehow she managed to undo the button on his jeans, slide down the zipper, and kiss him all at the same time. But she hated that she had to move away from him in order to touch him skin on skin. She tugged at his pants, then took him into her hand, his skin like velvet, his desire like steel.

"Stop," Newland rasped.

Stop? She couldn't stop. She needed this, wanted this, had to have this. Had to have him if for only one night. She might not ever feel this way again in her entire life. But at least she would feel that way tonight.

"Please tell me you didn't just say that." Somehow she managed to keep her voice even, but it took almost more effort than she had.

He brushed her hair back from her face, his touch gentle and sweet even though his fingers trembled. "We don't have a condom. I didn't bring my wallet out here. I came out here to look for bootleggers." He said the last word on a small laugh.

Natalie tucked her hair behind her ear suddenly embarrassed, suddenly shy as if she'd been caught doing something she shouldn't have been doing. Then she pushed off him once more. She reached into her pocket and fished out the tiny package. "I've got one."

The surprise on his face was priceless. "You've got one." The implication was obvious.

He grabbed the leg of her pants and pulled her to him, easing them down at the same time. When she was free of the offending fabric, she dropped down beside him and rolled the condom into place. He watched, still as she straddled him once again, this time impaling herself on his hard length.

She loved the feeling of being in control but yet not. The passion simmered just below the surface, just under the façade of control. Then she realized that he was going to let her dictate the rhythm, set the pace. She gasped as she took his length, then wiggled a bit for good measure.

He groaned and fisted his hands in the grass at his sides. This was insane, but when had anything with Newland been normal? Somehow, she liked it that way.

"You need to move," he said. His eyes were closed, his fingers still knotted in the blades of grass. His teeth were clenched, and she thought for a moment he was in pain. Maybe he was. She wiggled again. His groan grew louder.

"That's not what I meant." Eyes still closed.

She was in control. It was a heady feeling to know that she could feel so full, so fulfilled, so complete and yet have the power to make him crazy.

She gave a small laugh, pushed herself up on her knees just enough to move up his length and still retain their connection. She pushed down again, slower this time, and the feeling was beyond compare.

"I can't take much more of this, Natalie." His voice was perfect proof that he was close to the end of his self-control.

Maybe that was what she wanted all along. Maybe she wanted him to lose control, to be pushed over the edge, to not know if he would be able to take another breath if for some reason this stopped.

She raised herself up, slowly, almost to the tip before easing down once again, taking all of him deep inside.

"That's it."

The next thing she knew, she was flat on her back in the cool summer grass. She wrapped her legs around his waist as he pumped into her harder and harder still, taking her to the brink of someplace she had never been, not even in his arms.

He snaked one hand under her hips and lifted her higher, giving one last thrust before he stiffened and cried out her name.

She was close. So close. And she couldn't let it stop. She bucked against him again, grinding herself to him, holding him to her, her legs locked around his hips. As if sensing her need, he thrust again and again even though his climax had passed. Again and again, over and over until the pressure building inside her burst into a thousand pieces of stardust.

She heard a strangled cry, realized it came from her own lips, and still she couldn't let him go. She held herself pressed against him, heels locked around his back, needing this moment to go on forever and ever and ever.

"Oh God, oh God," she chanted. Never, *never* before had she experienced anything like this.

Finally, still locked together, he rolled to one side pulling her on top of him.

She lay sprawled across his chest, their bodies pressed close as she tried to gain back her breath. Not even knowing if she wanted it.

"Have I died and gone to heaven?" she breathed into the sweaty skin on his chest.

He chuckled. "That's about the tritest thing anyone has ever said to me."

She leaned up on her elbows, her mouth inches from his. "Is that bad?"

He pulled her in for a swift kiss. "No, it's the best thing ever."

"Tritest?" she asked. "Is that a word?"

He laughed, still holding her close. "It's a word."

CHAPTER EIGHTEEN

Natalie couldn't stop her smile all the next day. After their foray in the grass, they'd spent the rest of the night ensconced in his room exploring each other until dawn.

She should have been exhausted, wiped out, and dead on her feet. Instead she felt exhilarated. Never before in her life had she felt so alive. With Newland, she had been in control, she had lost control, she had given up control, and she had taken it back. He had given as well as taken and showed her an equal partnership and love that she hadn't known could exist. But even after all that, one thing was left unsaid. Gerald. But maybe no one mentioned him because Newland knew he was leaving after Thursday night. But she wasn't going to worry about that right now. She was going to pull a page from Scarlet's book and worry about all that tomorrow. Or the next day. Whichever was convenient.

She let herself into the house just after six, praying that Aubie had come home like he was supposed to. Home. Had she really started to feel that way about Bitty's house? She had moved out to prove her self-worth, but hadn't she done that? Couldn't she move back, she and Aubie, and help Aunt Bitty?

She and Newland both knew there was no ghost, as did Aubie. But if she and her brother were there, they could help Bitty and wouldn't have to worry about her leaving the stove on and the refrigerator door open. Someone would be there shortly to help take care of things. Her aunt loved to cook and loved to feed people, and Natalie would hate to take that away from her. Then again hadn't she taken some of that away when she and Aubie moved out?

Natalie shook her head and pushed those thoughts away. This was home now, and she would be moving in soon. For good.

She wasn't sure how Aubie would take that. He hated the duplex and thought they should buy a house, but he had never mentioned moving in with their aunt. Perhaps they could make him an attic room where he could have his office, privacy, and his big screen TV and game consoles. If he had come home.

She hadn't texted him like she did when school was out to make sure he knew he had to be there. But she was trying to do what he asked. She was trying to let him grow up, make his own decisions, and make the decisions he knew he needed to make.

Oskar barked out his welcome as she entered the house and set her purse by the door.

"Hello, baby." She picked up the pooch and got a bunch of puppy kisses in return.

Aubie poked his head out of the parlor, then turned back toward the room, saying, "It's just Nat."

Natalie set Oskar at her feet and together the two of them clicked down the hallway to the parlor.

It was card night. She had forgotten about that. Everyone was in attendance including Newland and Aubie.

Her aunt had pulled out the octagonal card tabletop that had once belonged to Natalie's father. She'd forgotten he'd even owned the thing. The last time he used it she was in high school. But it had been stored at Bitty's, someplace in this big rambling house.

She looked to the stack of change in front of her brother. "I don't think—" she started, but Newland shook his head.

Right. It was just poker. All between friends and nickel ante. She could do this. She could relinquish some control, enjoy her life a bit more and allow those around her to make their own mistakes.

She walked to the coffee table where two pizza boxes stood half open. She flipped one up, found a piece of veggie pizza, and nearly moaned with pleasure at the first bite. How long had it been since she'd eaten pizza? Way too long. She chewed the bite with ecstasy, then turned to find Newland watching her, his face an odd mixture of laughter and desire.

She chewed a little slower, suddenly hit with the fact that in two days he would be gone. She had gotten used to him being around. And it wasn't just the great sex. It was him playing cards with the Fab Four, him fixing the steps to the cellar, and him walking around with Mr. Piddles cradled in his arms. There was so much more to Newland than she'd thought when she first met him. She was going to miss him when he was gone.

She swallowed hard, suddenly uncomfortable with the idea.

As if sensing her turmoil, Newland mouthed, "What's wrong?"

She shook her head, unable to even whisper the words back. There was a lot that was wrong. And come Friday morning, her life would never be the same again.

****

"I've got a theory," Newland said as they walked around the side of the house and down toward the cellar. The idea had come to him while he was playing cards with the girls and Aubie. Right about the same time that Natalie's attitude had shifted.

At first she had seemed happy, jubilant even, but then as if someone had dropped the curtain, her expression changed, became troubled and clouded over with something akin to despair. At the time he thought it might have something to do with the fact that Aubie was playing poker or maybe even the fact that she was eating pizza like it was about to give her an orgasm. Just the thought made him shift in his seat. She really needed to treat herself a little more, and not worry so much about making sure everyone's life was nothing but smooth sailing. She thought she had everything all neatly lined up, but *that* was the hitch in her life. She wasn't even living it.

"So what's this theory?"

Newland opened the cellar doors and started down inside. He turned on the light and motioned for Natalie to follow. Thankfully when he told her to put on something more comfortable and come with him to the cellar she had actually donned those incredible blue jeans and followed him out the door.

"I think this is just a storage facility for Gilbert and Darrell."

She shoved her hands into the back pockets of her jeans, seemingly unaware of what the action did to emphasize certain parts of her.

Newland dragged his gaze away from her breasts and back to her face. "Uh, where was I?"

"Darrell and Gilbert use this as a storage facility. I thought we'd already decided that."

Newland nodded. "I think tomorrow night, they'll come to move all this out of here."

"Why tomorrow night?"

"That's the brilliance of it all."

Natalie shook her head. "I've never heard anyone mention Gilbert, Darrell, and brilliance all in the same conversation."

"I can see that. That's why I think somebody else is in charge of all this."

"Like who?" Natalie frowned.

"Well, I was hoping you might have some theories on that. You know the town. Who in Turtle Creek is smart enough to run a moonshine business of this magnitude?" He pointed toward the increasing number of crates stacked in the cellar.

Natalie thought about it for a moment. "Most of the businesses here are small. They don't make a great deal of money, but they do okay. No one's driving around in a new car or has a new Rolex or anything like that. And I can't imagine anyone here doing something like this."

"I guess they could be from another town close by. Any ideas?"

She shook her head. "They could be from anywhere in the county. Maybe even in Tishomingo County."

Newland nodded thoughtfully. He'd really hoped she would have some idea who might be behind the operation.

"So what makes you think that it's all going to disappear tomorrow?"

Newland immediately perked up. "The ghost. Whoever's behind this is using the ghost as a decoy, a distraction."

"That's brilliant," Natalie said.

"And now you know why I think somebody else is behind it."

Natalie couldn't stop her laugh. "Absolutely." She stopped for a minute then turned back to him. "So what do we do now? Get the sheriff?"

"I don't think the sheriff is the answer. If he's one of their best customers, I'm not sure he'll care too much about this. And if I'm wrong…"

"Right," Natalie said. "So what's our answer? Leave it alone? Tell Aunt Bitty that her ghost is a fake?"

Newland couldn't have that. He needed this story. This story was going to get him back in business.

Suddenly that didn't seem quite as important as it did a week ago. But that was before… Natalie. "I say we stake it out."

Her eyes grew wide. "Are you serious?"

"As a heart attack. If we stake it out, take some pictures, get some video, maybe even some audio. Then we have something to take to the higher authorities." And he would have a story. Otherwise it was just a Scooby-Doo ghost in a county-run moonshine ring.

"This sounds dangerous." She took a step closer to him and suddenly Newland was more aware of her presence than ever before.

"Are you worried about me?" He leaned back against one of the crates, testing its sturdiness.

"Maybe a little." She came closer still until he could reach out with ease, snake one arm around her, and pull her into the V of his thighs.

"Does that mean you'll protect me?" he asked.

She gasped as he buried his face in the crook of her neck. "With my life."

He kissed the line from the hollow of her throat to her waiting mouth. "Let's hope it doesn't come to that."

CHAPTER NINETEEN

"Can I go too?" Aubie asked.

It was nine-fifteen Thursday night.

As darkness had fallen, Natalie's heart began to pound. What if this was dangerous? Where would they turn for help? Contacting the sheriff wouldn't do much good if he was the one behind it all.

She shook her head to clear that thought. Whoever masterminded this plan was extremely intelligent. She had gone to school with Buster Riley, and though he had a good heart, as good as anybody, he was not an evil genius.

"No," she and Newland said at the same time.

"It is exciting though, you have to admit." Aunt Bitty's eyes sparkled. "Though I don't think the ghost has anything to do with this moonshine business."

Natalie refused to roll her eyes at her favorite aunt. But if she wanted to believe in the ghost, there was nothing Natalie could do to stop her.

"Awh, why not?" Aubie protested.

"Aside from the fact that it's a school night, you are the mayor and the mayor should not be involved directly in moonshine stings," Natalie said.

Newland frowned at her. "You can't go because she said you can't go."

Aubie seemed stunned for a moment, blinking as if trying to put everything into focus. "Yeah. Okay."

It was Natalie's turn to blink. What had just happened? Why had she never tried that? She made a mental note to add "because I said so" to the list of reasons why Aubie couldn't do something and pulled the black ski cap from her back pocket.

"You're not really going to wear that are you?" Newland asked.

"Isn't this what people wear to a sting operation?"

"This is not a sting operation, it's a stakeout. We're going to get information, which we will turn over to the authorities. I'm loving life just a little too much to try and take down moonshiners all on my own," Newland said.

"He's a smart man, dear," Aunt Bitty said. "You should listen to him."

"I can't go to a stakeout without being camouflaged. My hair is not as dark as yours and my skin isn't as dark as yours. I'm afraid I'll stand out more than the ghost."

"Suit yourself. It's just ninety-five degrees out there."

"You should probably use the lint brush before you go. You have cat hair all over you." She nodded to where Newland cradled Mr. Piddles in his arms. She wasn't sure what the cat was going to do when Newland finally left.

That makes two of us.

"Again, this is a stakeout. Not the Governor's Ball."

Aunt Bitty clapped her hands in excitement. "Should I pack you some snacks?"

Natalie and Newland turned to her in unison. "No," they both said.

"Are you ready to go?" Newland asked.

Natalie's heart gave a hard pound. Was she ready? She wasn't, she decided. But not because they were headed into a potentially dangerous situation if they got caught observing this moonshine run. But because this was the end. After tonight, after Newland proved that the ghost was a product of a distraction to keep people from noticing that moonshine was being carted out by the crate, then he wouldn't have a reason to stay in Turtle Creek. She wasn't prepared for that. Not by far.

"Let's go," she said.

They walked out the door to the wishes of *good luck* and *be careful* from both Aubie and Aunt Bitty.

Newland stopped on the porch and turned back to both of them, a stern look on his face. "Stay away from the cellar, and don't come to the cemetery. We'll be back in a little while. Got it?" He looked at each of them in turn.

They nodded in unison, then smiled and patted him on the back once again.

"Now remember," Newland started, "we're just two young lovers out for an evening stroll."

Natalie ignored the way the word "lovers" made her heart pound a bit faster. "And we just so happen to be wearing all black."

"It would help if you would take off the ski mask."

Natalie pulled the knit hat from her head and stuffed it into her back pocket, shaking her hair out and trying to rub down some of the static electricity.

"You remember the plan?" he asked. He took her hand into his, and Natalie tried not to read too much into the situation. They'd had three very sexy encounters in three very odd places—not counting the night in his room—and though she knew his body intimately, holding hands with him somehow seemed special.

"We're going to cut across Selma's yard to the side of the cemetery opposite the big mound of dirt."

"Right. Everyone says that the ghost appears on that side of the graveyard. If my theory is correct the ghost is there to keep everybody's eyes trained to that side of the cemetery while they unload all the moonshine into a truck on the other side."

"And if your theory isn't right?"

"It has to be. There are too many factors in place. A ghost where there is no body, secret tunnels, and stashed moonshine. I just wish I knew who was in charge of it all."

Natalie swallowed hard. "I think we're going to find that out soon enough."

As they had planned, they cut across Selma's yard, going around the back side and heading along the far cemetery fence.

They jumped the fence and duck-walked to the second row of gravestones.

"I think your ghost should be showing up anytime now."

Despite the fact that she knew—at least thought—that the ghost was a projected image, a chill ran through her. "Have I ever told you I don't like to be in cemeteries after dark?"

He shot her a look that clearly said *Be quiet*. "Nobody likes to be in cemeteries after dark. And bingo." He pointed toward the next row of graves where a lone figure walked toward them.

The man glowed as if a light was emanating from him and limped a little as if whatever battle he had served in had sustained him an injury. There was no moaning or groaning to go with his solitary walk, but Natalie was certain she could hear the rattle of chains. Which was ridiculous. Or maybe it was the rattle of the gate banging in the wind. Except there really wasn't much of a wind tonight.

"He looks so real," she whispered to Newland.

"Didn't you say that people in this town did reenactments?"

"Yeah. Lots of them."

"Does he look familiar?"

As the ghost drew closer to them, Natalie realized she did know that face. It was Harvey Johnson who staggered along dressed as a Confederate soldier wounded in battle, now left to haunt a grave that was no longer there.

"It's Harvey Johnson," she said. "But I know from my aunt's house she can't tell that."

"It's ingenious. You think he's behind all this?"

"He can't be. He's no smarter than Gilbert and Darrell put together."

"So our mastermind is still out there."

Natalie nodded. A bit of movement across the cemetery caught her eye. It seemed their trick worked. She'd been so busy watching the ghost that she hadn't immediately noticed movement by the big oak tree.

"They're moving them out now."

Newland raised the binoculars to his eyes. "I wish I had night vision goggles."

"Me too." So the ghost was fake and the wind was playing tricks on her ears. But it was still creepy to be out in the cemetery in the middle of night. She would love to be able to see what was going on across the way to help ease her mind that there were no real ghosts out there. She shook away the thought.

"Are those—" Newland stopped. "Here. You take a look." He handed her the binoculars.

It took a second for her eyes to adjust to seeing so far in the distance. Her vision was a tad blurry. She blinked a couple of times to clear it. "Oh my lord! That's a coffin." She was ready to hand the binoculars back to Newland when they stacked it on the bed of the truck. That rattle sounded again, and Natalie knew that it wasn't the sound of chains but the dull clink of glass cushioned with hay against the inside of a coffin.

"Yeah, I guess they put the moonshine in the coffins and move the coffins out. Who's really going to check them?"

Natalie shuddered again. She raised the binoculars back to her eyes and watched as Gilbert and Darrell continued to stack case upon case of moonshine into plain wooden coffins and stack those onto the back of the truck. "It's ingenious."

"Why thank you."

They whirled around to find Gerald Davenport standing behind them.

It took Natalie a full five seconds to realize that Gerald wasn't there because she was lying in the grass in the cemetery with another man, but because he was the mastermind behind the whole moonshine ring.

"You!" She pushed herself to her feet. "What are you doing?"

"Awh, Natalie. You and your old money. I'm securing my future. There's a lot of money in moonshine."

"But people bottle and sell moonshine all over—legally," Natalie told him.

"And let the government have all my profits? Not likely. I've sort of gotten used to my lifestyle, and this helps finance it quite well."

"Of course if you had just left everything well enough alone and talked Bitty into moving into the nursing home, we wouldn't be standing here right now."

"What?" Was he saying what she thought he was saying?

"Yes, that's right. I wanted the house to secure that tunnel. Not to put it on the historic registry. What a joke. Who even cares about such things anyway?"

Natalie felt the heat rise and her cheeks. "I do. That house is almost two hundred years old. And all you care about is how it can make you money. What about me?"

He gave her a pathetic little smile. "What about you?"

"I thought you loved me."

Her stomach fell as he threw back his head and laughed. "You thought I loved you?"

The way he said it made it sound absurd. But once upon a time she had thought... "I thought you were going to ask me to marry you."

She was barely aware of Newland pushing to his feet and brushing himself off. He came to stand beside her, a little behind and a little to the side as if he were protecting her.

"Well, you thought wrong. All I wanted was the house. And now that I can't have that..."

"What are you going to do?" Newland's voice was low and flat. He seemed almost scared, but he didn't know Gerald like she did. Gerald wasn't about to hurt them. Surely Newland could see that.

"The cufflink!" she said pointing at Gerald once again. "The cufflink was yours."

"You found it?" he asked dryly. "Good, good, it'll be nice to have that set back together again. They belonged to my grandfather, you know."

His grandfather, Phineas Charles.

"To answer your question." He pointed to Newland and sighed. "It goes against my original plans, but as I see it, my only option at this point is multi-murder-suicide."

"What?" Natalie cried. Surely she had heard him wrong. "Gerald, don't joke about things like that. It's not funny."

Newland leaned down, closer to her ear. "I don't think he's joking."

"You played into my hands perfectly. Taking a stranger as a lover—"

Natalie gasped. "You know?"

"Sugar, you should know by now that nothing goes on in this town without me knowing about it."

She hated his tone, self-serving and arrogant. What had she ever seen in him?

"You invited a stranger into your aunt's home, then took the man into your bed. Now all I have to do is shoot everybody in the house, stage his suicide, and we have a stranger who brings tragedy to our poor little town."

"I'm not listening to this anymore," Natalie said. "You're crazy." She turned to go. "Come on, Newland."

"I wouldn't do that if I were you," Gerald said. Even in the dark she could see him raise a gun— a big one.

"You have a gun?"

"This is a dangerous business, Natalie." He smirked at her once again. "I really did like you though."

"Whatever."

His words still hadn't sunk through. Even though he held a gun, his threats of murder-suicide seemed ridiculous at best. This was Gerald, who raised money for St. Jude's Hospital and supported dolphin-free tuna and all sorts of other environmentally-sound, save-the-whales and help-the-children benefits. How could he kill all of them? It didn't make sense.

"All righty then," Gerald started. "Let's get this show on the road." He motioned with his gun for Natalie and Newland to move ahead of him. "To the house."

****

Newland had never been more scared in his life. It was evident that Gerald Davenport was greedy and a little off balance and would stop at nothing to secure his seven-figure future. Thankfully Natalie seemed to take Davenport threats with a grain of salt, but Newland wasn't so sure. At least she wasn't crying hysterically. He needed her to be strong; they were going to get out of this alive.

But they needed a plan. *Think, Tran. Think.* The main thing was not going to the house. Davenport might be desperate, but Newland was betting he wasn't desperate enough to shoot them point blank in the street. It was a slim bet, but it was all that he had at the moment. No, he couldn't go into the house, and neither could Natalie. They had to keep Davenport outside.

But the closer they got to the house without a solid plan in his mind, the more nervous Newland got. He had to do something, and he had to do it quickly.

They neared the sycamore tree in Bitty's front yard. He didn't have to look to know they were close. The sidewalk was already becoming buckled.

Then the idea struck. He leaned a little closer to Natalie. "Do you still have your mask?"

"He's not going to shoot us, is he?"

He hated the fear he heard in her voice. Just a few minutes ago she had seemed incredulous over Davenport's solution to them finding out about his nefarious activities, and now she sounded downright scared.

"Not if I can help it," he said. "The mask?"

"In my back pocket."

"I need you to follow my lead," he said. "Can you do that?"

She gave a small nod. But he could tell she was terrified.

"I do not want to get shot and killed by that pantywaist, stuffed shirt. Just trust me on this, Natty."

He saw something in her eyes, something more than trust. But he couldn't think about that right now.

The sidewalk had started to become uneven. He slowed his steps and urged Natalie to do the same. The five or so feet that had been between them and Davenport narrowed to around three. Newland hated having the gun that close to them, that close to

Natalie. But it was necessary if he was going to pull this off.

"I'm sorry," he said. Then stuck one foot out and tripped Natalie.

He grabbed the mask from her back pocket as she started to fall, then stuck out his foot to trip Gerald as well. Natalie screamed as she fell. He said a small prayer that she didn't skin herself up too badly. But it was better by far than getting shot.

Newland lunged at Davenport, using his superior height to pull Natalie's ski mask over Davenport's head, throwing him off guard. As he suspected and feared, the gun went off, the bullet flying upward at an odd angle. Natalie screamed again.

Newland fell on top of Davenport and rolled to the side hoping to gain power over the handgun. Instead, he just got a jab in the ribs from one buckled piece of sidewalk.

Noise erupted around them. And light. People started coming out onto their porches to see what was going on. They turned on their porch lights and slammed screen doors. Dogs started barking and the whole neighborhood seemed to be talking at once.

He had to get that gun. But for all his stuffed shirted-ness, Davenport was surprisingly strong. Newland supposed there was something to be said about gym muscles. But he wasn't about to let them get the best of him.

He twisted the gun in Davenport's hands.

The man yelped in pain and surprise but hung firm to the weapon. They rolled the other way and stars filled Newland's vision as his head hit another uneven piece of sidewalk.

Dammit! If he got out of this alive, he was making Aubie fix this stupid sidewalk.

"Newland!" Natalie cried.

"Get away!" Newland shouted. He couldn't have her too close. Fighting over a gun with a madman was not a good idea on any occasion, surely not in the dark, rolling around on an uneven sidewalk. But he had to get the weapon if he was going to save them all.

"Natalie, is that you?" Bitty called from the porch.

"Stay up there, Aunt Bitty," Natalie demanded. As Newland lost his grip on the gun, Davenport executed some kind of Indian wrestling move that flipped Newland over onto his back.

He groaned as another jagged edge of sidewalk tore into his side. He was going be lucky if he came out of this with anything less than all his ribs broken.

"Enough!" Davenport pushed to his feet, yanking the ski mask from his head as he wobbled the gun between Newland and Natalie.

Natalie!

She moved to stand in front of him and cut Davenport's direct aim. "Gerald, put the gun down."

"Natalie!" Newland said. "What are you doing? Get out of here."

"You're not getting away with this," Gerald said.

"You're mistaken," Natalie continued in that soft, level voice. She really should get a job as a hostage negotiator. The thought threaded through his worry and concern for her.

"Natalie, seriously."

Newland pushed to his feet, but she was there, standing in front of him. They were so close together that any shot that Gerald might let off would run through them both.

"It's all easy when your money has been there for generations. I have a standard to uphold. Don't you know?"

"Put the gun down, Gerald."

She took a step toward him, and Newland grabbed the waistband of her jeans to pull her back next to him. She swatted his hand away without looking and started for Gerald once more. "There's no need for anybody to get hurt, Gerald. It's over."

In the distance, a siren sounded. The sheriff was on his way. It was just a matter of time before he got there. But until then, Davenport still had his gun pointed directly at Natalie.

He went to move around her, but she moved in front of him still. Why was she protecting him like this? She was going to end up hurt. And he couldn't take it.

Never in his life had he loved anybody the way he loved Natalie Coleman. And she was putting herself in harm's way for him. He wouldn't be able to live with himself if she got hurt.

"Gerald Davenport, is that you?"

All eyes turned as Myrtle came striding across the street, her purple Crocs almost on fire with the speed at which she moved. "What do you mean standing out here holding a gun on these people?"

Whether she held some power over him or it was simply shock, Gerald turned as Myrtle came up behind him. With one swift karate kick she knocked the gun free and before Newland could take another breath, she had Gerald's arm twisted behind his back and him face first over the hood of Newland's car.

"Ow! Ow! You're going to break my arm!"

"I should spank your bee-hind," Myrtle said. "You were the brightest student in your class and this is how you show your potential?"

"Did that just happen?" Newland asked as the sheriff pulled up on Sycamore Lane, lights blaring, twirling, siren blaring.

"I think it did," Natalie said. She turned toward him then, and he saw the fear that he hadn't seen before.

"I don't feel so good," she said, and with that she collapsed into his arms.

CHAPTER TWENTY

Two hours later, Sycamore Lane was quiet once more. Though Natalie had a feeling that everyone was still awake, talking about the most exciting thing to happen in Turtle Creek since Rodney Montrose caught that alligator out in Ray Clement's pond.

"Here you go, dear." Aunt Bitty took her flask from inside her dress and poured a big dollop of brandy into each of their teas. Natalie wasn't sure exactly how brandy would taste in Earl Grey, but hopefully the snort of an adult beverage would take some of the tremor out of her hands.

"That was the coolest thing I have ever seen!" Aubie said, his blue eyes sparkling. "First thing tomorrow morning I'm putting Myrtle in for Citizen of the Year."

Natalie smiled, though she felt tears threaten. Myrtle coming to the rescue was more than heaven sent. Who knew the retired English teacher had it in her?

"That was incredible," Newland said. He sat across from her in one of those antique Louis the Something chairs, and Natalie wanted desperately for him to come sit next to her. Somehow she could feel a distance starting between them.

The mystery of the ghost was solved. They'd had a near brush with death and had come out on top. But everything had changed. Everything.

The sheriff had taken Gerald away on charges of attempted murder, but Natalie knew that once the county prosecutor got ahold of it, there would be a laundry list of misdeeds.

"They started to teach tae kwon do at the senior center," Aunt Bitty said. "It was our suggestion."

Surprise me. Natalie shook her head. "I still can't believe…" She wasn't sure what to finish that sentence with first. She still couldn't believe Gerald was behind it all, that he was going kill them—surely he wasn't really going to kill them—that Myrtle knew tae kwon do, that Natalie loved Newland Tran enough to get between him and an armed madman. On all levels, the thoughts were scary. The last one doubly so. How could she have given her heart to a man she wouldn't see past tomorrow? That just went to show what lack of control did for a person. She had taken a chance, let loose, let her hair down as they say, and all she was going to get for it was heartache.

And she knew he was leaving. He had to be. He had his story, a story bigger than the Civil War ghost in an old lady's home. This was a story worthy of any major newspaper across the country.

"Would you like another snort, dear?" Aunt Bitty asked, her gaze trained on Newland. He held his cup toward her.

He hadn't looked at Natalie since he had come in. She had no idea what was going on behind those exotic eyes.

Aunt Bitty uncapped her flask and started to pour. "Say when."

"When." Then Newland groaned as Mr. Piddles jumped into his lap.

Somehow, Aunt Bitty managed to save Newland's tea from being spilled all over the floor as Newland doubled over in pain.

"Are you hurt?" Bitty moved to set Newland's drink on the coffee table then shooed Mr. Piddles out of his lap. "Let me see," she demanded, pulling him gingerly to his feet.

That's when Natalie saw it, the pain glazed over in his eyes. He was hurting. Badly. Her heart fell to the ground. "Did you get shot?" The words were nothing more than a desperate whisper.

He shook his head. "Sidewalk," he gasped as Bitty grabbed his shirttail and pulled it over his head. He was a roadmap of scratches and bruises. And he had one knot on his left side that looked like it needed medical attention immediately.

"You need a doctor," Bitty said.

"I'll be fine," Newland said. The man and his pride.

She wanted to run to him, press little kisses to all those bruises and cuts. But something kept her in her seat. He wasn't hers. He never had been. And even though he didn't belong to another, he would never be as foolish as to give his heart to a conservative yet bossy Southern Belle.

"Aubie, run over to Josephine's and see if her new boyfriend is there. He's a retired doctor. I'm sure he can help."

For once Aubie didn't protest and did as he was asked.

When the doctor came in, Natalie used that time to slip upstairs unnoticed. Nursing a broken heart required rest and solitude, and right now she needed both.

****

Stiff was not the word to describe how he felt the following morning. Hit by a truck might work. Mauled by a sidewalk would also suffice but didn't have quite the same visual.

Newland tried to take a deep breath, but the pain in his ribs sent a white light flashing behind his eyes. For now he would just have to settle with whatever air he could manage to drag into his lungs before he passed out from pain.

Josephine's new boyfriend/retired doctor had taken one look at his ribs and promptly wrapped them as tight as Newland could stand. Then he pumped him full of ibuprofen and told him to get some rest for a couple of days.

Like that was going to happen.

Aside from wondering where this crazy love for Natalie Coleman might lead, he had a helluva story running though his mind. And it was surely a better thing to think about than how she wouldn't want anything to do with a vagrant like him.

Yep, he'd blown it bigtime. He had fallen in love with the wrong woman. Hell, he'd fallen in love with them all—Natalie, Bitty, Aubie, Mr. Piddles. There wasn't a one of them he wouldn't miss like crazy when he was gone.

Instead of thinking about misplaced love, he stayed up half the night writing his story. He would present it as a series of articles. One of the unbelievable secrets of the small southern town with a moonshine ring bigger than anybody ever believed and players more crooked than the sidewalk on Sycamore Lane. It was a great story, a great idea, and he was lucky to have found it.

Friday morning, he managed to pull his T-shirt over his head, without blacking out, but decided to forgo his jacket. It wasn't worth the effort. Then he let himself out of his room and gingerly made his way down the stairs. His torso had taken the brunt of it and he had a goose egg on the back of his head that was as big as his hand. He had managed to cut both knees and had a bruise in his calf muscle that cramped every time he tried to walk. All in all he felt like hell. But the main thing, the absolute best thing of all, was that Natalie was safe. Natalie, Bitty, and Aubie. No one had gotten hurt at Davenport's hands. And that was worth every bruise, every cut, every pain he had this morning.

"There you are!" Bitty exclaimed, hurrying toward him as he entered the dining room. She had been seated, serving her own plate when he arrived, but she dropped all that to take a hold of his elbow and lead him toward his place at the table.

"I'm fine, Bitty. Really."

He looked around the table. Aubie was sitting across from him eating breakfast as he prepared to go to school.

"Do I really have to go to school today?" he whined.

"A good education builds a good mind," Bitty quoted.

Newland shook his head. What exactly did that mean?

"But so much has happened," Aubie said.

"Aubie," Newland said. "Go to school today. Just think of all the stories you can tell at lunch."

Aubie's eyes lit up. "Okay then. Fine."

Bitty shot him a thankful glance, and Newland nodded in return. Aubie was a good boy; he just needed someone to direct him. Thank heavens that someone wasn't going to be Gerald Davenport.

And it's not going to be you either.

He pushed that voice away. As much as he wanted it to be him, it couldn't be. How could he stay there in Turtle Creek? The one thing that had been holding him and Natalie together was gone. There was no ghost on Bitty's property, the moonshine ring had been taken down, his story was written, and life went on.

He'd loved his time there in Turtle Creek, Mississippi. But he couldn't borrow someone else's life. He loved having Aunt Bitty to fuss over him and Aubie to help with school and manly things. He loved having Natalie sit across from him at the dinner table, hand tools down into the cellar, and cry out his name in ecstasy underneath him. But this wasn't his family. That was all he wanted his entire life: a family of his very own. Yet as much as he wished these fine people were that family, they weren't. And the sooner he realized that the sooner he could mend his broken heart, his broken ribs, and get on with the business of living his life. Not someone else's.

He looked to Natalie's empty seat. A part of him wanted to ask where she was, but there was another part that knew she had gone about her business. Their time together was over. She'd gone to work like she had every day this week. She had a foundation to run. Wasn't that what she was always telling him? She had businesses to take care of, lots of people to boss around, and money to oversee.

He eased into his chair as Bitty passed him a plate full of biscuits. "Grab yourself a couple, dear. Then I'll hand you the butter."

Newland made his plate, realizing this was probably the last time he would have a breakfast like this. How often would he make it to the South where he could eat biscuits every day with homemade jelly, bacon or sausage, eggs, and all the other wonderful stuff that was in front of him?

Okay so he could get bacon and sausage in the North too. The main thing was the company. This would be the last time he would sit across from Bitty, sit next to Aubie, and stare at Natalie's empty chair.

Somehow he managed to squeeze his breakfast past the lump in his throat. He took his time eating, hoping that Natalie would show up.

His bag was packed on his bed, his laptop all put away. Letters had all been sent, proposals and storylines. Now all he had to do was go on back to Chicago.

The thought of his empty apartment saddened him. Okay, it made him downright miserable. But what was a guy to do?

He lingered as long as he could, then stood. "I guess I better hit the road."

Bitty was on her feet in an instant. "Hit the road? To where?"

"Chicago."

Aubie stood as well. "Will you come back?"

Newland squelched the urge to ruffle Aubie's hair. First of all, he was far too big for that, and second of all, Newland wasn't sure that one should ruffle the mayor's hair.

"I'm not." Somehow the words were spoken, by him. Maybe it was one of the miracles of the New World. But he did say it and managed to say it without his voice cracking. Not even once.

"Are you kidding?" Aubie asked.

Newland shook his head.

"Why that's just silliness," Bitty said. "You can't go back to Chicago forever."

"I sort of have to. See, that's where my apartment is. All my stuff is there." Yeah his stuff. A closet full of concert T-shirts and an extra razor in the bathroom cabinet. That was about all that was left in Chicago. It was all he had.

"You can't leave," Aubie said.

"Is that a decree from the mayor?"

"No, it's a request from a friend." Aubie's voice turned sad and soft.

Newland's heart hurt. Who knew leaving would cause so much pain?

"I wish it were that simple, buddy," he said. "But it's time I left." Without waiting for anyone else to protest or say another word, Newland retrieved his bags from his room and started out the front door.

He hardened his heart as Bitty and Aubie followed him outside.

The day was turning out beautiful, a perfect day in the South. A perfect day to be driving around in a fancy little red convertible Jag.

Natalie pulled up, tires squealing as she ran over the curb and braked.

She got out, car still running, and ran over to where Bitty and Aubie stood on the thick concrete steps leading to the house. "What's wrong? What's wrong? I came as fast as I could."

Aubie had the decency to turn bright pink. "Fire?"

She smacked her brother on the arm. "Don't ever do that to me again. Why did you call me and tell me that we have a huge emergency, then when I get here I find out there's no emergency at all?"

"But there is an emergency," Bitty said.

Newland tore his gaze from the scene and threw his duffel bag into the backseat. He couldn't stay here a minute more. This morning he had wanted the opportunity to say goodbye to Natalie. And now that he had it, he didn't want it. He didn't want to tell her goodbye. That was just something he couldn't do.

"Emergency? What emergency?"

Newland slipped into his car and started the engine.

"Newland's leaving," Bitty said.

Natalie stopped and turned to face him. Newland gave her a jaunty little salute and pulled his car out of the drive.

He checked his rearview mirror to make sure it was in the sweet spot, only to see Natalie running after him. He braked. "What the hell?" Thank goodness for small towns. He put the car into *park* and waited on her to catch up with him. It took a few minutes considering she was running in four-inch heels. But he had time. Even though he didn't want to tell her goodbye, he really couldn't leave without seeing her one last time.

She was breathless when she reached the window. "What are you doing?"

"Sitting here?"

She smacked him on the arm. "Why are you leaving?"

"Because I don't live here." He said the words without his voice cracking, which was good, but he knew he couldn't mask the pain of his expression. He wanted to live here. He wanted to belong here, to be a part of this silly little town, to worry about school mascots and Harvey Johnson's hound dog. He wanted to live in a town with the sixteen-year-old mayor and buckled sidewalks and haunted cemeteries and a sheriff who supported illegal moonshine. Never before had he been to a place like Turtle Creek. But more than that, more than Aubie and Aunt Bitty and Selma and Myrtle and Josephine, more than all of that combined, he wanted the woman in front of him.

"Will you get out of there and talk to me?"

He shook his head.

"Why not?"

The truth was always the best way to go, right? "Because if I get out of this car, I don't know if I can get back in it."

"Newland," she breathed. Her voice changed from urgent to pleading. His gaze searched her face. "I love you."

****

Natalie sighed as she said the words. It was the only thing she could say to make him stay. And she wasn't even sure that would work. He seemed convinced that he didn't belong in Turtle Creek. That he belonged somewhere up north. But couldn't he see how much they needed him, how much Turtle Creek needed him? And beyond just need, there was love.

"What?"

"I said I love you." Her voice grew stronger as she said the words out loud. "I love you, I love you, I love you!" She grinned from ear to ear, her heart feeling light for the first time in a long, long time. "I love you, Newland Tran, and I don't want you to leave."

She opened the door to his car and held it for him. He seemed to think about it a minute and in that instance her heart constricted. Then he slipped out of the car, shut the door behind him, and pressed her into the front fender.

Arms braced behind her, he leaned in close. "You love me?" His eyes twinkled.

Natalie nodded. "Yeah, I do."

"Really?"

Natalie slipped her arms around his neck and held him close. "Really. Now what do we do about it?"

He swooped in and captured her mouth with his, kissing her until she lost all breath. "How about that?"

Natalie's eyes fluttered open and she stared at him, this man she had fallen in love with. How strange love was and how wondrous and joyful and exciting. "Does that mean you love me back?"

He pressed his forehead to hers. "Yeah, it does. I love you, Natalie Coleman, even though you try to boss everybody around and run everything and make everything perfect and crazy. I love you."

"And you're not leaving." It wasn't a question. She needed to hear him say the words, that he was staying there in Turtle Creek with her forever and ever.

"I do need to go get my stuff from Chicago…"

"That can wait." She pulled his mouth back to hers for another soul-searching, love-binding kiss that curled her toes and made her want him even more.

"There's just one thing," he said, breaking their kiss.

"What's that?"

"If I stay here, you're going to have to marry me."

Natalie had never heard sweeter words. "Of course."

"And we're going to stay with Bitty, Mr. Piddles, and Aubie, and Bitty won't go to a home."

"And maybe in a couple years we can have a baby?" She pinkened at the thought. But it had been one of her most secret desires for as long as she could remember. A little baby all her own with the man she loved. What could be better than that?

Newland nodded. "Okay," he said, "but let's give it five years. I'm sure by then you'll need somebody new to boss around."

She started to reprimand him, but he kissed her instead. And she decided that was a more satisfactory way to end the conversation.

EPILOGUE

His first Christmas in Turtle Creek. Newland couldn't wipe the smile from his face as he lugged the freshly cut pine across the buckled sidewalk and up the concrete steps leading to Bitty's house. Well, their house now. Just as he'd wanted, he and Natalie had moved in with Bitty, bringing Aubie with them. It'd taken a little while. He'd moved to Turtle Creek and taken up in her apartment until they could officially get married. Bitty insisted. Newland sort of liked the idea of living apart until they actually became man and wife. Now two weeks into married bliss, he was more than ready to see his wife again.

He juggled the tree and managed to open the door. "I'm home!" He loved saying those words. Loved knowing that his family was on the other side of that door.

The first one to greet him was Mr. Piddles. Bitty said it was a shame that he seemed to love Newland more than he loved her, but as far as Newland could tell that was just the way of cats. They did what they wanted to do when they wanted to do it. Which sounded a lot like Bitty herself.

"Do you have the Christmas tree?" Aubie stuck his head out of the parlor. He was dressed in an ugly green Christmas sweater and tan corduroy slacks.

"I do, but I don't understand why we need the tree for pictures. It's not even going to be decorated."

"Trust me on this. It'll still give the feeling of Christmas to have a pine tree behind us."

Newland supposed he came by it honestly. Just look at his sister. But as mayor Aubie did spend a lot of time bossing people around. Newland forgave him.

He lugged the tree into the parlor where everyone waited. Bitty was there wearing her own patchwork Christmas cardigan that was even uglier than the reindeer sweater that Aubie wore. And his Natalie. He smiled as she came toward him brandishing a twig of the mistletoe. "It's good to have you home, hubby."

"It's good to be home." And it surely was. Never in a million years had he dreamed that all this could be his.

"Now," Natalie started in that voice he knew all too well. "Aubie will set up the tree. You need to go change into your sweater."

He started to protest but she cut him off with one swift "hup" and he decided that putting on the ugly sweater for the Christmas picture was not worth sleeping on the couch tonight if he didn't.

He loped up the stairs, grabbed the sweater, and pulled it over his head as he ran back down. How he had managed to get the ugliest sweater of them all he wasn't certain. But the red snowflake-covered monstrosity that he had been presented with was definitely the worst sweater of them all.

"Why do we have to do this again?" he asked, smoothing down his hair as he came back into the room. Natalie's sweater was baby blue and strewn with crystals, which on paper sounded okay enough. Except the crystals were part of the white Santa Claus beard on her shirt.

"Because all families take a Christmas picture," Bitty told him. That was one thing they were doing, teaching him how to be a part of a real family. Though Newland was sure most real families weren't as eccentric as his. But he didn't care. They were his and that was all that mattered.

"Yeah but why ugly sweaters?"

"Because I said." Aubie grinned. "And I am the mayor."

"Touché," Newland returned.

Bitty waved everybody over to the divan that had been pushed against the bookcase, the freshly cut tree squished in between. "Everybody on the sofa. I've got the timer set. Aubie, all you have to do is hit this button here and then come around the front and sit down in front of Newland. You got that?"

Aubie nodded and waited until everyone arranged themselves on the divan.

Newland had Natalie half in his lap and Bitty beside him. He felt like the luckiest man in the world.

"Everybody ready?" Aubie asked.

"Yes," they all said through clenched smiles.

"Everybody say sex," Aubie said, staring down into the camera screen.

"Aubie, hit the button and get over here," Natalie grumped.

"Right. Here we go." Aubie hit the button and raced around just getting in front of the camera before the timer went off.

"I hope that's a good one." Natalie popped off of Newland's lap. He hated to see her go, but he knew it was for the best. They still had the picture to deal with and dinner to eat before they could head upstairs to be by themselves.

Aubie grabbed the camera off the tripod and examined the digital picture.

"Hmmm," he said looking at the image.

"What is it?" Bitty asked. "It should have taken four pictures right in a row. Did it not?"

Aubie thumbed through them, an odd look on his face.

"It did but…" He didn't finish as he started thumbing through the pictures once again.

Newland went to stand by Bitty as she took the camera from Aubie. Natalie squeezed between, staring at the tiny screen. "Well, I'll be," she said.

"Is that—" Newland asked, unable to even say the words.

"Yep," Bitty said, her tone matter of fact. "That's the ghost." She hummed a little as she walked away leaving Aubie, Newland, and Natalie to stare at the four pictures on the tiny screen.

Newland thumbed through them one more time just to make sure that he was in all the pictures. A small, dark-skinned boy no more than eight in full Union uniform blue smiling at the camera.

Natalie turned her gaze to Newland. "Is that a ghost?"

Newland flipped through the pictures again. "I think it is."

"Wow," Aubie said.

Bitty took that minute to pop back into the parlor, a sweet and self-satisfied smirk on her face. "I told you he was real."

Newland laughed and hugged Natalie close. "So you did," he said. As real as the love they shared.

EXCLUSIVE, MONTHLY GIVEAWAYS
INSIDER KNOWLEDGE ON NEW
RELEASES
AND FUN STUFF IN EACH EDITION

Sign-up for the Amy Lillard Newsletter. The best email you'll get all month guaranteed. (Well, I can't really guarantee, the newsletter, but I do think you'll enjoy it!)

To sign up visit Amy's website: www.amywritesromance.com

ABOUT THE AUTHOR

Amy Lillard is the award-winning, best-selling author of over sixty books and novellas in a variety of genres.

A transplanted Southern belle, Amy was born and raised in Mississippi and now lives in Oklahoma with her husband of a billion years. They have one (almost) adult son whom they are embarrassingly proud of. These days their 'empty nest' is rounded out with two spoiled cats who always seem to want to be fed when she's hit her writing stride for the day. But such is life with felines. >^..^<

Amy loves to hear from her readers. She can be reached at amylillard918@gmail.com or found on the web at www.amywritesromance.com & www.amywritesmysteries.com.

DID YOU LOVE THIS BOOK?
I LOVE REVIEWS!

Hey, reader. If you enjoyed this book, please take the time to leave a review on your favorite online bookseller's site or Goodreads. Seriously, authors adore this sort of thing!

Thanks!

CPSIA information can be obtained
at www.ICGtesting.com
Printed in the USA
LVHW110252060722
722857LV00006B/275